IMPRINT

IMPRINT

PAUL L. BATES

Five Star • Waterville, Maine

First Edition, Second Printing

Published in 2005 in conjunction with Tekno Books and Ed Gorman.

Set in 11 pt. Plantin by Minnie B. Raven.

Printed in the United States on permanent paper.

Library of Congress Cataloging-in-Publication Data

Bates, Paul L.
    Imprint / by Paul L. Bates.—1st ed.
      p. cm.
    ISBN 1-59414-312-9 (hc : alk. paper)
    1. People with disabilities—Fiction.   2. City and town life—Fiction.   3. Missing persons—Fiction.
    4. Street cleaners—Fiction.   I. Title.
PS3602.A865I48 2005
    813'.6—dc22   2005006638

This book is dedicated to the memory of Nancy.
You are sorely missed.

CHAPTER 1

In his dreaming, a child screams piteously. Face down inside a utility crate, it is soiled, dirty, hungry, goes ignored. The child screams louder. Something in his awareness responds with: *That is not the voice of a child.* The image fades quickly, but the sound does not. *That is the sound of an animal.*

He awakens on the dirty cot by simply opening his eyes and staring at the dingy wall. More of the faded yellow paper has peeled loose in the sweltering August night. He takes a deep breath, takes stock of his life, as he does every morning, lest he lose any more of it.

It's Monday morning, the rats are fighting again in the hall. They have invaded my dreaming for the third night in a row.

He listens to the sounds of their skittering feet within the hollow walls. He moves his eyes to the right, focuses his attention on the wand sitting on the crate beside the cot. Reaching over his chest with his right hand, he notices that his left arm has melted into a gelatinous pool beside him, seeping into the stained sheet. He lets out his breath. The wand seems to hum with delight as he closes his fingers about it. He does not move his torso, lest he lose contact with the missing arm, then points the wand at the gaping rat hole on the other side of the room.

There is a red glint somewhere in the darkness beyond the peeling wallpaper. He aims the wand and gently presses the discharge stud. An arcing bolt of vibrant purple flashes across the room, illuminating the startled rat for the briefest

7

instant. Another hideous scream fills the morning, as the bolt incinerates the rat. The cockroaches clustered under the table scatter and vanish into their crevasses beneath the baseboard. He sets the wand back on the plastic crate that serves him as a night table.

His heart is racing, like it does every time he kills a rat. It reminds him of the sweep. It also reminds him that his morning litany has been disrupted. He looks at the clock Rachel has given him. It is five after nine.

Damn, I've overslept again.

In the corridor, another one of the rats resumes its shrieking. It sounds just like a baby dying. He hears the other rats rushing toward the sound, knows that a struggle within their social order has just been resolved. Those who were neutral are now siding with the winner, pouncing upon the loser, tearing him to pieces. The shrieking becomes deafening before the silence.

He shuts his eyes. In this self-inflicted darkness, he remembers his left arm, all of it. He remembers the bones, the muscles, the sinews, the arteries, the veins. He feels the spongy mass at his side starting to reconfigure. He concentrates completely on the task at hand, for he knows that if his attention wavers, he'll have to do it over again—worse yet, he might lose the arm altogether.

Ignoring the lancing pain and all the awful tickling, he builds the arm cell by cell, layer by layer. Soon he is remembering the pink skin and the blond hair follicles. There is a tattoo of an ancient Celtic glyph, but he decides to do away with it. Tattoos are no longer in vogue, they are now a liability—the mark of a loser—just a way for the authorities to keep tabs on him. When his fingers begin to tingle and ache, he remolds the swirls on their tips. These, too, will have new patterns.

For a long while he remains still in the darkness, feeling the pain subsiding. He wiggles his fingers, to make certain he has regained control over the arm. Balling his hand, he makes a fist and smashes it down on the mattress. It bounces, he laughs.

He sits up, opens his eyes to admire his handiwork.

Not bad. It looks a bit more muscular than last time. The skin is a bit pale, but it will have to do. It's getting easier, each time I do that.

Then he starts over.

It's Monday. Jennie has gone missing for fifteen days now. Yesterday Rachel gave me a blank look when I mentioned her name. Even Tom, who used to follow her about like a puppy, has forgotten her. Everyone in this block knows there never was a Jennie—everyone except me. Her roommate has relocated. Someone new has moved into her flat. A fat man with dark, mean eyes, bald head, cheap tattoos bleeding into one another all over his hairy arms, a spider on the back of his neck, a teardrop below his left eye.

I remember Jennie. I remember her bright blue eyes, her thick red hair, her soft tight skin. I remember her touch. I miss her so much I want to scream. I will never forget Jennie. I will remember her today. I will remember her every day.

I will remember them all. I remember Rafe, Wiffle, Splash, and Kirsten. I remember Hans, Effie, Weggie, and Rikki. I remember Crash and Flicker, Winston and The Elf. I remember all the missing. I remember them to keep them alive inside me.

He stops to picture every face, every expression, every laugh, and every frustration that reminds him of them. There were others—so many others, but these had been his friends. It has only been a month since he has resolved not to let himself be swept away by the general malaise. So many gone in a month. He hears Rikki laughing, brushing her short blond hair from her face. Then he sees Jennie again, handing him an ale over the black granite bar.

He begins sobbing loudly, turning himself over and burying his face in his pillow. Was there no way out? Was there no hope? Jennie believed in hope. His memory of her keeps his hope alive. It gives him the courage to do those things that get him out of the flat, get his mind off the dead end looming before him like an icy abyss.

He loses himself in a tidal wave of self-pity, blubbering like an infant, before he finds the resolve to pull himself free from its strength-sapping embrace. He wipes the tears from his eyes and blows his nose loudly into an old shirt he keeps in the crate for that purpose. He forces himself to rise, staggers to one of the three broken chairs surrounding the small, square table overlooking the city street.

Slumping down into the only chair with four level legs, he wonders if all of the missing have just melted away like his left arm, or if there are even more sinister forces at work here.

It is so hard not knowing. It is so hard being the only one who remembers—who wants to remember. It is so hard not just letting it all slip away.

His rambling thoughts are interrupted by a sharp staccato rapping on the hall door.

He winces, recognizing the sound, hoping that if he remains still, it will just stop, that she will just go away.

"Wyatt? Are you up? I heard you shoot that rat. Please don't ignore me. You have no idea how much that hurts me."

It is Rachel. Rachel who is trying to make herself indispensable. Rachel who changes effortlessly with every flux in their surroundings. Rachel who remembers nothing that is not of today. Rachel who does not want to remember. Rachel who pretends not to notice him changing his own reality in ways that are not in keeping with the tide sweeping them all out to sea. Rachel who will not go away. Rachel who holds the key to his escaping the abyss.

The rapping starts up again.

"Wyatt? I'd rather you shoot me with that wand than do this to me—really I would."

He looks at the wand upon the crate, wonders if he could get away with it. Just shoot her and be done with it. The thought makes him smile. The smile gives him the strength to get up to do what he must: unbolt the locks that gird the steel door, let Rachel into his life.

He looks down into the white face with the hard brown eyes, the long curved nose, the thick purple lips, the little pink tongue darting over the perfect white teeth like a sensor, making sure that she is always alluring. Her tan blouse is pulled tight around her large breasts that seem to levitate with the aid of a push-up bra, her lustrous jet-black hair is pulled back behind her head where it seems to turn inward like a cresting wave. Gently, she clasps him by the arms, causing the tender new left arm to ache. He winces.

Rachel pretends not to notice, pushes those pointed breasts into his chest like soft daggers. Her breath smells of fresh basil. She blows the sweet smell softly into his face.

"My cousin will take you on for the day again, Wyatt. I know you need the credits and it will do you good to get out. Besides, Curtis says you are a good worker. He could use more just like you. You need to be there by eleven thirty-five. That gives us enough time, if you like."

Jennie's name bubbles to his lips, like the last spent breath of a drowning man, but Rachel's forefinger presses hard against them, lest he speak the spell of banishment.

"Don't spoil it Wyatt," Rachel whispers.

11

Her large nose makes her resemble an Egyptian goddess for a moment—one with a young woman's curvaceous body and the head of a raptor. The bright red talon on the end of her finger completes the image. His eyes probe hers and find a vast ocean of feeling and comfort, beckoning to him to lose himself therein. He has resisted her for weeks. But she holds the key to so many of his needs. They both know he will resist no more.

"I understand, Wyatt, really I do. Your need for privacy, your need to remember those you have left behind. But please don't keep throwing them up at me as if they were just here. Please don't pretend around me. It's hard enough the way it is. Don't make it any harder."

Her hand slips from his face to the back of his neck as she pulls his head down. She is on her tiptoes, pressing hard against his lips and loins. Her need is infectious. It becomes his need. He hates himself for his weakness. He hates himself for giving in to her. He tries to conjure the image of Jennie, but there is only Rachel, with her little pink tongue darting everywhere, her tan blouse unraveling like a streamer, her strong Egyptian goddess legs rubbing against his thighs, then coiling about him.

His hands begin finding all the parts of her, paying homage to each. She bares her neck for him to kiss. He cannot refuse her. Later he will consider shooting her with the wand again, but not now. Now he is whimpering as she rakes his chest with her talons. Now he is clinging to her as his only remaining hold upon this reality.

CHAPTER 2

Wyatt slouches against the soft plastic seat, does his best to think of nothing. The taste of basil lingers on his lips, the bright pink scratches crisscrossing his chest sting. He holds fast to both sensations, peering through the acrylic walls of the train into the hazy cityscape darting past. His backbone feels like jelly, his loins feel drained. The physical satisfaction has nullified the emotional vacuum. He touches the cool curved wall, listening to the whooshing sound of the train gliding through its tube. It reminds him of a lonely turd in a flush toilet, descending into the bowels of the city. He smiles, as he is flushed through the city.

The compartment seats six. It is a warm gray plastic. Today it seems unreal. He is alone with only one other passenger. Across the seat facing him, a tall tight-lipped man in his late thirties with a flat face, a small nose, and the posture of a Heartlander flicks an imaginary crumb from his black silk lapel and glances over at Wyatt as if he were that crumb. His light brown hair is impeccable.

"Down on your luck, boy?" the man says and smiles.

The glint of sunlight on sterling silver teeth momentarily blinds him.

Wyatt glares at his traveling companion. His first thought is to clamp his fingers on the man's throat to squeeze the life from the thick Adam's apple, his second is a vivid image of crackling shock prods and the two long nights spent in a crowded dank cell following his last angry outburst. Dim lights illuminating dented beds layered in slick epoxy three tiers high against gray metal walls, and the company of broken men hacking into the night. Blotchy shadows hovering like vultures, accented by a few predatory nothing-to-lose stone-cold souls with glinting rats' eyes in the vapid darkness. Leering smiles, drooping slack-jawed scowls, missing teeth, and bloodshot vacuous eyes. The memories are vivid enough to be real. *Repeat offenders simply disappear,* he hears the night warden telling him as he is pushed into the bleak rain-splattered street. The unwelcome recollection includes the smell of stale urine and regurgitated chipped soy protein on dry brown bread, making him gasp for air.

"No need for pride," his traveling companion continues. The voice is a distant drone that suddenly snaps him upright in the seat. "Pride is the undoing of the faithless. Your luck may have just changed for the better, boy—I'm an important man."

Wyatt sighs, braces himself for the coming ordeal.

"So what need have I for such as yourself, you're wondering, eh?"

"No," Wyatt whispers, "actually I'm wondering why you don't have anything better to do than to empty yourself on me, you being so holy and all."

"But I do," the man protests, leaning toward him. "It's just that I've learned that one must always give back to life when one takes from it. So if you mind your manners, talk real nice, you'll be the beneficiary of my faith."

Wyatt shuts his eyes, nods his head, and leans back. There will be no escaping this prattling fool unless he is willing to find another compartment—but that requires more effort than he is willing to expend. He is saving his strength for Rachel's cousin. The rent is due, the cupboard is bare. Rachel is right, as always—he does need the credit balance. Three months with a zero balance makes you a drossie. Drossies get swept. Better to be a sweeper than a drossie.

"Do tell," he whispers.

"You are laughing at me, boy. But I don't mind. You'll be thanking me before we're through with each other. You'll be fluttering around me like a butterfly drunk on the nectar of a poppy."

Wyatt has no idea what either a butterfly or a poppy is. He glares at the man, who seems to take neither notice nor offense at his resentment.

Taking a silver case from his inside breast pocket, the man removes a metal toothpick and begins cleaning slivers of real meat from his teeth. He pauses to inspect them, turning them over as if they were strands of pearls on the end of the pick, making certain that Wyatt sees them for what they are, before popping them back into his mouth.

"How old are you, boy? Twenty-one? Twenty-two?"

"Close enough," Wyatt says with a smile. He will not give the man the satisfaction of saying his name is Wyatt, not boy, and that he is twenty-three years old. There is already a nervousness in the man's pale blue eyes, announcing that Wyatt has deviated from the expected responses. The man is improvising now. That makes it almost real.

"Do you know what I was doing when I was twenty-two?"

"Turning tricks in gaytown's my guess, at least until some face shoved yours in front of a ten-watt bulb, which transmogrified your sorry butt forever—right?"

The man glares at Wyatt and puts the toothpick back in its case.

"That's right, boy. You see what's in front of you. Not

15

many do, you know. With bright eyes like yours, you ought to be wearing natural fabrics, not oil derivatives. You must be wasting yourself away, crying into your pillow every night, trying to remember the faces that just disappeared. You probably sit in bed for hours making up ways to fit all the scattered pieces of your life together, trying to make logic out of nonsense. Some kind of sad-assed loser you are, by any standard. I'm willing to change all that for you."

Wyatt and the man glare at one another without saying anything as the transport glides to a smooth stop at the next station. A voice announces the station. Wyatt stands up and the man pushes a thin plastic card into his curled fingers.

"Come see me when you wake up, boy. But don't wait too long. You won't stay awake without help, you know. This whole conversation could turn into another one of your scrambled memories before you can scratch yourself again."

The man laughs, watching Wyatt make his way from the stuffy compartment to the end of the train. As Wyatt steps out onto the platform, he feels the man's card biting into his hand. He pushes it deep into his shirt pocket without reading it, buttons the flap to keep it there.

Who knows, maybe I can use him, too.

Behind him, the train vanishes in a surge of magnetic force. The platform is crowded with lumbering civil guards in their gray ceramic armor, herding clusters of uninspired day workers just putting in their time toward the transport chutes. Nobody loiters, nobody pauses. Wyatt walks slowly, looking around at the thinning crowd. Thick hands, a bulging Adam's apple, and small hips—a transvestite posing as a housewife on a shopping spree stands out from the others. Wyatt sees the man lost within the gaudy body of the faux-woman.

He moves on before he attracts any undue attention on himself. He hears the two warning blasts, announcing the sweep. A civil guard shoves a long barrel across his chest.

"Why you packing a wand?" the guard demands, tapping the bulge in Wyatt's vest pocket.

"For the sweep," Wyatt says. "I pick up the little pieces."

The guard grins, showing sparkling teeth of cubic zirconium.

Wyatt mimics the smile, flashing his own teeth.

"Better hurry, you got six minutes before you get swept yourself, little sweeper."

Wyatt nods and walks as fast as he can to the transport chute. His stomach churns as the weightlessness overtakes him and he is sucked up, then to the right, and finally down, deep into the recycling works. He holds his breath, feeling something ice cold reaching out to him. His eyes are still shut tight when he hears the familiar cackle on the other end of the ride.

He looks up into a cherubic face, smiling good-naturedly at his awkward aversion to the transport chutes.

"Hey, Louie," Wyatt says, stumbling the two steps it takes to find his balance.

"Hey, Wyatt. How's Rachel of the lovely pontoons?" the fat man asks, his eyes wide in anticipation.

"All too necessary, Louie."

The fat man laughs, sweeping away the stray lock of thinning blond hair that perpetually falls over his left eye.

"Ain't they all, Wyatt. Ain't they all. Ya better push on. Curtis wants you near the front on this one. I think yer gonna be family before long."

Shoulders like ham hocks heave and fall.

Wyatt nods and jogs across the slick sky-blue epoxy floor

toward the office. With bright red numbers over a meter high, a large clock above the black door proclaims it is eleven thirty-two. Wyatt knocks once.

A smallish man with a dark narrow mustache above his thick lips, wearing a spotless tan uniform and black helmet-headset, steps out, tosses him a set of white coveralls with a flaring helmet, stands ready to hand him a long barrel. Wyatt scrambles into the suit, adjusts the helmet's controls to *blocking*. He accepts the weapon, flicking the activation switch to *live*.

"You taking good care of Rachel?" the man demands, looking at the clock. The helmet turns Curtis' voice into a gargle.

"She was smiling when I left her."

"Good. She's my mother's sister's favorite. Nothing's too good for Rachel. She's living outside the Heartland because she thinks she should live like *real* people. You be real for her, Wyatt—she's special. You be real for her and I'll make it up to you."

Wyatt nods as he presses the coveralls shut.

Curtis leads him to a hover pod outside the office door. They both climb aboard. Silently the disk glides upward while Wyatt clings to the thin tubular handrail, sucks in a deep breath.

The clock below reads eleven thirty-five when they reach the small opening in the ceiling and continue rising upward into the stale city air. Spiderweb streets twist and angle in all directions, radiating and intersecting at regular intervals around the recycling center. The piercing sweep sound begins, but the helmet muffles just enough of it to keep Wyatt from wanting to leap off the hover pod. Sweat beads break out on Wyatt's forehead as Curtis sets the controls to auto-pilot. Well below them, Wyatt estimates two hundred civil guards hover in small clusters like wingless beetles three stories above the maze of angular streets, while countless day workers wearing helmeted white coveralls and holding shock prods outline the perimeter of the sweep.

A pair of drossies break cover from the shadow of a doorway, run wildly for the next intersection. Two sweepers break ranks to drive them back. Ripples of blue force knock the drossies from their feet. They bounce like rubber balls. Scrambling back to their feet, they turn tail, staggering back toward the center, followed by a stream of brown that breaks to flow around them. Rats by the hundreds and roaches by the thousands, escaping the sound boring into their skulls, outpace the staggering drossies, all making for the center, where they will be recycled for the productive members of society.

Moments later, a second wave follows the first one. Then a third and a fourth.

"Over there, by the delivery tube," Curtis yells and points.

One of the drossies stands proud, with a self-made helmet protecting him from the lethal sound. He points a stolen long barrel skyward at the hover pod.

Wyatt sees movement in the shadows. He aims, fires, using nothing but reflex. A lancing arc of blue crackles from the pod toward the tube. It incinerates everything organic within a two-foot radius, leaving only a pile of rags and the stolen long barrel clanging on the ground. Another sweeper scrambles toward the spot to retrieve it.

Gradually all the white suits with mirrored faceplates converge upon the iris opening into which the rats, mice, cockroaches, stray lizards, dogs, cats, and the surging crowd of drossies have fled. Following them come the high-wheelers manned by more day workers, filling the big trucks with empty food containers and other assorted inorganic waste that had littered the streets. The swarm of civil guards continues to hover above the opening until the living tide is swallowed whole. Nothing will be wasted. All is returned to the source. Everything will be made new. All will be forgotten.

CHAPTER 3

Her name is Frieda; she hands him an ale. She was once Jennie's roommate and best friend, but now Frieda can't even remember her. Wyatt still wants to ask Frieda about Jennie, but he is thankful that she can't recall the other two times he asked. Her hair is brown silk, clipped just above her shoulders. She wears a thin pink top that wraps her small breasts so tightly that Wyatt can see the fine definition at the edge of her nipples. Jennie once offered to make it a threesome with Frieda, but Wyatt refused. Now, looking at Frieda and feeling her need, he wonders why.

"Thanks," he says, taking the plastic mug. The Wurlitzer plays a rocking piece that makes him feel like strutting. He moves his head back and forth in time with the music. Frieda smiles.

"Louie says you got a big promo," Frieda says, making conversation. There is a music in her voice that says she's made no plans for the early evening. Her eyes linger on his, searching, while her small mouth sings the words.

"Yeah, I got a new long barrel, a high ride with the boss, and a clean shot at some poor bastard who just wanted to live," Wyatt says and turns his empty stare on her.

He does not mean to put her off, only to show himself to her.

Frieda looks at the black granite bar for a moment, then answers another call farther down the line. He watches her move, sees only the struggle for identity in her quick hurried steps, her slightly awkward gestures. He

21

cannot picture himself clinging to her.

Wyatt shuts his eyes and sees Weggie, an athletic young man with wiry white hair, laughing black eyes. Weggie is doing an effortless handstand on the top of the concrete retainer at the reservoir. The water level is down two-thirds—only the Heartland is getting unrestricted use. A commotion on the opposite side will soon turn into a cluster of civil guards swarming to investigate them. Weggie vaults to his feet and the two friends continue their leisurely walk along the bank as six guards fly across the mirrored surface of the water in formation to challenge them. A soft blue sky devoid of clouds lingers above and below. Weggie makes a joke, does a little dance, and soon the civil guards are all laughing. They fly off a few minutes later after checking their I-Dents.

What really became of Weggie? He had a steady gig—he didn't get swept. He always had at least 2000 reserve credits. Did he get disappeared?

"You want another ale?" Frieda asks him. Wyatt notices that the mug he holds is empty, the music has changed on the Wurlitzer, the music is gone from Frieda's voice.

"Naw, I gotta get my credits before I'm a drossie," Wyatt says. "See ya next time?"

"Yeah."

Frieda looks at him with large gray eyes that seem to apologize for not remembering what he wants her to. Wyatt smiles and wonders what Frieda would feel like wrapped around him as tightly as her top. Then he remembers Jennie. They met like this, only it had been electric from the start. Every moment magic.

Back at the office, Curtis is smiling broadly, with his little dark mouth puckered as if he had just sucked down a lemon whole.

"Good tally?" Wyatt asks.

"We beat the quota," Curtis admits. "You did real well. You're my new full-time shooter, Wyatt. That drossie would have fried us in another second."

"I just wanted to live a little bit more than he did. Maybe I had more to live for."

"Rachel told my sister you were a philosopher. Now I see why."

Wyatt wonders what a philosopher is, but only smiles.

"Here," Curtis says, handing him a magnetic voucher. "Deposit this and then show Rachel a good time. You've got nowhere to go but up. Just don't forget what I told you about Rachel. We want her back in the Heartland, smiling. Now get going."

"Thanks."

"It's all right. See you in two weeks."

"Right."

Wyatt takes the voucher to the office depository next to the door. It is usually reserved for Curtis, his clerks, the lead sweepers. The lines are forty deep at the depositories near the transport chute. Wyatt does not feel like waiting.

The thin-faced clerk looks up from her screen and stares at him. He smiles back. Her face looks like a spade with small eyes, nose, and mouth drawn on it. She glares at Wyatt for a moment, then looks back at the panel. A flicker of red and blue lights ripple across her features as she resumes her imputing. She glowers at the screen.

Wyatt pushes the buttons, inserts the magnetic card Curtis has given him, watches, waits. On the screen, his recent credit history appears slowly.

Previous balance: 40 credits.
Voucher: 1000 credits.

Taxes: minus 450 credits.

Outstanding claims:

    60 days rent: minus 240 credits.

    60 days commissary usage: minus 150 credits.

    One ale: minus 1 credit.

Balance: 199 credits.

We appreciate your business. Make time to laugh.

Wyatt grimaces at the homily. Curtis has left. The office clerk looks up, scowls at him again. She wants him gone. Wyatt wonders what she will do when she is alone. He smiles and waves to the woman as he opens the black door. His last voucher was for 500 credits. Rachel must have big plans for them both. Or else Cousin Curtis does.

The taste of basil is gone, and his chest is starting to itch.

In the train he thinks about Rachel. She will be waiting for him. She will want him to stay the night. *What if she sees me change?* He shuts his eyes and pushes himself back into the seat as the city whooshes by beyond the plastic tube. Wyatt has memorized all of the red and blue towers with their black faceless windows. For no reason his teeth begin to chatter. He opens his eyes. Three vacuous faces sharing the gray plastic compartment with him are searching his for signs of an impending emotional breakdown. His arms feel cold. He begins rubbing them, trying to stimulate the circulation. A pair of hovering civil guards appear just beyond the tube for a second and vanish. He shuts his eyes again.

I love you, Wyatt, he hears Jennie whispering to him in the dark. Beyond the fiber walls he hears Frieda's bed springs moaning faster and faster, as Wiffle lets out a whoop of ecstasy. *Whatever happens, remember that. This is what is real, Wyatt. All the rest of it is insanity. Sooner or later we all get swept away, one way or another. When it's your turn to get swept, you come back here for me, Wyatt. I'll always be here waiting for you. Keep me alive in your memory—not many can do that. I know you're one of them.*

He wants to stay here with her now. To hell with all the rest of it. He reaches for Jennie in his mind. They embrace. Her touch is perfect. Self-confident, but not crushing— yielding but not surrendering. *I'm here now, Jennie. I've come back for you. No need to wait to get swept, love.* The image fades in spite of his efforts to maintain it.

Wyatt feels the hot tears running down his cheeks, the three pair of eyes boring into his face. The other passengers expect to watch him let go. The two women are cringing, afraid that he might attack them. One has gone all white, while the other presses herself against the curved wall, as if that might make her invisible. The man beside them is just waiting for Wyatt to curl into a helpless ball of quivering manflesh upon the floor. There is a faint smile at the corners of his puffy mouth as the train comes to a smooth stop.

"Sorry to disappoint," Wyatt says, as he stands up and brushes past them.

In the street, the faint smell of ozone lingers. The old woman is setting up the fruit stand at the corner, with her two children playing at her feet. Wyatt guesses she must be forty. *Not many make it that far outside the Heartland, not that you could guess their age anyway.*

The boy looks up at him and Wyatt feels his heart leap as a wave of terror washes over him. The girl stands up and asks him what he wants.

Still trembling, he buys some bananas and a bouquet of sweet-smelling hybrids.

He does not remember leaving the fruit stand until he suddenly finds himself standing outside Rachel's building.

It is much more imposing than his own. Two flat-faced security guards with thick arms folded across their chests eye him with disdain as he stares into the small black glass monitor. The motionless black mechanical pupil glints, watching him like a hungry predator. Wyatt holds his features steady, lest the invisible beast lurking within pounce upon him.

"Is that you, Wyatt?" Rachel's disembodied voice asks. "I'm in the bathroom."

"It's me."

"Let him in."

The doors fly open and the transport tube sucks him upward. He twists and turns, gripping the flowers, clutching the bananas, squeezing his eyes shut.

Rachel appears, her long black hair swathed in a towel, her muscular legs showing beneath a bright red cotton robe. "For me? How sweet."

Awkwardly, he hands her both.

"I'm running you a bath—you need one. Why don't you stuff your clothes into the recycler? I've got you some new ones anyway."

"Is it all like . . . like this . . . in the Heartland?" Wyatt asks her timidly.

"Like what?" Rachel says with a smile.

"Recyclers, talkies, bathtubs, flush toilets, no rats, no sweeps."

Rachel's forehead becomes a pattern of wavy lines as her dark eyes narrow. He thinks he sees something akin to rage distort her features.

"It's nothing like this. Everything is easy. Everything is impossible. Nobody can feel anything. Everybody is what they are expected to be. Nothing is real. There is too much of everything. I hated it so much I used to cry myself to sleep."

She turns toward the large lexan wall, peering into the hexagonal pattern of the city grid, her fingers tracing the pattern on the lexan.

"You shouldn't have to cry, ever," he says.

Rachel puts the hybrids into a blue and white vase, adds water. She sprinkles some white powder into the mouth. The pale pinks and yellows intensify at once, as the flowers seem to take on a new presence. Absently, she picks a ripe banana from the bunch and peels it. Her robe seems to open by itself, revealing the top of her pale pink torso.

Wyatt stands naked on the granite tile floor and touches the smooth sides of the tub like a dreamer. Crystal clear water, hot to the touch, it is only the third time he has taken a bath. He steps in and watches the water discolor around his foot before submerging all of himself. Out of breath, he lifts his head above the water. The scratches on his chest are festering. He takes a quick glance to be sure Rachel is not watching, and then concentrates on removing them. Three rows of four red and pink lines shrink and then vanish. He reaches for the bottle of Castile soap. The mint fragrance is intoxicating as he lathers his face and hair. He submerges again, running his fingers through his hair until the soap is gone. When he surfaces, Rachel is handing him a piece of banana. The robe is completely open now, and he watches her firm breasts rise and fall with her quiet breathing.

"What happened to your tattoo?" she asks.

Wyatt hesitates. "I had it removed."

"I liked it."

"I didn't."

"Don't be too long. The concert starts in two hours."

He watches her glide toward the bedroom, shedding the robe on the way. The small of her back is so gracefully curved he wants to bury his face there.

With rivulets of water surging all around him, Wyatt stands up to lather the rest of himself. The smell of Rachel fills his nose, the sound of her voice is in his ears, the memory of her clinging to him this morning is obliterating everything else. He stands stark still. For a moment, he wants to run for the transport tube as fast as he can.

Minutes later he is caressing that pale pink skin, kissing all of her, touching all of her, clinging to her like a motherless child plucked from the raging storm, as she sinks her perfect white teeth into his lower lip, splattering both of them with tiny droplets of warm blood.

CHAPTER 4

The lyrics are inane. The rhythms are simple, repetitious, numbing. The melodies are lean and tinny. Every song sounds exactly the same as the last one to Wyatt. Even the verses are indistinguishable from one another. Yet the crowd roars at every song; the strutting figures in the glittering silver and blue costumes prance back and forth across the stage, eating up all the adoration. Wyatt sits bored, with his right arm about Rachel, who roars along with the crowd.

He still tastes the blood where she bit his lower lip, and he leans over to inhale her scent.

"You don't much feel them, do you?" she asks later when they sip cappuccino in the streetside cafe up the block from the Downtown Odeum.

"Not much."

Rachel pouts. "*The Mimis* bring out the defiant spirit in me," she says. "What do you hear, Wyatt?"

"Noise."

"What do you see?"

"Uptown children."

Rachel frowns, leans back from the table, brushes the hair from her face.

On the avenue across from the cafe, something strikes the pavement with a dull thud. Scurrying people cry out in surprise and flee. Moments later, a silent crowd converges warily around the spot.

"Jumper," Wyatt says calmly, taking another sip. "I

guess he went alone. Bad shot."

Rachel trembles. Her face is ashen and drawn as she pushes herself from the table as far back into her rattan chair as she can get.

A swarm of civil guards drops from the shadow of the night above the well-lit street. The crowd disperses as quickly as it formed. A clean white recycling truck lumbers onto the scene within minutes. Faceless figures in white coveralls and mirrored helmets emerge; moving meticulously, they carefully scrape up every bit of the mess. It is placed into a white container that opens wide from the side of the truck. Other sweepers douse the spot with bright blue stain remover shot from high-pressure hoses. The terror on the few faces who brave watching the process is distorted in the curved mirrors of the faceless sweepers.

Is that the big plan Curtis has waiting for me? Is my next promo sweeping jumpers? I can hardly wait. He's just a drone— what can he offer me?

Wyatt gestures for the waiter to bring the pastry cart.

Rachel watches him in silent disbelief. She can see he is obviously enjoying this street performance more than the concert.

City-real ain't quite what you thought, is it, Rachel?

Wyatt picks a rum baba for himself and a Napoleon for her.

The recycling truck creeps off, signaling the crowd to gradually fill the avenue.

Wyatt smiles as the color returns to Rachel's cheeks.

"What's wrong with them?" she asks.

"What's wrong with who? The crowd?"

"*The Mimis.*"

Wyatt stares at her. "*The Mimis?*"

"Yes. Why don't you like them?"

"They play like they've been swept."

Rachel grimaces. "They're the most popular band in the world, you know," she informs him.

"Until tomorrow, when nobody will remember them."

"What?"

"They'll be just like that jumper."

"What jumper?"

Wyatt laughs in spite of himself.

"Don't laugh at me, Wyatt," Rachel whispers. "I know I've led a sheltered life, but I don't deserve your ridicule. I've given myself to you. There will never be anyone else but you for me. I don't even feel alive if I haven't touched you. So please don't laugh at me. You have no cause to hurt me. You say the strangest things sometimes. I just want to know what you mean. We are one, Wyatt. Don't talk as if I'm not even here, please."

Wyatt feels the blood rushing to his cheeks. He wants to tell her she has just proven his point, but he knows he will never convince her there was a jumper, much less that she has already forgotten him.

"I would never hurt you," he whispers back instead. "But I can't hold back the laughter. It's not you I laugh at. It's all this."

He makes a sweeping gesture with his left arm. "It all looks so real," he adds. "Sometimes I almost believe in it."

Rachel is growing angry. He can see that she thinks he is baiting her. The distance between them seems to elongate as she shuts herself off from him. Nothing else he says can reach her. She might as well be on the rooftop across the street, waiting to jump onto some hapless soul passing below. For a moment, he is standing in the middle of the street watching her drop onto him. Her lacy white dress spreads, making her look like a snowflake with legs as she gets bigger and bigger. He knows they will both die in the impact.

"Take me home," Rachel whispers. Her voice is a winter wind.

The transport chute outside the cafe sucks her up. For a moment, Wyatt is tempted to simply walk away. He feels naked and alone without her. On the train she waits for him to sit, then sits opposite him, careful not to let her legs touch his. He reaches for her—she pulls away. Wyatt can see the tears welling in her large brown eyes. Silently she stares at her own reflection in the tube while he starts two half-hearted conversations. She does not answer him. When the train stops, Rachel struts out in front of him. She brushes past the tube in the station, takes the concrete steps two at a time. Wyatt must jog to catch up with her in the street. They nearly run the two blocks to her tower.

"I love you, Wyatt Weston," she hisses outside the door, avoids his kiss, slips away when he reaches for her.

Wyatt is thankful that Rachel says goodnight in the narrow vestibule with the two dog-faced security men looking on. He will not have to chance her seeing some part of him dissolve in the night. She will get over it, he is certain. He is feeling awkward, too tired for any more of her moodiness, too exhausted to tryst with her again.

The evening has cost him most of his remaining credits, but it was worth it, even if *The Mimis* were terrible. By next week they will have disappeared, at least from memory. Rachel will not recall them in a month. She will have forgotten about the concert in a few days. He laughs out loud as he walks back into the night, running his fingers across the row of black steel bars that resemble spears protecting the small forecourt in front of Rachel's tower.

He walks the fourteen blocks back to his tenement,

feeling the swelling on his lower lip, smelling her scent all over him, listening to the sounds of the night. The walk will help him to sleep, make him too tired to think, too tired to remember Jennie.

The new clothes Rachel bought him fit and feel much better than his old ones, and the wand feels snug in its new silk holster below his left arm. The new vest is contoured around it, so as not to reveal a bulge. The new shoes are especially nice. Soft leather, instead of plastic, they do not pinch his toes nor do they squeak when he walks.

Wyatt thinks about spending a night with Rachel. It might be fun to wake up in the middle of the night and find her there: hot, soft, needing.

And in the morning? Would she panic if she saw me change? Would she prevent me from repairing the damage? Would she throw me out, and tell Cousin Curtis to can me? Would she even remember once the fix was done? It's still too big a risk. Oh, Rachel—so good and still so bad. How long can we keep this going? What's going to spoil it all for me? What's going to end this little trip into the real for you?

Above his head, another train shoots through the plastic tube hurtling northward, toward the Heartland. He stops to watch it dart and slither around the intersections.

Rachel could get us there. I'd like to try too much of everything, even if it wasn't real. What could be more unreal than this? But she'd never go back. I can see it in her pretty brown eyes, hear it in that loud voice of hers. What am I going to do with her?

The streets become narrower, with smaller street lamps shining downward. The daylight white becomes a pasty yellow.

Rats would be out and about, except for the sweep. Another few days before the new ones show up from the utility tunnels. I wonder if Curtis lets a few of them go, just to make sure he's got something else to sweep the next time? I wouldn't put anything past that little bastard.

The thinning crowds have all gone. It is mostly second-shift day workers trudging home from the stations in twos and threes. The occasional drunken reveler stumbles by, tempting the civil guards.

No drossies either on the night after a sweep. All gone the drossies.

It becomes a sing-song phrase, *all gone the drossies*, repeating itself over and over again in his mind, like the lyrics of *The Mimis*, fading from his memory.

Soon he is home alone again, unbolting the locks on the dented gray door, only to bolt them anew from the other side, trying to ignore the acidic rancid smell that lingers everywhere. There is no sound of scurrying feet within the walls tonight; there will be no screaming rat voices to invade his dreams tonight.

He stares at the filthy mattress. For the first time, the thought of spending another night alone in this dismal flat disgusts him. Rummaging through the pile on the floor of the single small closet, he finds the package of cotton sheets Rachel gave him last week. He flips the mattress over, then encases it within the zippered bottom sheet. He stuffs the top sheet under the bottom edge and undresses himself in the dark. He lays the wand gently atop the plastic crate, kicks his new shoes under the table, lays his new clothes neatly over the back of one of the chairs.

I haven't forgotten you, Jennie. Or you, Weg. I will remember. But I can't go on like this, if I'm going to stay behind. I've got to move uptown.

By the faint light of the street lamps, he rinses his mouth over the sink. Antiseptic stings his lip. He spits, and specs of pastry dot the bowl. He tries the tap. The water is running. Enough to rinse out the sink and half-fill it before it shuts off by itself. He splashes his face and lathers it with the soap Rachel gave him. It makes his skin feel cool. Reluctantly he washes it off, climbs into bed before the water dries.

Staring at the gray ceiling splashed yellow by the flickering street light, he wishes he had stayed with Rachel. His own world depresses him. He struggles with the idea of going back to her for a few minutes before he drops off to sleep.

CHAPTER 5

Terror binds him to the darkness. He cannot remember how to open his eyes. His mind is awash with a deluge of fears and imaginings, each vying for his attention, each sucking him down a gaping black maelstrom of no return. When his fear is spent, he realizes the problem. His face is gone. There are no eyes to open. He can feel himself shaking as he balls his fists. He wants to touch where his face should be, feel whatever is left there, know exactly what is missing by touch—but he knows better. Once again, the floodgates open and his fear sends his mind reeling into the abyss. Again his imagination runs riot until everything is spent. He lies still, bathed in perspiration, the chaos replaced by a numbness that distances him from what is left of his body, until he hears himself breathing, feels the blood gushing through his veins and arteries, hears the whooshing sound of it as his mind turns inward.

Finally he remembers the face he wore to the concert, the one he saw in the mirror behind the bed, when Rachel's strong legs flowed around him like a river of milk and honey, when her knees rocked up and down against his ribs. He remembers the face with the bloody lower lip. He remembers it in great detail: hair follicles, pores, lesions, and lines. He decides to do without the wound or the blemishes.

He starts with muscles, builds them piece by piece until he feels them taut. He adds the skin resting on the muscles that wrap the bones. He moves on to the eyes, the gray-green eyes that stare without blinking. Cell by cell, he con-

36

structs two eyes. Then the light brown eyebrows, the ones that rise to express doubt and narrow for anger and concern. The nose he changes slightly, removing the bump near the top. He also straightens the canine tooth that overlaps the incisor on the left side of his jaw. Atom by atom, he rebuilds his entire face.

When there is nothing left to remember, he tries the eyelids. Gradually they rise, like curtains before the play of life. The dirty walls reappear from the dark around him, as the blackness gives way to a blurry yellow that slowly defines itself as the ceiling above his bed.

Wyatt gasps for air and blinks. He listens to his heart racing until it is calm once again. He sits up and hugs his knees.

A pale sunlight floods the apartment as he repeats the litany of names.

It's Tuesday morning. I cannot remember dreaming. Jennie has gone missing for sixteen days now. It's like she never existed. I remembered Jennie yesterday—I saw her in my mind. I remember all of Jennie. I remember her bright blue eyes, her thick red hair, her soft tight skin.

I remember the way she touched me. When Jennie touched me, I laughed. When she touched me, I cried. Her touch made me real.

I touched Rachel that way yesterday and she bit me. Rachel says we are one, but she cannot even admit she saw a jumper. How can she see me? If she can't even see me, how can I let her be me?

I will never forget Jennie. I will remember her today and every day.

I will remember them all. I remember Rafe, Wiffle, and Kirsten. I remember Hans, Effie, Weggie, and Rikki. I remember Crash and Flicker, Winston and The Elf.

He builds every face in his mind's eye, just as he rebuilt his own. He spends the better part of the morning remembering the events that made each of these people special to him, until his stomach begins to churn and rumble. Then he sits up on the clean sheets Rachel gave him, cursing her name.

Damn you, Rachel! Why must I need you? Why can't I do it without you? Why must I numb myself to be in your world? Why do I need your damn relatives? Why do I need your damn body? Why do I put myself through this shit every time I'm with you?

Wyatt forces a laugh and gets out of bed. He knows that Rachel will not come calling today. Their lovemaking will contain her for at least two days, maybe three. He wonders if she is still brooding or if that stops the moment he is out of sight. He knows she will have forgotten about her anger by the time he sees her again.

Opening the dirty metal door on the dented kitchen cupboard, he reaches for a large tin of dried food, begins fumbling with the hasp. There are small abrasions all along the ridges, where hungry rats have gnawed it unsuccessfully. He wonders how they know it contains food.

Staring at the dingy red building across the narrow street, he can make out shadowy figures moving behind three of the windows. He tries to remember who they are but cannot. He had once spent two days memorizing every face in every apartment in his own building and in that one. Within a week, ten of them had changed.

What if everyone else just melted away in the night? What if we are all just waiting to disappear into our sheets? What if everyone was too scared to admit it, too dumb to talk about it, too far gone to do anything about it? What if that's all there is to it?

The thought leaves him shivering, yet comforted at the same time. Then he remembers the nights he spent with

Jennie, waking up before her to reassemble melted digits and limbs. It was the only thing about himself he had not shared with her.

She never melted. Neither did any of the others before her. Back then the changes were small. They only happened once or twice every few weeks. Now it's almost every night. I don't think Jennie just melted away. I don't think they all melted away.

He opens the tin and shakes some of the small beige flakes into a red ceramic bowl. He inspects the tap water to make sure it is running clear before thrusting the bowl beneath it. A few slow stirs with a spoon and the flakes begin to swell into a soft gray tasteless mush than will sustain him for most of the day. Wyatt keeps his mind occupied as he scoops the stuff into his new mouth. He tries not to let the disgusting texture keep him from swallowing.

Rachel would probably like it if he showed up at her place.

Not yet. Maybe not ever.

Something nags at the back of his mind. Something trivial, yet somehow important. He shuts his eyes as he chews the last spoon of mush. The image of a plastic card appears. Absently he reaches for his shirt pocket. It is empty and he remembers the pushy face on the morning train, picking its silver teeth and telling him personal truths. That card might have been a ticket to the Heartland, but he never even looked at it. It went into the recycler with the old clothes. Nothing for it now. Wyatt curses softly and opens his eyes. He leaves the dirty utensils in the sink and wonders what to do with the day.

The summer heat has abated slightly. He feels the need to get out, dresses in haste. He slips on the new silk holster. The wand disappears beneath his left armpit when he adds the vest. It gives him great comfort. On the street in front of the tenement he notices a faint cluster of darker half-moons and small circles forming a larger circular pattern. He has stepped across it nearly every morning since he can remember. Could it be . . .

He begins retracing his steps from the night before. The streets are sparsely populated this morning. He passes carts and stands that form the makeshift market on the corner. Wyatt hears customers haggling with the vendors. He moves to the middle of the street.

Blocks later, he finds himself coming to a major intersection in the web of streets. He stops at a tall fence around a two-story brick building with narrow windows and a small yard filled with climbing apparatus. The children are all inside now, studying in their classrooms, learning discipline, respect, fear. He reads the maroon sign over the door and makes the words with his lips, remembering the school-house, even though he has not been this way in years. Trembling, he watches forty or fifty children march two abreast, surrounded by six supervisory adults. He knows he marched just like that once. Why can't he remember?

Wyatt is still working his mouth without speaking when the two civil guards drop down from the overcast sky on either side of him.

"What we got here?" one asks the other.

"Looks like a perv to me."

"What?" Wyatt demands angrily. They have maneuvered him against the fence with nowhere to go. They obviously do not notice the wand in its concealing holster.

"My friend says you a perv, bright eyes. What you say to that?"

"I'm a sweeper," Wyatt growls back. "I'm no damn perv."

"A sweeper, huh? You know the drill. Gimme your fingers."

The civil guard opens a compartment in the left forearm of his gray ceramic armor. He expects Wyatt to press the fingers of his right hand over the five black pads.

Oh shit. I changed them yesterday. No, it was my left.

"Come on, do it," the other civil guard snaps, prodding Wyatt with a long barrel.

Reluctantly Wyatt presses the soft round pads as the first civil guard grasps his wrist, holding his hand in place for five seconds.

"Hey, he is a sweeper. Sweeper Four, come yesterday. How you get from Sweeper One to Sweeper Four in a day, huh?"

"What sector?" the other civil guard asks. There is an eagerness in his voice.

"Sixteen."

"Hey, that's Curtis Void's center. What you do, boy? Bend over on old Curtis' desk for a quick poke or something?"

Both civil guards laugh.

"Hey, get this," the first civil guard says with amazement, staring at his wrist prompter. "No priors and he's keeping Curtis' cousin Rachel warm. He's a poker, not a pokee!"

The second civil guard gives Wyatt a good-natured slap across the shoulders. "Hey, the kid's a mover."

The first civil guard winks. "So, what you doing here anyway?"

"I went to school here," Wyatt says. "I was trying to remember."

The two guards exchange glances.

"Go see Rachel, boy. Never mind remember."

Wyatt watches them lift off. They rise above the sixth story of the nearest tenement, disappearing behind the

41

rooftop. He has two priors. Both D&D—drunk and disorderly. That makes him a felon. They could have disappeared him for loitering here. He shakes his head, looks around, hurries off. *Could they have missed my record?*

Disoriented, he jogs out of the residential sector, crossing into an industrial one before he realizes he has gone the wrong way. Long low yellow buildings without windows clustered around a smaller block of pubs, betting parlors, and brothels remind him of some of his lesser day jobs. He turns sharply back toward Sector Fourteen, lest another pair of civil guards spot him doubling back and challenge him anew. He does not feel like pressing his luck today.

Two blocks later, he notices another pattern in the street like the one outside his tenement. He pauses to inspect it. He finds six more over the next four blocks, before he is standing nervously over the spot where the jumper landed just beyond the cafe the night before. It is exactly the same as the others, only smaller. Dark blotches and half-moons in a circle.

He looks up to meet the eyes of someone watching him from an umbrella-covered table at the cafe. There is something familiar about the chewing face. Cautiously Wyatt crosses the street, walks past the pair of fragrant cedar sentries in their gaily painted ceramic pots.

It is the pushy face from the train grinning broadly at him.

"Counting jumpers, boy?"

"Something like that."

"You lose a friend last night?"

"What are you doing here?"

"Having breakfast." The face smiles and waves an arm at the cane chair opposite him. "I told you we'd meet again, boy. You have no idea how lucky you are."

"Don't start that shit again," Wyatt says.

"How would you like to spend the afternoon in the Heartland?"

"Doing what?"

"Doing what you dream about doing, boy. Getting out of here, getting real, getting mean, getting rich, getting yours while you can."

Wyatt sits down slowly. The waiter rushes over to present him with a steaming cup of coffee and a small pitcher of cream.

"Get my friend an order of eggs with potatoes," the face says. "Hollandaise sauce on the side, toasted oregano bread, fresh squeezed citrus juice."

The waiter hurriedly disappears back into the open doorway.

"What's in it for you, swami?" Wyatt asks.

The man grins, flashing his silver teeth. "Like I told you on the train, it's part of my religion."

"Right. What else?"

"I need someone I can depend on to watch my back."

CHAPTER 6

"Ever been this far west?" the man asks.

The question is a subtle weapon. Wyatt sees it in the man's laughing blue eyes. He winces as a sharp pain suddenly lances across the left side of his head, branches out like the veining in a leaf, sizzles like a lightning bolt across his face, shoots up to the top of his head. He snaps his head back, squints involuntarily. The man grins at him—Wyatt knows for certain that his knee-jerk reaction was anticipated. He glares helplessly back, says nothing, taking comfort in the nearness of the wand below his left armpit.

Towers of mirrored steel ablaze with shafts of reflected sunlight sail past the transparent tube at fifteen-second intervals as the train hurtles closer and closer to the Heartland. Clusters of ornate trees form a rich green canopy below them, filling in the spaces between the towers; the cloudless blue sky is alive with birds. He cannot recall seeing so many birds or trees at once. The sight of them is unnerving.

"The memory escapes me," Wyatt says as amicably as he can. He does not wish the other to enjoy or even see his pain. His voice is a low growl.

The man laughs loudly, slaps his knee. "Damn, I like you, boy."

"So what do you know that I don't, Victor?" Wyatt says as the pain subsides.

The guards at the transfer station had called him Mr. Crist. The station master simply called him Victor, as if

44

they were old friends, or at least family. Everyone made a fuss or kept a respectful distance. Everyone was alert. Victor wasn't lying about one thing—he was an important man, at least in the eyes of the station crew and the civil guards.

"A lot, Wyatt. And you'd best not forget it."

It was Wyatt's turn to laugh. "So what are you afraid of, Victor? You think I might get a little crazy, bite you on the shinbone or something?"

"I think you might get a lot crazy and shit it all away for both of us, until you get a solid handle on it, boy. How good are you with that wand you wear like a lover's token?"

"I hit what I aim at."

"Well that's the idea, isn't it?"

"You afraid I'm going to point it at you?"

"If you're half as quick as I hope you are, you'll be pointing it at anyone you think might mean me ill, boy. And if you're not, we'll both be well past caring soon enough."

"You putting your life in my hands, are you?"

"Let's look at it like this. I've got your balls in my hand and you've got mine. Now we've got to convince each other that we're neither one of us going to squeeze or rip. Then we've got to convince ourselves that it's really in our own best interest not to."

Wyatt squints as a shaft of sunlight washes across his face. The train comes to a smooth stop at the next station. A face ripples across the door of their compartment, surveys them, and moves on. Victor Crist looks up at the face, winks at Wyatt, smiles for no particular reason. The train eases into a quick start. Soon the towers are sailing past again, only this time there are wide open spaces between them. The trees are smaller, ornate, defining walking paths. Moments later, all of it is gone; a choppy blue panorama takes its place, rolling on for miles. Wyatt turns to stare across the lake, not believing what he is seeing.

Another image replaces the windswept surface. Effie takes a long swig on his ale and then wipes the foam off his dark face. *You ever been swimmin'?* he asks Wyatt with a grin. Wyatt knows this is meant as the beginning of a love story, but he has no idea what Effie means. *Don't think so,* he admits. *Don't think so?* Effie repeats and laughs. *Either you have or you haven't. Which is it?* Wyatt turns an angry face at his friend. *Well, that would depend on what swimming is, now wouldn't it?* Effie takes another long swig on the ale and shakes his head. *Damn, Wyatt, you really live around here all your life?* For no particular reason, Wyatt begins to tremble. He wants to shout at Effie. He wants to grab his friend by the vest and shake. But he manages to control himself. He knows his reaction has nothing whatever to do with Effie and he will not punish his friend for his own madness. *What's swimming?* he whispers. *Swimming is moving through water—lots of it. It's fun. Almost as good as sex. Great with it.* Wyatt just stares at Effie, wondering where, besides the reservoir, one would find lots of water.

"We're here," Victor Crist announces.

Wyatt blinks and turns away from the tube. The lake is gone, the sun is directly overhead. Everything should be bathed in white light, with tiny black shadows huddling under everyone's feet. Vibrant blue sky has gone pale. For some reason he cannot focus his eyes on whatever lies beyond the tube.

"What is it?" he asks. The words are gasped, his mouth is as dry as sawdust.

"The Heartland, boy. It's the Heartland."

"It's inside another tube?" Wyatt asks, looking at the distortions of the midday sun on the smooth curved surface.

"It's inside a dome, boy. Nice and cozy-safe from all the bad shit that can make you old, make you sick, make you crazy, make you dead because you're too stupid and too far gone to know any better. It's the place where dreams come true for the strong, where nightmares are born for the weak. Welcome to paradise."

Victor stands up as the door to their compartment draws open by itself.

"Last stop. Everybody out," Victor says, smiling at Wyatt.

Like a sleepwalker, Wyatt rises to his feet. He steps slowly into the corridor, as if the air had become dense, resistant, just in time to watch the last of the other passengers disembarking. They are all well-dressed men in their thirties, moving with a lively gait. On the platform, a few dozen men eye one another quickly and carefully. All make for the exit singly or in pairs. The hovering civil guards here wear green ceramic body armor, and carry stunted long barrels. They seem more alert and humorless than the ones in the city. Wyatt senses they're making sure that no one who does not belong here gets past them.

"Welcome back, Mr. Crist," one of them says loudly.

"Good to see you, Charlie."

"Your personal transport is at bay eleven."

"Thanks, Charlie."

Wyatt follows Victor closely, like a young dog, feeling hard eyes boring into his back. Together they pass through the open gateway onto a wide concourse that opens into smaller private compartments, shielded from one another by black plastic walls twice the height of a man. Victor leads him to a small iris gateway that opens as they draw near. Unseen insects are singing in the tall grass beyond. Wyatt stops to listen.

"You awake, boy?" Victor asks.

"Yeah."

"You kinda faded out on me over the lake."

Wyatt says nothing as Victor stares into his eyes.

"You better be awake, boy, or we're going to have one short bumpy ride."

The personal transport is shiny reflective silver, with curved sides that mirror two rubber men on the platform. It hovers above the pavement silently, four doors open upward like the wings of a dragonfly. It seats four, two abreast, with plush contoured seats and restraining harnesses. Victor points at the rear seat, Wyatt climbs in.

The doors shut with a comforting click as the soft hum of interior climate control replaces the eerie sounds of chirping insects. They sit and watch the other vehicles leave their private bays in twos and threes, making off into the lush green beyond. For twenty seconds, violet lights outline the entire interior of the vehicle, while another hum seems to pass through every part of Wyatt.

"What was that?" he asks.

"Bioscan and filter," Victor replies. "Can't let any organic nasties into the Heartland, you know."

A panel filled with glowing red, amber, and blue lines, and points of green and orange light, flickers in front of Victor, who studies it with great care. When the last one is gone, Victor guides the craft into the open, keeps it hovering about ten feet above the ground.

They glide forward, banking left, cutting a smooth arc into the air above the tree line. Around them, Wyatt counts seven other craft disappearing in different directions. Their transport suddenly rolls hard to the right just as another craft shoots past them, nearly sending them careening into the treetops. Victor compensates quickly. He cuts back to the left, accelerates below the other craft, gaining steadily on it. The first craft veers sharply right, but Victor anticipates the move, rising directly beneath them. The other craft is spinning end-over-end through the air. Victor slows, loops smoothly up and over, coming down just behind them just as the other driver regains control.

Wyatt is certain they will crash, but the other transport bounces wildly before the two come into physical contact. Once again, Victor anticipates the recovery point. He makes for the top of the vehicle, driving it downward into the foliage, breaking off the chase as the other driver scurries downward, weaving and darting between the trees.

"You all right?" Victor demands. His eyes are wild, his face aglow, his silver teeth glint in the sunlight.

"Yeah, great. What the hell are you doing?"

"Celebrating life, boy. Only the strong survive."

Once again Victor accelerates, soaring high above the trees, circling like a hawk, one eye on the flickering panel, the other on the foliage below. He rolls the vehicle back on its side as a shaft of red light slices soundlessly past them. It strikes the dome above with a whine, and bounces downward, once again narrowly missing them. The second vehicle breaks through the tree cover, making directly for them. Wyatt stares at the squat tubular weapon mounted on the roof that was not there moments before.

"You got one of those?" he asks.

"No—they're illegal. I've got something better."

A silver dish grows on the nose of the transport, catching the next shot, bouncing it back the way it came. The other vehicle plunges low, breaking off its assault as an elm below them shudders and drops one of its stout branches. Victor accelerates head-on toward the other craft. The dish disappears before he catches the second craft in mid-turn and strikes it broadside. Once again, there is no physical contact. Both transports bounce away from one another, only Victor maintains control while the other tumbles over and over until Victor strikes it broadside again, driving it down into a clearing, where it bounces off the ground. Shrubs bend flat and small rocks fly off in all directions. The other driver is still struggling to regain control when Victor strikes him on the roof, forcing him into a skid that sends him spinning just above the ground until the transport becomes wedged upside-down between a pair of oaks.

Victor lands in the clearing about ten yards away. The transport's doors fly open at once. Wyatt and Victor unsnap their harnesses and jump out on the left side together.

"Finish it," Victor shouts to Wyatt.

The doors pop open in the other vehicle, two men tumble out onto the ground. One is still ensnared in part of his restraining harness, while the second scrambles quickly to his feet, reaching into his vest as he orientates himself.

Wyatt presses the stud on the wand before he is even aware he has removed it from its holster. The purple arc undulates as it reaches across the field, incinerating the standing man just as he draws his own weapon. A smoldering blackened carcass collapses into a heap.

"Now the other one!" Victor screams.

The second man is on his knees, trying unsuccessfully to rise. Wyatt hesitates.

"Shit," Victor says, drawing his own weapon.

A red-orange ball flies from the muzzle, engulfing the second man in a heartbeat. He erupts in a blinding pink flash, leaving only a wand, a belt buckle, and a clutch of brass buttons to fall upon the charred ground.

"Rule one, don't think," Victor snaps. "Just because he's helpless now, doesn't mean he will be later. Rule two, once you commit, you follow through."

Wyatt stares into Victor's wild features, swallows hard, says nothing.

Victor holsters his own weapon, pulls back his shirt cuff, presses a stud on his wristband. "Downer in Sector Seven, request cleanup."

Turning back to Wyatt, he smiles benignly. "All in all, not bad for your first outing. Let's go. I'm hungry."

CHAPTER 7

The women barely look up when Wyatt and Victor walk past the large open room. Wyatt notices that from the back they all look the same—petite, with shoulder-length blond hair, wearing red and purple silk saris, golden bangles at their wrists and ankles. In front of them is a large screen that resembles an entry into another room; only the wide picture windows looking onto the lake on either side betray the illusion. They sit on the edges of identical red leather ottomans, with their legs crossed, their elbows resting easily on their thighs. Deep red Oriental carpets accentuate their pale white skin. He sees three, but there may be more. They all look young, but it is hard to tell from the back, impossible to tell with Heartlanders as a rule.

On the screen, another young woman in her early twenties is discussing the hormonal cause of wrinkles. Her smooth skin has a yellow hue, her dark almond-shaped eyes sparkle when she speaks. Her straight black hair hangs down her back. She addresses someone unseen in a voice full of earnest authority. She is larger than life, another defect in the illusion of her presence. A second young woman appears on the screen to ask a question. Her hair is red and her face is covered with delicate freckles. There is an eagerness in her voice that belies the banality of the topic. One of the young women seated before the screen answers her. The first woman reappears, all smiles. She acknowledges the given answer and begins to elaborate on it.

Without a word of greeting to the women, Victor ushers

Wyatt into another room overlooking the lake. Stone piers
define the curved windows, a large stone fireplace domi-
nates the room. Victor had called the building a house. It
was big enough to be a school, or maybe a small workshop.
Monumental stone columns, a series of low sloping roofs,
large dark wooden decks make it look more than real. In the
distance, Wyatt sees several more of these palatial dwellings
dotting the curved tree-lined lakeshore at regular intervals.
Rachel was right. There was plenty in the Heartland.

Victor turns, stares hard at Wyatt.

"That was my wife and daughters. Key word here is *my*.
You look. You don't touch—unless I give one of them to
you. Are we absolutely clear on that point?"

Wyatt shakes his head in disbelief. "They're too fragile
for me, Victor. I really don't want to touch. So please don't
make me a gift of something I can't use."

Victor stands back and laughs. "Sit down," he says, motioning vaguely at the three comfortable-looking black
leather chairs that face the desk.

Wyatt selects the one that is closest to the wall.

Victor leans back against the desk, sighs, stares past
Wyatt at the calm surface of the lake. "How far did you get
in school?" he asks Wyatt.

"All the way. No trouble from me."

"I'll bet. What did you study?"

"The three m's—math, music appreciation, and machine
repair."

"Can you read and write?"

"I read. Don't have much need to write."

"You'll need to study a bit before I take you on. Can't
have you misunderstanding something, or drawing a lot of
attention to yourself. For a bright boy like you, studying
shouldn't be a hardship. That is, if you can spare some of

53

your valuable time from your present research on jumpers."

Wyatt feels his neck reddening. He glowers at Victor.

"Don't be so touchy, boy. Somebody will goad you into doing something rash, and that will be that. You'll reach for that wand at an inappropriate time, you'll get fried faster than the last drossie you dropped. Look, I know you're just trying to remember. That's what it's all about, isn't it? Memory is the key to the Heartland, boy. I'm giving you the keys to your memory. Part of the process is to get you cleaned up a bit—polished. I can't have you resenting the neighbors because they live here. I can't have you not knowing which fork to use. When someone says something that doesn't involve your immediate needs, I need you to understand what and why they said it. Where do you live?"

"Sector Nine."

Victor scowls. "What do you do for work?"

"I'm a sweeper," Wyatt answers, with just a little pride.

"Yeah? A sweeper what?"

"Four."

"Marksman—good. You make what—a thousand credits a sweep?"

"Something like that."

"How'd you like to make a thousand a day?"

"Shooting who?"

"Whoever gets in my way—our way."

"Not much different from being a sweeper—just a little more personal."

"You got it. That's what I like. For now, I'll pick up your room and board. Give you a small taste of why you're doing it. Then, when you're ready, you get the credits, as well. That'll be a little incentive for you to get ready fast."

"What's the catch?"

"There isn't any. You just study hard, get it right, show

me you want to learn. Forget your fears about becoming a drossie. I own a little real estate in the city. I've got a vacancy in Sector Thirty-Two. You got anything worth salvaging back at your place?"

Wyatt tries to remember what he has collected. He thinks of all the presents Rachel has given him. Sheets, soap, antiseptic, the clock, his clothes. He is wearing the clothes. There is nothing else worth having or remembering. "Nothing I can't live without."

"Good. I'll take care of everything. Anna will take you back to the train after dinner. You listen carefully to what she tells you. And remember . . ."

"Yeah, I remember—look, don't touch. They're yours. All of them."

Victor smiles, looks back at the lake, waves toward the door.

Dinner is served by a trio of female servants. Others come and go while they eat. Victor calls each by their first name. The three women dine with them. Apart from the color of their eyes, and certain small personal gestures, they could be the same woman. They watch Wyatt with amusement, doting on Victor's every pronouncement. After dinner, Victor beckons one of them to accompany him. She rises demurely like a cloud, floats to her father's side.

Her name is Anastasia; her eyes are as green as emeralds. Her face is almost expressionless, her pink lips seem pinched below her small upturned nose. She walks with her arm linked to Victor's, keeps looking back at her father's face. Unclasping her arm, she gestures toward the fleet of vehicles garaged beside the house and leads Wyatt to one of them.

With his first taste of roast lamb, basmati rice, fresh mint sauce still lingering on his lips, Wyatt climbs into the small silver two-seater beside her.

Her golden teeth flash a smile at her father before the doors close. She barely seems to notice Wyatt, who finds her obnoxious.

They ride in silence, save for the occasional tinkling of the bells at Anastasia's wrists and ankles. Wyatt scans the sky nervously for other drivers.

"What are you doing?" Anastasia demands.

"Watching for . . ." He does not know what to call them.

"No one is going to challenge us. Just relax."

Wyatt sighs, peering through the window at the perfect countryside unfolding below them. Rolling hills, small forests, babbling streams seem to simply drift past.

It is Anna who eventually breaks the silence. "Are you Daddy's new watchdog?"

"Something like that."

"Good. He needs protection."

"What happened to the last watchdog?"

"He got careless. Someone shot him."

"How many have there been?"

"You need to learn etiquette. One doesn't talk about such things."

"Yeah?"

"Do you have a screen at home?"

"No."

"Have you ever worked one?"

"No."

"Where did he find you?"

"On the train."

The conversation ends until the smooth sides of the dome suddenly drop down in front of them. Anna sets the transport into one of the parking bays beside the station.

"Listen. It's easy. Push the red button at the bottom.

The one marked *On.* Push it twice. Then just follow the instructions on the side of the screen. Daddy says you can read. I'll send you your lessons. Any questions?"

"Where am I going?"

"Didn't Daddy tell you?"

"Sector Thirty-Two."

"Take the south chute to number eight. Security will direct you from there."

The door on his side pops open and he climbs out. He looks back in time to see Anna pout, hear her bells tinkle one last time, dodge the dragonfly wing door as it snaps shut. The transport soars back above the tree line before he can walk away. It nearly knocks him down.

Don't touch them? Hell, don't shoot them would be better advice.

The sun is sinking low as the train hurtles back into the city. The mirrored towers that zip by at fifteen-second intervals are glowing orange. Wyatt stares into space, counting the stations.

So you really never been swimming before, Effie says good-naturedly. Wyatt orders another ale, shakes his head. Jennie leans over the bar and takes a few minutes to join in the conversation. Her eyes meet his. Wyatt swims in them. *I'll take you, Wyatt,* she says. *I know a few swimming holes just past the city where the civil guards will leave you alone for a case of ale or a quick tumble.* Wyatt blushes. Effie laughs, tells his story about soft black skin, cool clear water, the chirping frog chorus that sang love songs deep into the night while wavelets lapped at the shore.

Wyatt shakes his head, scrambles for the compartment door. He is not sure how he knows, but this is the Sector Thirty-Two Station. The transport chute sucks him down the street, around the corner, into the small lobby of a silver tower surrounded by trees. He is cringing, with his eyes clamped shut, in the lobby of his new flat. Real rosewood panels soar up in graceful curved shapes in front of him.

A flat-faced woman in her early thirties with curly black hair and angry brown eyes stares at him. She is a head taller than he is, displaying a wand upon her hip. "You Wyatt Weston?" she demands.

"Yeah."

"You're on forty, number seven. Take the second lift." She hands him a black plastic card. "Use that on the lock."

"Thanks."

The lift is walled with mirrors. In the reflection, he sees Jennie smiling at Effie's story. *I got Saturday off, Wyatt. We'll go swimming then*, she says, *just you and me. I'll give you a love story so good it'll make Effie's black face blush.* Her smile is mischievous, her smell intoxicating; she caresses the side of his face. By Friday, nobody could remember Jennie. Nobody but Wyatt. The tears are streaming down his cheeks when he uses the card to let himself into his new apartment. A large picture window looks westward. On the rim of the horizon he can just make out the top of the distant Heartland dome, crowned with spiked rays of orange sunlight.

CHAPTER 8

The sun is setting just above the dome on the western horizon; for a moment it looks to Wyatt as if the sun is really a figure-eight—infinity turned upon its head, the Heartland. Before this moment, the metaphor would have been wasted upon him. Wyatt squints at it from the balcony of his new apartment, feels a hot breeze blowing from the south. Only a few weak clouds, barely orange smears against the fading blue, cross the shimmering horizon. His head is throbbing from days without number spent interacting with the screen.

Mathematics—not so bad once you get the logic. Literature— the stuff nightmares are made of. Now history—how the hell can anyone remember all of it, and what difference does any of it make anyway? If it's not Caesar, it's Cyrus, Alexander, Genghis Khan, Napoleon, or Hitler. Meanwhile, somebody else designs a new collar, rifles a hollow metal cylinder, stares at the stars through a tube, retunes a piano, plays with chalk on a slateboard.

Wyatt holds his throbbing head. Anastasia seems to know just how much he can absorb at one sitting, always making a point of overdoing it. He must answer the anonymous questions she poses on the screen to her satisfaction, or the lesson will repeat itself. When he asks for clarification, she ignores him. When he tries to turn away, the volume increases. He spends his evenings thinking of ways to torture her.

Wyatt is aware that the air is denser here outside the

Heartland. It has a dirty taste he never noticed before. Now he cannot forget it. He leans over the balcony rail, drinks deeply of it anyway, listening to the hum of the climate controls behind him. The evening is pleasantly warm and dry. The civil guard drift by in twos and threes with little to do.

He has not been melting in the night since he moved into the new apartment.

Could it be something in that foul-tasting air? Something the purple lights in the lobby destroy? Maybe I had some sort of disease.

"Mr. Weston?" another disembodied voice asks from the living room.

"Yes."

"You have a guest."

"It's about time."

The voice cuts out. It was the flat-faced female security guard. Her tone is courteous and respectful. He wonders what she thinks he is. He wonders what he has agreed to become. In the hall, Wyatt can just hear the whoosh of the lift doors opening.

Expecting to see Victor Crist, Wyatt feels his moods swinging wildly, as he cannot decide if this new life is a boon or a curse. He listens expectantly but the thick carpet muffles the approaching footfalls. He answers the knock expectantly.

"Rachel!"

Her arms enwrap him like a vise as they press their lips together. She seems to be a thing of living fire, at once as firm as steel, yet yielding like the surface of the reservoir. He feels her body tremble. His answers with a tremble of its own. He feels her breasts pressing against his new silk shirt. He caresses her backside until she pulls away from him.

"You were expecting someone else, weren't you?"

"How did you find me?"

"Were you trying to hide from me, Wyatt? It's been over a week. Did you think I'd just forget you? Is that what you wanted? You leave without a word. You don't call. I thought I'd never see you again. I had to call my cousin to even find out your last name. I was lucky to find your new listing. Why didn't you call me?"

"I haven't learned how to use the talkie yet," Wyatt admits. His cheeks flush red.

"What are you doing here?"

"Studying."

"I don't understand any of this."

He takes her arm and pulls her into the apartment, shutting the door softly behind her. "It's kind of hard to explain, Rachel. But things are going to be better for us."

"Us?"

"Yeah, us. Or do you want me to be a sweeper forever?"

Rachel glares at him. Then she sees the large screen behind him hanging from the ceiling, blocking the panoramic view to the west. "What are you doing with that?"

"Learning."

Rachel shakes her head. "Not you, Wyatt," she says. "You're not going to become one of them. Promise me that, Wyatt. You're going to stay yourself."

The words seem to have more than one meaning. He looks at her askance.

Does she even notice the new nose? The teeth I fixed?

He reads the emotional storm in her eyes, realizes that it mirrors his own, and grabs her again. She does not resist. He peels the cloth wrappings from her body while she tears the shirt off his back. Her legs are wrapped around his hips when he walks her across the room, presses her into the leather couch.

"I hate you, Wyatt!" Rachel screams again and again, as she rakes his back with her nails.

He bites into her neck; her thighs lurch hard against him.

Later, they sit in the marble tub together, Rachel's backside soft against his front while he examines the perfect teeth marks he has left upon her graceful neck. The pale skin has already begun to bruise. He kisses the spot, wonders if she can remove it as easily as he can rid himself of the burning gashes across his back.

"My cousin wants you for the sweep tomorrow, Wyatt. Will you be there?"

"Yeah."

"What about all this?"

"I'm not getting paid yet, just room and board."

"Paid for what?"

"I'm going to be a bodyguard."

"For who?"

"Some big shot I met on the train. I think I remind him of who he wants to be."

"What are you studying?"

"Everything, I guess. Did you learn about mathematics, literature, and history back in the Heartland?"

"Yes."

"Did it make a difference in your life?"

"I don't know. I don't think about any of it anymore. But I guess coming to grips with all of it helped make me who I am. It probably convinced me to leave."

"What do you mean?"

"It seemed to me that all that struggling was for something a lot more real than the Heartland, Wyatt. I never felt anything before I left there. Now I feel everything. The Heartland just seems like one big comfortable nightmare I'm trying to forget."

"I might want to try the Heartland someday, Rachel."

"I know."

"I can't reject something I don't know."

"What about me?"

"You better teach me to use the talkie."

Rachel starts to laugh at him, so he pushes her head under the water, holding it there. She does not struggle. Wyatt realizes how much he still needs her. Water streams off her face when he lets her back up, gasping for air. Wyatt buries his face between her breasts, begins blubbering like a baby.

CHAPTER 9

"Sweet Rachel, look at you," Louie says and whistles. He pushes a lock of his long thinning blond hair back away from his eyes.

"Hey, Louie," Wyatt answers and smiles. "You looking good. You get lucky or something last night?"

"As a matter of fact. But, tingle and all, I'm still wearing the same shirt. You decide to be Curtis' new partner or something?"

The big man takes a step backwards cocking his head, as if that will put Wyatt's new clothes into a clearer perspective. The lock of hair falls back across his forehead.

"Who's the lucky? Anyone I know?" Wyatt presses, suddenly feeling a bit awkward.

"Yeah—Frieda. She got tired waiting for you. I see her need so I tell Bart shove off, start talking about you and Rachel, then suddenly, suddenly. No offense, Wyatt."

"None taken."

"You better get going. Curtis is all hot. Said for me to get you in there soon as you show. No smile this time. No more Cousin Curtis. Just one fuzzy twitch under his nose after another. Not good, Wyatt. Not good at all."

"Consider me got," Wyatt quips.

He saunters toward the office with the black door.

Other heads turn in the large hall as the lower-grade sweepers suit up and check their wands' and long barrels' power supplies. Wyatt feels a tension in the air when he crosses the slick epoxy floor. His new shoes squeak against it as he walks.

In the office, Curtis is waiting just inside the door. He says nothing but his eyes widen, looking at Wyatt's silk shirt and linen pants. Behind him the clerk smirks at Wyatt, leaves her screen, rests her pointed chin in the palm of her right hand.

Wyatt stands still. With a cocked head and friendly smile, he touches his forehead in greeting.

"I pay you too much," Curtis mutters at last.

"Not by half," Wyatt answers. "Louie said you want me early."

"What's up with you and Rachel?" Curtis demands.

"It's called love—a wonderful thing. Ever try it?"

"Don't smart-mouth me, Wyatt. I can turn you into a drossie in a rat's fart. Know what I mean, pretty boy?"

Curtis' small mustache begins to dance, as he nervously puckers and repuckers his purple lips. He stares at Wyatt, who glares back.

"Rachel calls me the other day, wanting to know what happened to you," Curtis growls. "She says you don't live in Sector Nine anymore. Wants to know did I move you uptown. Wants to know did I disappear you. Wants to know your last name so she can look you up. Then she starts crying her pretty brown eyes red. So I say again, Wyatt, what's up? No more mouth. Just tell it to me sweet and straight."

"And I say again, Curtis, love. New digs. Only I never had a talkie before. There's nobody to show me how to use it. You know? Never needed one before. So there it sits— life's big mystery. Now I got somebody special to call. That's love."

"So why don't you just foot it over to say, *Hey Rachel, I*

got new digs but *I'm just too butt stupid to talk to the wall?*
That's love, Wyatt. *Try and find me, you silly uptown tart—*
that's rat shit. Know what I mean?"

"You call her today?" Wyatt demands.

Curtis says nothing, but the scowl on his small dark lips
shows no sign of fading. "Nice shirt, Wyatt, but not what
Rachel would buy for you. Who buys your shirts today?"
Curtis demands.

"I do."

"Not on what I pay you."

"Now you're there, Curtis. Long way around, for certain, for sure, but there."

Curtis' scowl shows signs of breaking. He exhales loudly,
turns to the dour-faced clerk who has been watching the
confrontation with delight. He motions angrily for her to
get back to work. She lifts her face from her hand, buries it
in the glow of the display panel.

"You here to sweep today or you just come to flaunt?"
Curtis asks at last.

"I come to work—just like always."

"Then you better suit up. And you better not forget what
I told you about Rachel—she's my mother's sister's favorite
daughter. You hurt her—you disappear with much pain,
many screams, pissing and crying like a baby, silk shirts or
synths. You disappear right along with your memory. You
got that?"

He pokes his finger into his little mustache, scratches
hard, walks away without waiting for Wyatt to reply.

Wyatt finds himself back on the ground crew. The sweep
is uneventful. He is careful to keep Curtis and his new
shooter in sight at all times. Rats, roaches, strays, drossies
flow like a muddy river down the gray streets into the
gaping doors of the recycling center, while he searches un-

enthusiastically in the shadows for holdouts.

Where do they all come from? he wonders absently.

Curtis' new shooter takes no interest in him, the other sweepers avoid him, Curtis does not want to see him again after the sweep.

Standing in one of the long lines of day workers next to the transport tube, he is not surprised to find his credit balance increased by only five hundred credits once again. Back to Sweeper One. Curtis is still angry. Wyatt decides this will be his last sweep.

He skips the ale house, making the long walk back uptown alone.

The electric smell lingers in the air. The afternoon heat makes his new clothes stick to him. He feels the sweat rolling down the back of his head. Peddlers and vendors are setting up their carts and portable stands at the intersections. Customers are gathering to buy food, clothes, trinkets, and contraband. Uptown cafes, shops, and service parlors are opening as well.

Everyone with someplace to go has gone there. Now that the end-sweep is sounded, they come out again. How many just decide enough's enough and don't go home before the sweep? How many say a tingle and a tattoo just won't do it anymore? How many drossies are really drossies, and how many are citizens? Is that what happened to you, Jennie? Did another tingle with me just not do it for you? Did you just have enough of all of it?

A warm breeze washes over him, he shuts his eyes.

Jennie is standing before him. It's late, the ale house is closing as she entwines her long pale arm in his, leans her head softly on his shoulder. She smells of spilled ale and fried bread. He kisses her neck and watches the soft red hair flutter in a passing wind gust. *I love you, Jennie. You make it all real for me,* he says to her. Her eyes glisten and she smiles. *I'm tired, Wyatt. Take me home and show me again why I keep drawing ale. Tomorrow we can go up to the park and ride around like Heartlanders on a gawk. Tomorrow we can tell each other how we make it better than this, make it last forever. Tomorrow we figure how to get uptown, all the way uptown. Just you and me, Wyatt. Just you and me.*

There is no way she would have given up, he decides. There is no way she would just let herself get swept.

Are you there, Jennie? Are you already in that dome? Did you just go on ahead? Did you want me to follow you? Did you figure Rachel would make her move and I'd follow you there? Is that why I'm doing this? Am I going to find you when I get there? Are you hanging around some face's house, looking too fragile to touch, waiting for me to run his sorry ass out of the air, fry him on the grass? Are you there, giving him a tingle, sending me dreams I'm too stupid to remember? Are you more than a memory, Jennie? Are you still here?

Hot tears are running down his cheeks, people he passes are staring at him. He wipes at his eyes and walks faster.

He is back in the horse drawn cart, clopping around the park. Jennie fits perfectly inside his rounded arm. He doesn't ever want it to end, but he's only got fifteen credits left. Dinner will cost him ten. He keeps looking back to the meter, making sure they don't end up hungry. Jennie has her eyes shut. They never make those plans. They never talk about reaching the Heartland together. They just ride, touching and smelling one another. Her smile is enough for him. He would kill for that smile. But he never has to. Now he kills for Curtis' twitching mustache, for Victor's celebration of life. Nobody smiles at him for nothing anymore.

Wyatt has walked fifteen blocks lost in memory. He looks around, sees another school. A dozen civil guards are hovering near it.

Looking for pervs? he wonders. *We just swept them up.* Then he realizes there must be more to it. He tries to remember. His earliest memories are scattered bits of half-glimpsed actions, jumbled dreams. A big hand slapping his face. A mouth full of ebony teeth and a cruel smile. A thin-faced young woman with long auburn hair, pale blue eyes that sparkle, delicate fingers that kept potted flowers. She was kind to him. A ride in a transport chute that still makes him cringe.

He is trembling, standing before the iron gates. He remembers the last time, begins walking quickly past. *School memories?* he wonders. He is gasping for breath; his heart sounds like a fist pounding against the inside of his chest, demanding to get out. His vision blurs, making people and buildings indistinct shadow forms, menacing and imprecise. *School memories,* he decides. He digs his nails into the palms of his hands, trying to force the memories into focus—trying to force them into chronological order. Two of the civil guards take notice of him, hover closer. It will not do for him to be questioned twice near two different schools. That would get him a conviction. Might even be enough to get him disappeared, especially with Curtis angry. Back to Sweeper One would not impress the civil guards either.

He crosses the street, stops squeezing his hands. He lets the memories slip back into the abyss of forgetfulness. His vision clears.

Two blocks later, he stops shaking. His palms have deep half-moon gouges that sting. He is thinking about Jennie again. *Would Curtis have disappeared her?* he wonders. *Would Curtis have disappeared Jennie because Rachel wanted a taste of the real?*

He cannot decide. There is no way of knowing. The torment is worse than the memories brought on by the school-house. Then he is standing at the edge of the park. A sea of green grass, a trio of trees, the foot and cart paths. Six couples are tossing a ball, another group of eight are clustered about a musician sitting on the low stone wall playing a guitar.

A horse cart saunters by with a pair of uptown lovers lost in each other's eyes.

Wyatt stands there gasping for breath, watching them draw closer. Sadly, he turns to watch them go. Another pair of hovering civil guards appear above the trees. He hurries back toward the drab safety of the city streets. For the next ten blocks, he sees nothing but citizens and buildings flashing by him as he makes for his new sanctuary in Sector Thirty-Two.

CHAPTER 10

Dawn floods the beige bedroom with pale yellow, leaving a diffuse outline of his body against the wall. Wyatt cautiously opens his eyes. At first he is elated to see and feel both of his arms. He wiggles his fingers gleefully. He laughs softly, remembering his last dream, in which he had been walking expectantly behind Jennie.

Then he remembers that he had been unsuccessful in his attempt to catch up with her, was never able to overtake her no matter how fast he went. He could not even draw her attention by waving, shouting, calling out her name. They had walked from the park to the Heartland, where she had simply walked through the acrylic dome as if it had no substance. For him, it had been an unyielding sheet of cool clear plastic. He stood there shouting her name over and over, watching her disappear behind the trees and bushes beyond his reach.

He stops laughing, raises himself to his elbows. But when he tries to sit up, he notices that both his legs are gone. He draws a deep breath, shuts his eyes. His heart is racing. It has been over a week since any part of him has dissolved in the night. Now he must remember his legs in vivid detail. Smooth white bones, tiny cell by tiny cell, wrapped with layers of sinew and muscle, veins and arteries to feed them, skin and hair to encase them. He adds to the previous muscle tone, to facilitate his walking—no more cramps after the long ones. He breathes deliberately as the agonizing process goes on and on. The lancing pain is followed by a tickling sensation. He balls both hands, squeezes hard lest he is tempted to scratch.

The sun is full in his eyes by the time he can feel his legs without pain. He sighs and wriggles his toes, then drops back down onto his back, shutting his eyes softly once again.

It's Friday morning. Jennie is in my dreams, leading me on to the Heartland. She has gone missing forty-one days now. I have remembered her each and every one of those days. I remember her blue eyes—brighter than the sun—her thick red hair and her soft white skin. I remember when she smelled of ale and cooking oil, when she smelled of sweat and love. I am real because I touched Jennie. I will never forget her. I will find her, if she is still here. I will find out what happened to her, if she isn't.

I will remember all of them. I will remember all of those gone missing. I will not forget my friends. I remember Rafe, Effie, Weggie, and Kirsten. I remember Crash and Flicker, Winston and The Elf. They are still real, so long as I remember them.

Wyatt pictures each of them, says their names aloud, remembers the events that made these people special to him—little things, like a laugh, a way of walking, a story they told, a look, or a spontaneous moment of shared realization. Afterwards, he rises carefully on his new legs, walks slowly toward the shower.

The meter says there is just enough water to wet down and rinse off again after he lathers, if he shuts the water off in-between. He sets the shower controls accordingly.

For breakfast, he has citrus juice, cinnamon-raisin toast with raspberry jam. Having good-tasting food on hand is still a novelty. He delights in every mouthful.

"I love watching you eat."

Wyatt wipes his mouth, looks up at Anastasia's smirking face, filling the screen. She has painted a deep red band across both eyelids and over the bridge of her nose. Another across her upper lip, and a third intersecting them from the top of her forehead, down the ridge of her nose to the small cleft in her chin. He sees her long nails are painted the same color, as she steps back from the screen. Behind her looms the blue placid surface of the lake. Either she is alone or the others have stepped away from the screen. He wonders if her mother and sister have made themselves up the same way. He watches her brush an imaginary crumb from her chest, remembers Victor making the same gesture on the day they first met on the train.

"So glad I have some special place in your life, Anna," he says dryly. "What's it to be today? History and geography? Etiquette or math?"

"No class today, Wyatt. Daddy wants you to meet him tomorrow afternoon at the Sector Thirty-Two Station at four o'clock. Just bring your wand. You're going to spend a few days with us, to acclimate, if you can. Daddy wants to see how close to ready you are. You should go see to your girlfriend today. She's a little insecure. Might do herself a serious injury, if you're gone too long. Tell her that you love her—that you'll be back for her and all that. She really needs to hear that kind of stuff, you know. That's important to some women."

The screen goes blank. Wyatt finds he has lost his taste for cinnamon-raisin toast with raspberry jam.

Someday I'm going to shoot that little witch.

He puts his plate and cup into the recycler, raises the screen into the ceiling, wondering how much of his lovemaking with Rachel Anastasia and the others watched. Then he wonders if Rachel was aware they were being watched, if she added something extra to the performances. He is unsure if he really wants to call Rachel, especially after Anastasia's taunting. Then he remembers Curtis' warning about disappearing him. Reluctantly he presses the wall stud and the light goes on.

"Rachel Void, Sector Twenty-Two."

"Wyatt?"

"You busy?"

"As a matter of fact, I am."

"I thought we might do some Shakespeare tonight."

"You mean see *Romeo and Juliet* at the Downtown Odeum?"

"Yeah."

"How sweet. You're taking your education seriously."

"A whole new world, Rachel. It's making me wonder where I was all the while."

"I haven't seen it in years. Pick me up at six. I've got a surprise for you."

The light goes off. It is just a blank wall again. Wyatt doesn't feel much like walking, so he goes out onto the balcony. The summer air is thick, hard to breathe, so he comes back inside at once. He pulls the screen down again, stares at the glossy gray surface. Organizing his thoughts, he presses the *On* button twice. He reads the menu carefully. He has never used the screen for anything other than his studies.

"Search," he announces. "Privately," he adds quickly.

"Name?"

"Wyatt Weston."

"Identity confirmed. Your privacy clearance is limited to the public domain."

Undaunted, he blurts out the words he cannot forget. "Jennie Height."

"No such reference."

Wyatt stops to think. "Sector Sixteen Pub and Canteen employee listing."

74

A white screen appears with two dozen names, addresses, and job titles printed across it, with color images of the faces that go with the names. Wyatt recognizes Frieda, two of the other barmaids, six of the bouncers—all those working after the biweekly sweeps. Pouring through the names, looking for anything resembling Jennie Height, he pauses at Jane Hanks. Sector Seven and a round dark face that looks nothing like Jennie.

"Previous employees," he says.

"Insufficient clearance."

"Sector Ten listings."

"List is too extensive to display. Please narrow parameters."

"Jennie Height."

"No such listing."

"Eight Twenty-Second Street listings."

A list of all those living in the building where Frieda and Jennie lived appears, along with the faces. Jennie is not there, either.

"Previous tenants."

"Insufficient clearance."

Wyatt sighs, grinds his teeth, peers into the hazy landscape beyond the balcony. "Heartland listings."

"Insufficient clearance."

Exasperated, he shuts the screen off, returns it to its pocket in the ceiling.

He paces the floor for an hour, thinking of something he might be able to ask the screen that might give him any clue. He can think of nothing. He pulls the screen down again, calls up *Romeo and Juliet*, text version. He spends as much time with the lexicon as he does with the text. The reading is arduous, but it is the fourth time he has read it, the story is growing on him. He is even starting to remember some of the strange words. When he is finished, he wonders if he and Jennie are as doomed as the title characters.

He leaves early to buy some roses for Rachel.

The thought of using the transport chute is too much for him. He walks the four blocks to the train. The heat is oppressive. His silk shirt is clinging to him by the time he reaches the station. Outside, the clean-up crew is loading three charred bodies onto the rack in the back of a glossy white recycling van. Wyatt notices a nearby civil guard retrieving a wand from the pavement.

Somebody just had themselves a short spree.

The dark splotch on the station wall must be all that is left of him. Two-white suited workers, anonymous behind their round helmets and silver faces, remove most of the stain with a thick hose, spraying a caustic blue powder onto it.

Blue erases black.

Another pair suck up the scattered blue fragments. In a few moments, all but a few traces of the event are gone. The hoses are wound back into their compartments, the sweepers climb back onto the van's running boards. One thumps the side twice. The van rolls slowly down the street. Horrified onlookers grow calm, continue on their way as the civil guards disperse above the street. The middle lane suddenly ramps downward to swallow the van.

Four more gone without a trace. Is that what happened to you, Jennie? Am I just chasing a dream and a memory? Am I just as numb as the rest of them? Do I just lose myself in the details so I can miss the whole picture? Am I blocking it all out in my own way? Am I just too stupid to adjust? Did you become a stat I won't accept?

The uptown and downtown trains arrive simultaneously.

The small crowd is drawn into the tubes like the blue powder into the hose. Wyatt climbs aboard with the rest, clutching his flowers.

Their fragrance seems to purify the compartment while the city flashes by. None of the faces around him show any sign of remembering the street spree. Wyatt smiles to himself.

He shuts his eyes, pictures Rachel. He feels her strong legs closing about him. He can taste the basil, smell her scent, hear her voice scolding, taunting, then adoring him. He thinks no more about Jennie as he counts the stops.

CHAPTER 11

The play is a major disappointment. There is no electricity between Romeo and Juliet. The lines are spoken like empty words, the characters are silly, their movements are exaggerated and stiff, the audience laughs at the death of the poetry, no one cares about love found or lost. Shakespeare has been swept. Even Rachel admits it stinks. But the event is not a total waste. Wyatt recognizes one of the actors. He waits for the theater to empty, then leads Rachel cautiously backstage.

Two civil guards block the entrance to the dressing rooms.

"What you want?" one demands of Wyatt.

"Pay my respects," Wyatt says with an easy smile.

"Who to?"

"Old friend."

"Name?"

"Rafe."

"Hey, Rafe," the vocal civil guard shouts at the closed curtain. "Got company."

"Yeah? Who?"

"Hey, Rafe!" Wyatt shouts. "It's Wyatt."

A moment later, a surprised face appears through the curtain with half its makeup removed. Red and black smears over chafed skin, it looks like something from a bad dream come to life, gawking at Wyatt. The slow glint of recognition appears in the blue eyes. The face smiles.

"Hey, you moving uptown, sweeper boy?" Rafe says, and they both laugh.

"Hey, yourself," Wyatt answers. "I thought you got disappeared."

"Only Shakespeare got disappeared," Rafe says. "But he's back again next night to get disappeared again. Like magic. I'm itinerant these days. Bringing culture to the grade seven and above masses. Making sure they don't want too much of it. Taking a quick look at the world while I'm at it. Good to see you, Wyatt. Who's your vivacious friend?"

"Rachel, meet Rafe, itinerant actor and drossie understudy."

Rafe is a head taller than Wyatt. He is lean and muscular, with thick black hair and thin black mustache. He smiles wide for Rachel.

"Stay close," Rafe says by way of invitation, "cast party tonight."

The party is held in the theater basement. It is much better than the play, as the actors act out their lives with conviction. Rafe tells many dramatic stories, and everyone laughs. Wyatt can see that most of the others have heard them before.

Rafe likes touching Rachel, who is flattered but gives him no encouragement. Wyatt watches everyone, listening to their rapid-fire dialogue, their shared laughter, their endless bickering. Rafe produces two bottles of very smooth white wine; manufactures, then discusses, their lineage; slowly fills each of the clean stainless steel goblets eagerly held out to him.

When Wyatt gets up to use the chem-toi, Rachel stays behind. For a moment, he considers leaving her here. She almost fits in with the others. Wyatt wants to get Rafe alone to talk seriously, but Rafe seems glued to Rachel and a blond actress who rests her head on his shoulders, watching

Wyatt with liquid green eyes.

"Civil guards gone," someone announces from the corridor. An older actress opens a foot locker, lifts a large tray, rummages through it. Then she hands out joysticks.

Someone else produces thick white candles and matches. The vague glare above them gives way to twenty pinpoints of pale fire, flickering and haloed, bunched like stars on the tables, the foot lockers, and the masonry projections.

Everyone lights up. Soon Wyatt hears buzzing insect voices all around him. He leans over and bites Rachel on the shoulder. She turns her head and bites him on the ear. He winces, pulls her close to him. She buries her face in his neck. He feels her volcanic breath enveloping him, arousing him.

"Hey, Wyatt," Rafe's face says with a leering smile.

"Hey, yourself."

"Lemme borrow Rachel for a while. Daisy will keep you smiling."

Blond face with dancing green whirlpools for eyes appears.

Rachel's arms coil about his midsection like a pair of pythons, saying she will never let go.

"You go make Daisy smile, Rafe," Wyatt says. "Then maybe we can talk."

Rafe is laughing.

"Rafe keeps everybody smiling," the actor says. He slips one arm around Daisy's waist. They disappear into the candlelight and smoke.

Wyatt hears a guitar, base, thumping hand drums. Then slow deliberate breath blown through a bamboo flute. A woman's reedy voice—sounds without words—makes his backbone feel like mush.

"What do you want from him?" Rachel whispers.

"Memories."

"You always want memories."

"Key to success and happiness."

"Yours, maybe."

"You taste especially good tonight," he says, changing the subject.

"For you, Wyatt. All for you."

Wyatt knows it is Rachel he is holding, but he feels Jennie. They are hugging playfully, then they pull away, walking together hand-in-hand beside the reservoir. It is May, a cool wind is blowing, her thick red hair flies behind her like a banner as she walks. Jennie is telling him about two rowdy patrons at the pub. She is laughing as she relates how the pair lose control. They eventually have to be subdued by the bouncers, who sedate them. *They came in like a storm and went out like a summer shower,* Jennie says. She cannot stop laughing. Wyatt has never seen her like this before. They hug again. Jennie is shaking. She cannot stop crying. Later that night they lay in bed, just holding one another. They do not make love. *That's all of us, Wyatt, coming in on the wind and disappearing on the street.* He cannot sleep, listens to her breathing. Nestled in his left arm, she falls asleep with a quiver. He knows that from that moment on he can never leave her. The hours creep by like roaches in the kitchen. He falls asleep just before dawn. In the morning she is gone and so is his right hand.

There is a musty smell in the basement when Wyatt awakens on the old sofa. Rachel is still asleep in his arms. He is relieved to discover nothing has melted away in the night. What little light there is comes through a pair of dusty curtains from the hall. He can make out several other round forms that look like sleeping people. Someone is snoring lightly. He puts his hand under Rachel's blouse, feels her firm hard back. She snuggles against him, opens her eyes when he runs his hand down over the small of her back.

"Not here, Wyatt. Let's go to my place," she says.

"Yeah, it's closer than mine." Looking around, Wyatt doesn't recognize anyone he knows.

In the theater, an old man with a broom is sweeping the floor. "You Wyatt?" he asks.

"Yeah."

"Rafe said give you this."

A gnarled trembling hand passes a folded piece of paper to him. Wyatt takes it, puts it into his vest pocket without reading it.

"Your memories?" Rachel asks.

"Maybe."

CHAPTER 12

Wyatt awakens with a start. Rachel is making a series of loud gasping snorts in her sleep. Her left arm is draped across his chest, covering three of the perfect pink teeth patterns she has left there. He feels them stinging, remembers Rachel's ferocity that morning. His sides are bruised where her legs were. He pushes her arm away gently so as not to waken her, gets up, staggers to the bathroom. Wyatt uses the toilet. He watches the water spin everything away, marvels at it. He sits on the edge of the marble tub, musters the concentration to remove the twenty or so bite marks from his chest and back, the deep red scratches on his thighs.

When they are all gone, he fills the sink with warm water, washes his face and hands. It is late afternoon; his head is still swimming from the joysticks the night before. He has no appetite. Looking into the hazy day outside, he is tempted to go back to sleep.

Rachel sleeps on. He considers suffocating her with one of the pillows. Then he goes to the balcony to breathe some unfiltered air. Outside it is as hot and dry as it looked, with no wind to move the stale air about. After sleeping in the climate control, this feels like drowning.

Twelve stories below, the small manicured garden before the tower is thriving. Wyatt watches with amazement as the automatic sprinklers rise from the ground, spray water on the shrubs and ornamental trees for a few minutes, then disappear back into the ground once again. A small dog squeezes between the black iron bars, scampers across the garden. He begins lapping at one of the puddles slowly seeping into the earth.

The familiar sizzle of a wand incinerates it almost at once. One of the security men emerges from the lobby to kick the small smoldering black mass that is left of the dog beneath the lush foliage. A moment later, a middle-aged woman appears at the fence, calling her dog by name. After a few minutes, she backs slowly away, her face a portrait of confusion and despair.

Wyatt has had enough fresh air, goes back inside.

He realizes that it is the second time he has slept beside Rachel, and nothing has melted away.

In the living room, he sits on a white leather chair, begins his silent litany.

It's Saturday afternoon. I feel like I'm about to disintegrate. I dreamed about the Heartland. I was living in Victor Crist's house all by myself. I was alone and everyone else in the Heartland was coming for me. My wand was on low charge, someone was about to open the door. I was paralyzed by my fear.

I found Rafe yesterday. But I never got to ask him about Jennie. If Rafe is alive and well, maybe she is, too. He left me a note. Must not forget to read it. I don't want to share it with Rachel. I don't want to share Jennie with Rachel.

Jennie has gone missing forty-two days now. Sometimes I dream about her, sometimes I think about her. I have remembered her on each one of those forty-two days. I will continue to remember her. I remember how she made me alive. I remember how she made me feel things. I remember how I learned to remember by just being with her. My life has continuity because I love Jennie. I will never forget her. I will find her, wherever she is. I will remember her every day until I do.

I will remember all of them. I will remember all those gone missing. I remember Effie, Weggie, and Kirsten. I remember

Crash, Winston, and The Elf. They are still real, so long as I re-member them.

"Wyatt, what are you doing?" Rachel asks.

He opens his eyes and looks at her. "I'm remembering," he says quietly.

"What are you remembering?"

"My friends. The ones who disappeared."

Rachel looks at him askance. "Why?" she asks.

"Because they are part of me. Without them, I am less than whole."

"You are a strange one, Wyatt. Do I make you whole?"

"Yes."

"If I disappear, will you remember me?"

"Don't talk like that, Rachel," Wyatt says. His voice cracks and she smiles.

"Will you?" she demands.

"Yes," he whispers.

"Good," she says. She turns, walking toward the bath-room.

"What time is it?" he calls after her.

"Three thirty-two, why?"

"Shit. I've got to go."

"What?"

"I've got to run. I'm supposed to meet Victor at four. I almost forgot."

Wyatt hears the water running in the tub and finds him-self wanting to join Rachel.

What if I just walked away from Victor? What if I just stayed here?

He realizes that Rachel does not want him here all the time. He pulls on his clothes as fast as he can, holsters his wand, makes for the tube to the lobby. He stops, turns around, walks back slowly toward the bathroom. Rachel is reclining in the tub, staring at the ceiling. The water is halfway up her legs, still rushing in. She does not look back at him.

"Rachel?"

"What?"

"What was the surprise you told me about on the talkie?"

She turns her head toward him and he sees that she is crying. "I'm pregnant."

Wyatt blinks his eyes, staring at her. It is not a word he has heard before. He does not understand. "So?" he says at last.

"You don't know what that means, do you?"

Blushing, Wyatt looks at his feet.

Rachel begins to laugh, a hideous cackling sound. "It means," she says languidly, "that we're going to have a child, unless I get rid of it. Do you want me to just get rid of it, Wyatt?"

Wyatt staggers against the wall, then slides down it.

"A . . . child . . . ?" he stammers.

"Yes, a baby. A little person. They cry a lot and need endless attention. They're totally helpless. At first, they're totally dependent on us. And then they grow up to be just like us. We make them sometimes when we make love. Scary, huh?"

He hears the sarcasm in her voice. "Is this a good thing, Rachel?" Wyatt asks expectantly.

Rachel begins laughing again. "What do you think?" she demands.

"I don't know, Rachel. I think it could be a good thing. I mean, if we do it right."

Rachel stops laughing. "That's why I love you, Wyatt. You always do what's right sooner or later, and you're so real about it. So either tell me you want to do this together with me or drown me now. I'm serious, Wyatt. No love play."

She is staring at him. Her big brown eyes seem to pierce burning holes right through his chest that he cannot repair with an act of will.

He touches her pink cheek with a trembling hand. She guides the hand down her throat, over her breast to her belly. He feels her taut skin, her navel, the bubbling water soaking his sleeve.

"That's where it is, Wyatt. That's where it's growing, bit by bit until it shows. It won't show for a few months yet. It's a little piece of you, a little piece of me."

Wyatt shuts his eyes, presses his forehead against hers.

"I love you, Rachel," he says.

He is still trembling when he boards the train to meet Victor Crist.

CHAPTER 13

"You're late," Victor snaps, "and you look half-dead. I don't think you quite grasp the nature of our arrangement yet, boy. I need you alert, on time, focused, avid. You have to want what I want, anticipate my needs, take care of business first. You can't do that if you're half-gone dreaming or still entwined about Rachel Void. You've got to be all here. Got that?"

"Yeah," Wyatt says. "I'll remember that."

The towers fly by outside the tube. Wyatt sinks back into the seat.

"Anna made this little tête-à-tête sound important," he adds.

"It is. The Committee is meeting. I'll need you there. First you need to be approved."

Wyatt's eyes widen but he says nothing.

"You'll be spending a few days at my house to get yourself ready. That should keep you out of trouble."

"Swell. What's the Committee?"

Victor flicks another imaginary crumb from his lapel, frowns. "We are the ones who control the Heartland: the city, the farms, everything, boy. We are those who have say. We are those who make the laws, see to it they are enforced. We are those who are allowed to live our lives to the fullest for that contribution."

"I thought you wanted me here. What's this about approval?"

"You have to convince the others that you belong here."

"What the hell does that mean?"

"It means you know when to smile and when to shoot. You know who to smile at, who to shoot. It means you know how to anticipate orders as well as follow them."

Wyatt's head begins to throb. Victor is leaning into his face, occasionally spraying him with saliva. The silver teeth look as if they are about to devour him. Wyatt leans away and wipes his cheek. He peers out the curved tube, sees the lake beyond the last of the towers. He begins trembling. His mind starts forming dream images.

"Stay alert," Victor snaps. "Never mind the fetal posturing. It's only a lake."

Wyatt's jaw becomes slack, his lower lip starts to tremble. "You know what's happening to me, don't you?" he gasps

"That's right, boy. More to the point, I know what you have to do with it."

An image of Effie and The Elf beckons him from a dream, but Victor's leering face breaks through the picture, turning it into a cluster of bean-shaped shards that scatter and dissolve against the beige compartment. "What's happening to me?" Wyatt whispers.

"You're running away from your fears, boy."

"I'm running?"

"You're taking refuge in your dreams!" Victor shouts. "Wake up! Stay awake!"

Windswept waves rippling across the deep blue water, like a tide of rats bound for the recycling center, seize hold of Wyatt's attention and he cannot avert his eyes.

Here's today, there's no tomorrow, he hears Winston's voice just beyond the tube, *yesterday's just a dream. Lose yourself in the maiden's arms, envelop her with all your charms, make sweet music with her scream.*

"Do I have to scream to get through to you?" Victor demands.

Wyatt draws his thighs up against his torso and begins hugging his knees. "I can hear you," he cries. "I can hear you."

Satisfied, Victor sits back against his seat, removes his silver toothpick holder from an inside jacket pocket, pops open the cap, draws out the pick.

It takes all of Wyatt's will to keep his eyes from shutting. He stares at Victor's expressionless face without blinking until the train stops. Victor stands up. Still trembling, Wyatt releases his legs to find they are too numb to move. He begins vigorously massaging the life back into them. He wobbles when he stands.

Victor laughs and pushes Wyatt out of the compartment before him.

Still staggering on the station platform, his legs turn to jelly when a group of twenty children is herded by four dour-faced adults into the tube. Two of the girls are sobbing and one of the boys is fighting to get back off. A sharp slap sends the boy flying back into the train. Wyatt feels himself falling.

Victor catches him, holding him upright by the armpits. "What's the matter, boy? Fresh out of insightful quips at the moment, are you?"

"I . . . that boy . . . those children . . ." Wyatt stammers.

"That's right. Some of us get thrown out of paradise at an early age, while others get to stay. You and me got the boot. We have to earn our passage back. Are you with me, Wyatt? Are you here enough to follow what I'm telling you?"

Wyatt is gasping for breath as the train reverses direction, heading back toward the city. He rotates on his heel to watch it disappear behind the tall firs. He does not answer Victor until the train is gone. "I come from the Heartland?" he says at last.

"Only those who were born here are allowed back in, sonny. Consider that your first lesson in legalities. Now do you think you can stand up on your own, or do I have to carry you back to the transport?"

Wyatt frees himself from Victor's grasp. "Did you . . . ?" Wyatt asks, still unable to complete his thoughts.

"Hell, I pissed all over myself," Victor says, erupting into a fit of laughter.

Wyatt looks down to make certain he has not done the same, sending Victor into a fresh spasm of laughter. He is soaked in his own sweat, but he has not lost control of his bladder. Victor slaps his thigh and laughs again.

The green armored civil guards greet Victor, who greets them back by name. They look sympathetically at Wyatt, who realizes that they have witnessed this scene again and again. They dare not laugh lest he become someone important. He smiles at the thought. He wonders how many watchdogs are lost on the way to joining The Committee.

The ride back to Victor's house is uneventful. The soothing hum of the bioscan brings an end to his trembling. He begins taking deep breaths.

"Who taught you to do that?" Victor demands.

"Do what?"

"Breathe."

The question is meaningless. Wyatt does not answer. Victor keeps the transport high above the trees. They do not speak again for the rest of the ride.

A group of young men awaits them at the house. Wyatt notices that two of these bear a striking resemblance to Victor. Both eye him with disdain. Victor tells him to wait while he goes off to speak with the pair. A servant wearing a silver and yellow uniform takes Wyatt to the guest wing, draws him a bath.

Wyatt sinks down into the hot water and shuts his eyes. Winston and The Elf seem to be staring at him from the other side of the tub. *What are you guys doing here?*

Winston removes the dark blue watch cap he always wears, holding it before him in a mock gesture of humility. His dirty blond hair still bears the mark of the cap's edge. The Elf just lets his head droop on his long thin neck until it is almost resting on his right shoulder. Both of them are grinning. *We just came back to congratulate you,* Winston says. *Yeah,* The Elf echoes, lifting his head again.

Congratulate me for what?

For making it here.

So what happened to you guys?

Both just grin at him as they slowly disappear.

CHAPTER 14

"I would have expected to see at least five tattoos," Anna says dryly.

Wyatt opens his eyes, looks up into the pale peach face with its pink cheeks, its little upturned nose, its pinched pouting lips, and its green eyes, liquid for Victor, iced jade for him. The tub water is still bubbling, hot, circulating, but he can tell by his wrinkled fingers that he has been soaking for a long time, lost in thought and memory.

"Sorry to disappoint, Princess," Wyatt says.

He knows she wants him embarrassed at his nakedness before her. He knows that she expects some sort of shame reaction, like closing his knees, or widening his eyes as he sits up. He knows that Victor's dictum, *they're mine, don't touch,* is all too familiar to her, that she will play it for all she is worth.

How many other poor hungry fools with fast reflexes, good eyes, struggling to maintain their memories, have lain here soaking before this silly twat, on their way to dying as they cover Victor Crist's back?

"More than you could imagine," she says, her small mouth breaking into a wide leer.

Wyatt sees the golden teeth flashing behind the smile.

"So what did you tell your chesty girlfriend-in-heat, Wyatt?" she adds. "That you were coming to the Heartland to make your fortune but you'd be back for her? You know she would rather die than come back here, don't you? You know she wasn't willing to play the loving daughter until she got auctioned off to the highest bidder among the old bulls and young studs in The Committee. Or do you know anything at all yet?"

Anastasia's bitterness seems to chill the bath water. Wyatt sits up and yanks the billowing terrycloth towel from the warmer.

"At least Rachel has her own teeth," he says quietly.

Anna flings her head back laughing, as if his response was even less than she had expected from a sweeper.

"What do you want, Anna? Did Victor send you here on some errand?" he asks as he dries his hair.

"As a matter of fact, he did. He wants me to find out if you can defend yourself without that little toy wand you take to bed with you. Meet me in the dojo in fifteen minutes. That should give you enough time to pick out some appropriate clothes, remember a few more of your loser friends, and set yourself up for a big fall."

"What's appropriate?"

"Comfortable and nonbinding. Some prefer tights, others baggies."

"Where and what's a dojo?"

"Left outside your door, end of the hall, down two flights. It's a big room with a maple floor and lots of mats for your face to fall into."

She flashes Wyatt another gilded grin, turns agilely on her heels, seemingly floats out of the guest suite.

What ugly teeth.

He stands before the recycler, wondering what to wear. Then he remembers the note the old sweeper in the theater basement handed him. His eyes scan the room for a screen or a black mechanical eye watching him. He finds nothing, but it gives him small comfort. The tech in the Heartland is much better than anything he has seen in the city. Cautiously he takes the shirt on the chair back, reaches into the pocket. He finds the small folded scrap of brown paper. Hunching over it lest an invisible eye watches him from above or behind, he opens it. On it are scrawled three lines in a bold hand.

Thursday water deliveries in Sector Thirty-Two.
Ask for Freddie Boy.
Don't wait—sooner or later, everyone disappears.

Wyatt reads, rereads the message. It is etched upon his memory. He shreds it into tiny pieces, eats them a few at a time before pushing his old clothes into the recycler.

In the dojo, Anna is waiting on the far side of the room. She wears white tights that make her look like a little boy with a girl's face and small breasts. Wyatt laughs when he sees her.

"Leave the wand on the ledge," she says.

"Why?"

"Don't want you blowing a hole in the wall or shooting your own foot off by accident, do we? At least Daddy doesn't."

"Right."

"Fine, draw it and try to shoot me, then."

"I don't think Victor would take too kindly to that, Princess."

"If you don't, I'm going to take it away from you and castrate you with it."

The wand is in his hand before he realizes it. His knees are bent as he sights down his outstretched arm, all in one fluid gesture, only Anastasia has somehow crossed the room in the same heartbeat, has moved slightly to his right, so that he is sighting on a circular sword and dagger display adorning the bare white wall above the maple wainscot. A sharp pain lances through his wrist, an agile bare foot finds his crotch. The room tumbles above and below him, ending with a dainty elbow slamming into his solar plexus. Wyatt struggles to recover his breath before looking for the wand.

"Try not to puke on the mats," Anna says. "The stain's no problem, but the smell lasts a few days."

She puts the wand on the shelf near the door as Wyatt struggles to his knees.

"What a silly twat you are," Anna jeers. "I'll bet Rachel slams the crap out of you every time you touch her."

Her head goes back with a short laugh.

"Try it without the wand this time," she commands him. "Just attack me."

Wyatt is on one foot and one knee. He is still gasping for breath as he rubs the sensation back into his right wrist. The ache in his groin is still debilitating. His knee begins to wobble when he tries to stand.

"Take your time," Anna adds. "And do give it your best shot this time. That last move was something short of pathetic."

Wyatt stands slowly, takes a cautious step forward. He tries to ball his right hand but the fingers will not close all the way. He approaches Anastasia with a slow limping gait. She steps forward, away from the wall, dances deftly to his left, remaining just out of reach. He glances at the wand, hoping she will lunge for it, but she keeps moving to his left.

You're faster than I am, aren't you? I'll never catch you with speed, will I?

Wyatt sidles to his left but makes no overt movements with his hands or arms.

"Are you trying to overcome me with your smell?"

Anastasia asks. "I had something a bit more physical in mind when I asked you to attack me."

It is Wyatt's turn to grin at Anna. He matches her slow fluid measured steps, curves his elbows just as she does, continues moving to her left.

"So you're not quite as stupid as you look," she says.

They circle one another around the room, never coming within contact distance, as Wyatt feels his strength slowly returning. Anna takes a quick step toward him. He gives ground at once, prompting her to laugh aloud.

"Maybe we should just move on to my attacking you," she says.

Her left hand flicks out faster than he can follow, raking his right cheek with four stinging electrical slashes. He feels his face swelling from the glancing blow.

The image of another smallish woman suddenly overlaps Anastasia. Wyatt cannot remember her name, but the slap that sends him reeling is all too familiar. He rolls across the mat, springs to his feet. Both women occupy the same body, leap at him. A dainty bare foot catches him on the chest, sending him crashing onto his backside. Anna is sitting on his hips, leaning over his chest, her left forearm hard across his throat, her right hand pressing below his left clavicle with two fingers. A sudden rage envelops him; Anna flies off, barely landing upon her feet. For the merest instant, Wyatt sees the fear flicker across her eyes.

"It's really too bad you can't do that at will," she says and laughs again.

Wyatt scrambles back to his feet.

Let's give it a try.

The two female faces are superimposed once again. Wyatt feels the anger and hatred welling up within him. He focuses it on Anna. She staggers backward as he presses slowly forward. Her eyes remain riveted upon his, peering through that other pinched blond face, green ice damning him. They never see the balled fist that catches her flush on the left cheek, knocks her to the mat. But her right heel finds his groin at once, followed by her right fist suddenly halfway through his gut before he can follow up on his momentary advantage. She disappears and the next kick is on his posterior, sending him flat on his face.

Wyatt groans.

"Not too bad," Anna says, flexing her jaw and working it with her left hand. "Not too good, either. Now get up and try it again."

Wyatt rolls himself into a ball, clutching his midsection with both hands.

"Don't get too comfortable," Anna chides him. "Your next session will be with my brothers. They can't wait to get their hands on you."

Wyatt sucks in a mouthful of air, pushes himself to his knees. The room is reeling. Everything has become a series of images superimposed upon themselves. He glimpses something gold on the mat, and realizes he has knocked one of the metal teeth from Anna's mouth. He laughs softly to himself, sits back on his calves.

"Come on, get up," Anna shouts.

Wyatt shakes his head, more to dispel the double image than as an answer to Anna. He looks at her, thinking, *I don't think so.*

She turns away from him in disgust, walks over to the sword display on the far wall. She draws a single-edged long-bladed dagger with a sharp angled tip from its sheath. She places her left foot softly on his right shoulder and pushes hard.

Wyatt finds himself once again sprawled upon his back.

Anna stands over him, the dagger in her right hand, the blade resting against her left palm. There is a flash of light against polished steel. He blinks, feels something flick across his loins, gasps. The horrifying ripping sound has him propped up upon his elbows, looking down at the slice across the front of his trousers. Anna coaxes him back down by pressing the blade's tip against his throat.

A moment later her face is in his groin, the blade still pressing into his neck. Her wet mouth envelops him. He feels himself becoming aroused in spite of the pain. She wriggles easily out of her tights, straddles him, holding the dagger steady all the while. She begins riding up and down slowly. Her face remains expressionless.

"If you move, I'll kill you," she says with a hard-edged seriousness.

Wyatt does not doubt her veracity for an instant.

CHAPTER 15

Wyatt lets the four red gashes remain upon his right cheek, even though they sting mercilessly. He decides there is no need to draw any undue attention toward himself by prematurely removing them.

Victor cocks his head, notes Wyatt's limp, then examines the face wounds with a mixture of curiosity and amusement. The small red dagger imprint on his throat brings a genuine smile.

"Anna says you're a diamond in the rough," Victor observes.

"Oh yeah?"

"It means you have potential, boy. Don't be too long in developing it. I've got enemies who will test you at first opportunity. One wrong move, someone calls for clean-up."

"Something to look forward to."

Victor lets go something midway between a grunt and a laugh. "You hungry?"

"Yeah."

"Good. After dinner you and I can go for a spin. There are a few people who want to meet you, boy. Important people. Important for me, important for you."

"I thought I had a few days before your Committee gets their go at me."

"You do. These are my friends."

"Somehow I don't picture you as having friends," Wyatt muses.

Victor laughs again.

They dine with Anastasia, her sister, her mother. Wyatt wants to ask why Victor's sons don't join them but he holds his tongue. The left side of Anna's face is red and swollen where he punched her. She does not look at him, keeping her green eyes fixed adoringly upon her father, twittering with his every witticism, gushing between twitters. Wyatt tries to hide his disbelief. He watches everyone with short glances across the table. All the women ignore him while constantly fawning over Victor. Wyatt tries to see which tooth he knocked from Anna's mouth, but he can't find the telltale gap anywhere. Wyatt is disappointed.

"Sonja," Victor announces after dinner, "I want you and your mother to join me later tonight. Anna, do something about your face, please. Wyatt, meet me at the transport park in ten minutes."

Victor gets up, tosses his napkin across his plate, leaves the room. The women all wait for Wyatt to follow before speaking with one another.

Three of the larger transports have their lift-up doors agape. Bright silver, they look like diving fish or winged ingots. Victor is waiting in the lead vehicle. He motions for Wyatt to join him. The two young men with Victor's face each drive one of the other transports. There are two silver- and yellow-clad servants armed with stunted long barrels sitting in the back seats of each. The familiar hum of the bioscan, against the soft whooshing of the climate control as the doors click shut, lasts for fifteen seconds before Victor clears the overhang. With a sudden burst of acceleration, he turns the transport steeply upward.

"Expecting trouble?" Wyatt muses.

Victor merely smiles without looking at him.

Wyatt turns his head, thinking to see the other two transports directly behind them, but he sees only the treetops covering the rolling hills that surround the lake. On the screen in front of Victor, four pulsing dots appear, two pink and two orange.

"The pink is our escort," Victor announces.

"So the orange must be your fans," Wyatt mutters.

"My dessert," Victor growls. "Now shut up."

Wyatt watches the pink and orange dots weave a dance about one another, growing ever smaller and fainter as Victor keeps the transport flying straight and steady. First one of the orange dots fades, then a pink one, and finally the second orange dot blinks out. The trees flashing by below them slow down long enough for the remaining transport to catch up with them. It assumes a position to their left, slightly above and behind them.

"What's the score?" Victor asks.

"Two down, one out," a voice announces from the panel.

"Theirs?"

"Theirs. Anastasia's on her way to pick up survivors."

"I told you to keep her out of it," Victor snaps.

"Then you tell her next time," the voice says with exasperation. "She likes to play. You know she won't take orders from anyone but you."

Victor grins, says nothing.

Wyatt squirms in his seat.

"Can they hear me?" he asks after a long silence. He gestures with his thumb at the other transport.

"No."

"You've got them—what do you need me for?"

"Either one of them can replace me as head of the family. You can't."

"If you're afraid of them, why don't you just send them away?"

"You mean like you and I were sent away?" Victor asks, momentarily turning his head from the screen to stare into Wyatt's eyes.

"I guess that's what I mean."

"It's not in my religion, boy. You think I'm having you on about that, don't you?"

"I don't know what to think," Wyatt admits. "It's all new to me, remember."

"Then keep your mouth shut, watch, listen, because it's no joke. Either you learn what to think, what to believe, or you don't last very long."

"Someone once explained to me having religion meant you believed something fantastic without question. You make it sound like believe it or else."

"Same thing, only you've got the reason why confused. You think I'll kill you if you don't agree with me, because I won't tolerate a dissenting opinion and that's that. But what I actually mean is if you have no faith, you'll lack the motivation to generate the focus needed to perform at your peak, which is really what we're all about. Only the best survive. We tolerate your failings while you're a learner. You learn quick, or you're dead. Pure and simple. Our faith is empirical, not wishful thinking, not clinging to ancient wisdom."

Wyatt makes a mental note to ask the screen what *empirical* means.

"Empirical means," Victor says with a sigh, "that our faith is based upon direct experience and observation, not hearsay or psychological need."

"Got it."

Three small green dots suddenly appear on the screen. Wyatt tenses.

"My friends," Victor announces. "Relax."

CHAPTER 16

Wyatt waits with the servants in the large foyer. Victor and his son have vanished behind closed doors over an hour ago. The servants sit around a large table amusing themselves by gambling, drinking ale, telling bawdy stories, while Wyatt sits beyond them at the window seat peering past his own reflection into the formal gardens within the spacious atrium of the house. No one offers him an ale. He does not feel like socializing. He stares into the forced beauty beyond the window. Shrubs and small trees have been trimmed into odd geometric shapes—spheres atop pyramids, cones balanced tip to tip, large canted prisms, mounded cylinders, truncated pyramids—with gracefully curved foot paths of white marble chips weaving around and between them. It is both stark and inviting.

Crash's wide face appears superimposed over one of the sculpted shrubs, a stack of spheres of varying diameters. *Hey, Wyatt, let's jump a couple of civil guards, steal their uniforms, fly around for a while, cause a little panic. It'll be fun to hover.* Wyatt laughs, never certain whether or not to take his friend seriously. *Think you can operate one?* he asks. Crash laughs. *If those feather-brains can.* Wyatt decides to go along with him. *But how long for them to learn?* Crash scratches his ribs and pats his ponderous belly. *At least you didn't tell me it'd take two suits to lift me off like Effie did.* Both laugh and stroll uptown toward the park. *How we gonna jump them?* Wyatt presses. *Them being above us all the time.* Crash smiles again. *Easy—we start on the rooftop or we do something to draw them down.* Wyatt shakes his head. *Don't think so. Bugboys land, outnumbering you two to one or better, if they think you're a perp.* Crash and Wyatt walk on in silence for a while, until Crash stops in front of him, smiling. *Then the trick is to get them down not thinking we're a couple of perps.*

"Are you Wyatt?"

For a moment his eyes bulge. *It can't be. It must be a trick of the light. It's Jennie. My Jennie, here.* Thick red hair, sky blue eyes, a pale freckled face atop a tall thin frame. Moving like the breeze, fluid like the lake. As she draws closer, looking sympathetically at him, Wyatt sees it isn't Jennie, only someone who looks and acts very much like her. *Her sister? Did they kick Jennie out of the Heartland too?* He gasps for breath.

"Are you Wyatt Weston?" she asks again.

"Yeah."

"You can go in now."

He nods. Then as an afterthought, he asks, "What's your name?"

The young woman smiles but does not answer. She leads him past the gambling servants toward a pair of rich brown wooden doors whose veneers seem to contain a fathomless depth all their own. She thrusts her graceful chin toward the doors.

"They're waiting for you. Best not to keep them too long," she says quietly.

"Thank you," he says, looking back at her.

She smiles, disappears into a side corridor.

Wyatt opens the door into a darkened room whose walls are sheathed in shadow. Somewhere near the center there is a single overhead floodlight illuminating a red leather chair on a black and white marble checkerboard floor.

"Sit down, Wyatt," Victor Crist says quietly from his left.

Wyatt does as he is told.

There is a long silence.

"Do you know anything of your own history, Wyatt Weston?" someone asks. The voice is hard, broken like stone chips.

"What do you mean?" he asks.

"What is the first thing you remember?"

"I . . . I remember getting on the train, with other children," he says, his voice cracking.

"How well do you remember that?"

"I remember a few details."

"Such as?"

"A big man, with a square chin, cleft, I think you call it. Black teeth and large hands. He liked to touch the children, push them, slap them. And there was a woman who did that, too."

"You said *the children*. Why didn't you say *us?*"

"I don't know. I guess it seems like somebody else back there, only I know it was me."

There is another silence.

"How many men have you killed, Wyatt?" a woman asks him calmly.

He is surprised to hear a woman's voice. "You mean one-on-one? Lots die in the sweeps, but I don't kill them personally."

"I mean one-on-one."

"Two."

"Why did you kill them?"

"It was my job."

"That's all?"

"Well, they were about to shoot me. I got them first."

There is another silence. It is broken by someone coughing. Wyatt rubs his throat.

106

"What do you believe in?" a man asks him. The voice is high-pitched.

"What does that mean?"

"Where do you place your faith?"

"In myself, I guess. I've never thought about it."

"You don't rely on anyone else?"

"I rely on lots of people. But I know when to move on."

There is some quiet laughter. Wyatt counts six, maybe seven voices. Victor Crist's is not among them.

"Why did you agree to accompany Victor to the Heartland?" another man asks.

"It seemed like a good idea at the time."

"Really, why?"

"His offer was better than my other prospect."

"Do you mean working for Curtis Void?"

"Yeah. I sweep for him."

"What did you expect there?"

"I don't know. I went from Sweeper One to Sweeper Four, so things looked promising."

"Because of Rachel?"

Wyatt feels his face reddening. "What's she got to do with this?" he demands.

"Maybe nothing, maybe everything."

There is another silence.

"Did Victor explain to you why you are here?" a new voice asks.

"To meet his friends."

"Did he tell you anything else?"

"No."

"Do you understand why you were sent away from here as a child?"

"No."

"Have you ever heard of the census?"

"No."

"Then someone needs to explain it to you. There is only enough for so many of us. When the new come in, the old must go. If the new are unfit, they are not admitted. If there are too many, some must be culled. Both new and old are culled. The sweeps in the cities do much, but not enough. We don't have sweeps in the Heartland, but only so many of us can stay. You were sent away to give you a chance, Wyatt. Slow learners and the unwanted leave the Heartland. You would have been killed had you remained here. Only learners have time."

"Victor told me that."

"Tonight there is room for one more. Three are here vying for that one place."

Wyatt swallows hard. He feels his wand pressing softly against his ribs, fully charged. He takes comfort from it.

"Below this room is a maze. You and the other learners will enter it from different paths. Only one may leave it. Wands are not permitted. Leave yours on the table behind you, then select one of the other weapons available for your use."

The overhead light goes out. Wyatt stands up. Another light goes on behind him. For an instant, he considers drawing the wand, shooting it as many times as he can at random into the shadows, making room for many more. Instead, he turns cautiously, walks slowly toward the freshly illuminated long sideboard. He parts with his wand reluctantly, leaving it in a silk-lined wicker basket beside two others. He wonders what a maze is.

The table contains a selection of clubs, daggers, spiked knuckles, a garrote, several other bladed items whose proper use he does not understand. None of them look appealing. For no particular reason, he selects a long slender club with a cushioned grip. The light over the sideboard goes out at the instant he touches it. Another light to his far right goes on, illuminating a flight of stone steps descending into the checkerboard floor.

With a sigh, Wyatt takes the first step downward. The overhead light fades as smaller dim lights near his feet illuminate the steps themselves. His footfalls echo, he does his best to muffle them. At the bottom, he finds himself standing on a concrete floor in a basement space more than twice his own height. Straight and curving concrete block walls higher than his head disappear into shadow, creating the maze. Like the stairs, they are faintly illuminated by dim lights along the bottom, spaced five feet apart. Everything is either pools of light or gaping shadow. He has three initial choices, two on level ground, one ramping upward. He slips out of his shoes, darts up the ramp, gripping his club tightly. One of his ankles makes a popping noise. He stops at once. Somewhere in the distance, he hears the clopping of someone else's shoes.

His heart begins pounding, sweat gushing from his forehead trickles into his eyes. Angrily, he wipes them. He removes his shirt, with some difficulty tears off a sleeve. The sound is deafening. Kneeling out of the light, he wraps the torn sleeve around his forehead to keep his own fears from blinding him. He ties the ends securely behind his head, tucks them snugly into the back of his shirt before refastening it.

A noise from another direction startles him. He retrieves his club from the floor. Slowly he makes his way forward, hesitating every few paces to listen. Now and then he hears movement, sometimes close, sometimes far. The ramp up forks, then forks again, the second time offering him three paths. He keeps to his right, avoids paths that appear to slope back downward. On a whim, he tucks the club into his belt behind him, jumps upward, his hands held high. He feels the top edge of the wall. He jumps again, catching it. Cautiously he pulls himself upward, wary lest he strike his head on the ceiling or on an unseen beam. The wall is almost two feet thick. Wyatt manages to pull himself onto it without losing the club.

Peering over the edge, he can see much of the maze below. One dark figure is in sight, far to his left, approaching barefoot, halting, listening, approaching again, a long dagger with spiked knuckles on its grip held before him. Turning his head, Wyatt can see most of the rest of the maze. A second, smaller shadow is approaching from the other side. Wyatt sees no weapon. He swallows hard, monitors their progress.

Twice they pass within one wall of one another, each listening to what he perceives, neither able to locate the other. Eventually they select intersecting paths. They move on until the inevitable confrontation takes place. It is over so quickly, Wyatt barely witnesses it. Something flies from the hand of the smaller candidate, strikes the dagger wielder in the throat. A gurgle, the clatter of the falling dagger, a soft thud. The winner retrieves both weapons and resumes his search for Wyatt.

Wyatt watches his perspiration falling into the small circle of light below him. He wipes his forehead and moves backward down the wall, so as not to give himself away. His torn shirt is clinging to his torso. Reaching upward to gauge the ceiling height, he finds no obstruction there. Rising to his knees, he waits in the dark.

The wait is exasperating. Once, Wyatt loses sight of the remaining candidate altogether for several minutes. Three times this one goes off in the wrong direction, once stumbling over the still body of his first victim. When, at long last, the shadow appears on the path below him, it stops, sniffing at the air, looking upward. Wyatt lies still, clutching his club, hoping the other cannot hear his pounding heart, smell his acidic fear.

The shadow takes three cautious steps forward, jabbing upward with the dagger. Wyatt swings downward with all his strength. A loud crack announces the meeting of weighted club and skull. Wyatt leaps off the wall, and strikes twice more. A pool of blood pours into the small circle of yellow light. A pool of blood, and the thick red hair of the nameless girl who took his breath away in the foyer.

CHAPTER 17

The fist comes from nowhere, breaks Wyatt's nose. He is already off-balance from a flat hand to the chest, so his head snaps back sharply, sending a lancing pain down both sides of his neck, across his shoulders, down his back before he hits the mat. Deep red blood runs over his lips, his chin, onto his shirt, splattering the mat. Floyd's grinning face does not make it easier.

Wyatt rolls over, cupping his left hand beneath his gushing nose. He shuts his eyes, repairs the break as swiftly as he can, stemming the blood flow, restoring the air flow, then relieving the pressure on his neck.

Floyd draws closer, leaning over him from the back.

"You're pretty good beating up on the girls . . ." Floyd spits.

Wyatt's right foot shoots back, catching Victor's son in the groin. The left foot follows, cutting a short arc, catching Floyd behind the knees. Floyd comes crashing down beside Wyatt. He just blocks Wyatt's open hand before it smashes his windpipe.

Both men are on their feet at the same time, but Floyd's eyes hold disbelief.

"I broke your nose," he says. "How'd you stop the bleeding?"

"Go play with your brother's ass," Wyatt spits.

"Not bad for your fourth session, Wyatt," Anastasia says from the open door. "You two can finish killing each other later. Victor wants Wyatt to get ready now. A bath, a shave, a haircut, your finest threads. Time to meet The Committee."

There is a music in her voice. Her smallish pinched mouth twists into a smile.

Wyatt's eyes never leave Floyd.

Victor's eldest son's eyes burn pure hatred, staggering Wyatt.

Wyatt snarls, glaring back at his sparing partner.

Back in his room, he begins trembling. Still unnerved by the death of Jennie's look-alike at his hands, he sees Jennie's face every time he is alone. He does not have to wait long.

Wyatt, the apparition before him calls his name. It is Jennie, stooped and haggard. Her eyes are tired, her face worn. There are deep dark circles below her faded blue eyes, her cheeks sag like gray rags. He stops undressing and stares. *I'm waiting for you at our special place, but you're not there.* A single tear streams from his left eye. He shakes his head to dispel the image. *That's not you, Jennie. That's just me gone mad. I'll be there, but not like this. Not like some face before a jump.*

After his bath, he combs his newly-trimmed hair and recycles his clothes, selecting a loose-fitting silk shirt and jacket, with baggy linen trousers. He charges the wand, holsters it. His face is bruised in three places; two of his ribs are cracked. He heals the ribs but darkens the bruises.

"No escort?" he asks Victor in the transport.

"Attacks against Committee members attending and returning from Committee meetings are a capital offense. The entire house responsible is disappeared."

"Why's that?"

"Because The Committee makes and enforces the laws."

"Good law."

Victor smirks and looks at Wyatt. "You don't look too bad for a workout with Floyd," he says.

"I guess he went easy on me. Your doing?"

"I told him not to kill you."

Wyatt laughs.

"Why is that funny?"

"You're afraid he's going to kill you and you tell him not to kill me. That's funny."

"You're wrong on both counts. I'm not afraid. And Floyd won't kill me unless he thinks he can take my seat on The Committee. He's too weak to take over my house, so without me, he won't survive. Too much competition for houses. He's a good first son, but no leader."

"Does he know that?"

"He's been struggling with it for a while."

"What about the others?"

"What about them?"

"Anyone else gone after your Committee seat?"

"My second son. He's dead now. Nobody mentions his name, all record of him has been expunged from the data bank."

"I was wondering about that."

"About what?"

"About history stopping after the plagues and the holy wars."

"No need for more history. There is at least one example of every right and wrong thing already. Self-history simply promotes vanity, vanity breeds weakness."

"I thought it might be something like that."

"Good, you're learning."

"What now?"

"Now you watch my back and I pay you."

"I live at your house?"

"Of course not. You live in Sector Thirty-Two. You meet my train when I come into the city, you keep me company while I'm there. When I need you in the Heartland, I'll let you know, so you can tell your lady friend you'll be gone for a few days. You'll come here for workouts, Committee meetings, special occasions."

"Why does everyone bother about Rachel?"

"You're about to find out."

Victor eases the transport into a slow banking curve until it hovers about a foot above the grass in front of a large domed building. He backs it gently into a parking bay, opens the doors. Two men are waiting for him on the elevated walk. One looks to be about thirty-eight with an expression of serenity—obviously a Heartlander. The other appears to be in his early thirties. He is alert, muscular, and watches every move Wyatt makes.

"You look pleased with yourself, Edward," Victor says by way of greeting.

"Oh I am, Victor. I am very pleased."

The two men walk side by side, with Wyatt and the other young man following discreetly four paces behind them. Wyatt cannot hear all of the conversation. What he hears makes no sense whatsoever to him, so he emulates the other bodyguard, watching and listening to everything else around them.

The promenade surrounding the interior of the building ends at a large open foyer where another fifty or so people have gathered. These are easily identified as Committee members with their bodyguards. Most Committee members are men, seemingly in their thirties, with a few appearing older and more distinguished, and a smattering of thin-faced women. The bodyguards all look younger, mostly men with the occasional young woman, standing behind

115

their patrons. Wyatt has never seen so many people at their ease in his life. The Committee members speak informally with one another in groups of three to six, with everyone gradually circulating among the other groups. All of The Committee members are smiling, nodding, sometimes leaning forward to hear what someone else is saying amid the buzz of voices around them.

Victor makes the rounds with his friend, saying very little, smiling continually, nodding often. The friend does most of the talking.

Wyatt feels someone watching him. He turns to look. A very large dark-haired man who appears much older than the rest, with the steely eyes of a hungry eagle, stares past his own circle of Committee members to catch Wyatt's eye. The three bodyguards flanking him do likewise. Wyatt feels Victor's hand upon his arm.

"Don't," Victor says softly.

Wyatt suddenly realizes he is reaching for his wand.

Victor releases his grip and returns to his conversation.

Eventually the circulating brings Victor and his friend into the group dominated by the large man. His dark hair is extraordinarily thick, his black eyes have a few fine lines leading to his temples. This one is smiling broadly. He seems to take no further notice of Wyatt. Victor remains at the fringe of the group until someone else moves on. Then he steps closer to the large man. Wyatt follows closely behind his patron.

"How are you, Victor? It's been awhile since our last debate," the big man says.

"I'm fine, Chairman Void. It's a pleasure to see you looking so well."

CHAPTER 18

The Committee meeting is an education. After at least an hour of informal gathering in the anteroom, The Committee congregates in the center of the domed building, in a large amphitheater consisting of a gallery for the bodyguards, five rows of wide tiered seats for the members, a small stage at the center, where a single orator or a group of debaters descend to sway the minds of their contemporaries.

Wyatt struggles to understand what is being said, what it all means. It is like Shakespeare—he has never heard or seen many of the words, but the gist is plain.

Census figures are first and foremost on everybody's mind. The population has held steady for two decades, but is on the rise again. This sparks a debate over building an arena in the city for monthly gladitorials as a means to further contain the population. This is sponsored by the realty/construction interests, to which Victor Crist belongs.

He and his friend, Edward, however, do not appear to agree with the others, but make no effort to argue against them.

Another group, the medical/pharmaceutical interests, proposes controlling the population by placing additives in the drinking water to both still the sexual urges in the city as well as temporarily sterilize the population. Both arguments are defeated in debate. The former is considered likely to promote sedition, the latter to further weaken the gene pool as well as contaminate the food sources.

Wyatt does not understand the arguments, but the propositions are astounding.

Manufacturing/recycling interests, dominated by Chairman Void, wish to expand the consumer product availability in the city, but are vehemently opposed by the farming/ecological combine, who stress preserving dwindling resources. The transportation/distribution cartel clamors for more assistance from manufacturing/recycling, who, in turn, want concessions from air/water/energy management.

In the end, Wyatt simply stops listening, as the arguments give him the worst headache he has ever experienced. The meeting lasts for hours. When it is over, the sky is black, the transport bays are illuminated by low-intensity lights on the promenade, the air is cool. The fresh air is welcome, even if there is no real breeze to move it.

"Well?" Victor asks him inside the transport.

"Well what?"

"What did you learn today?"

"Long conversations cause headaches."

Victor breaks into a short laugh. "Those were my exact words, about thirty-five years ago."

"How old are you?"

Victor turns to smile at Wyatt, but does not answer the question.

"Tell me something, Victor," Wyatt says.

"You want to know who Chairman Void is to Rachel."

"Yeah."

"Adolph is her grandfather."

"Is that why I'm here?"

"No, but it is an added bonus."

"How?"

"The old boy is really smitten with his granddaughter.

He and I have never seen eye-to-eye before, so maybe we can find a common ground now, us being almost in-laws and all."

Wyatt says nothing. He stares into the twinkling stars above the dome. There seem to be many more above the Heartland than he noticed in the city.

"What's recycling got to do with property interests?" he asks after a long silence.

"Some of the sectors have gotten very rundown. Too many citizens are living in squalor. Most of these have too much time on their hands. We don't want too many drossies—it might start a panic. I'd like to recruit those at the bottom to rebuild the dilapidated sectors. Adolph favors keeping things as they are. He thinks poverty ensures strength and drive in the slow but capable learners—like you and me. He wants to make more toys available as a diversion for the rest. His theory is the weak are content to play while the strong always want more."

"What's your theory?"

"My theory is that if we each look after our own interests, the system works. When we start to get caught up in theory, the system breaks down. Rioting is usually the first sign of that breakdown. Poverty and hunger breed rioting. I like the system the way it is, with me at the top, a wide base at the bottom to support me. I want to make sure it stays that way."

Wyatt laughs.

They ride on in silence until the lights of Victor's house appear below them.

"Anna will give you one more workout tomorrow morning, before she drives you back to the train. Keep up with your lessons on the screen. I'll let you know when I'm coming back to the city. And give up your other job—

you don't need it anymore."

Wyatt has no appetite. He retires early.

In the morning, his right hand is gone. He rebuilds it quickly, wondering if there is any correlation between the parts of him that melt away and his tumultuous feelings.

Sitting up in bed, he shuts his eyes, remembering Jennie. Twice he has to dispel her haggard visage and replace it with the Jennie he knows and loves. His lower lip is quivering and the tears are streaming down his cheeks every time the image of the dead girl in the labyrinth reappears. Finally he gains control of his grief, begins his litany.

It is Thursday. I'm about to return to the city. The world is a very different place than it was three weeks ago. I know things I never guessed, I'm part of things I never wanted. There is no going back on any of it now.

Jennie has gone missing forty-seven days now. I killed someone who looks just like her—maybe her sister, maybe just another hungry city kid with quick moves. I know it wasn't Jennie, I know I had to kill her. But it's tearing me up.

I will remember Jennie. I will find Jennie. I will not let this Heartland swallow me. I will not let the things I have to do destroy me. I will not become like Victor Crist. I need Victor, just like I need Rachel Void. I will always remember Jennie.

I will remember all of them. I will remember all those gone missing. I remember Effie, Kristen, Crash, Winston, and The Elf. They are real, so long as I remember them.

Wyatt begins visualizing their faces in his mind. He listens to their voices, their laughter, their wisdom, their sarcasm. He feels more alive than he has for days.

Anastasia is waiting for him in the dojo.

She shows him how to turn, how to fall, how to parry, how to breathe as he moves. Then she teaches him a series of slow precise movements, like a dance. After repeating it a dozen times, Anastasia tells him he must practice them at least twice a day, morning and evening, until every movement has become reflexive. At the end of the workout, she tells him to sit with his legs crossed, his eyes closed, thinking of nothing. She sits facing him. An hour passes slowly. When he opens his eyes, she is watching him. Her face is expressionless. In that state, he is surprised to find her beautiful.

"What's all this about?" he asks her.

"This is about keeping Floyd from bashing your head in. You really got to him. He isn't likely to forgive you. You're no match for him now, but in time, who knows."

"Victor's orders?"

Anastasia's serene expression disintegrates into a mask of ire. "I should let him kill you, Wyatt. I should let him beat that stupid city face of yours into a bloody pulp before you wreck everything."

He reaches out to gently touch her cheek but she slaps his hand away as if it were some sort of lethal weapon. She is on her feet before him, dropping him with a kick to the solar plexus. Assuming a defensive posture, she waits for him to strike back at her.

Wyatt stands up slowly, still weakened by the ferocity of her attack.

"You're afraid I'll make you weak," he observes.

"I'm afraid of nothing," she says quietly. "And you're likely to be dead before you can do much damage anyway."

She sends a lightning quick jab toward his face, but he lets it miss him with a slight twist of his head. He has to duck the elbow that snaps back after the jab, pushes up under it, sending her sprawling head over heel. She is back on her feet before he can follow up on his momentary advantage. They begin circling one another slowly.

For another hour, they take turns attacking and defending, with Wyatt usually finding himself on the mat as Anastasia twists an arm until he cries out in pain or presses her foot against his throat until he thinks she really will kill him.

"That's enough for this trip," Anastasia says, walking toward the door. "Meet me at the transport park in fifteen minutes. Poor little Rachel must be out of her head by now."

CHAPTER 19

"I'm looking for Freddie Boy," Wyatt says to the dirty-faced, dull-eyed mechanic in the faded black overalls slowly opening the valves on the water main below his tower.

"What for?"

"You him?"

The mechanic wipes his nose, leaving a dark streak on his cheek in the process, then spits on the tunnel floor. He looks back at Wyatt's expressionless face, ponders something, then turns back to the tram cart parked on the rails on the next level down.

"Hey, Freddie Boy—you got a lovesick face up here asking for ya."

Wyatt laughs, walks toward the railing. Resting his elbows on it, he sees a tall muscular woman with short curly brown hair wearing dirty overalls looking back up at him, her grimy hands resting on her hips.

"You Wyatt?" she asks in a husky voice.

"I'm Wyatt. Rafe leave you a message?"

She motions for him to come down, then realizing that he has never been in the service tunnels before, she points with her thumb at the narrow stairs beyond the tram.

"Watch your mouth," she whispers by way of greeting as he draws near. "Howie's lucky to remember his way home at night, but these tunnels carry sound."

Her round cheeks are red, her face energetic, her large brown eyes probe his blatantly.

"Rafe's an old chum," Wyatt says softly. "I thought

123

he got disappeared, then I see him the other night. We party, he leaves me a note to ask for you. What's the deal here?"

"The deal here is that some of us don't want to get disappeared or swept, so we're doing something about it. What's a face like you hanging out with Rafe for?"

"I love you, too."

Freddie Boy laughs. "Rafe says you're a sweeper."

"Yeah. Was."

"Those naturals look too rich for a sweeper, and this ain't no sweeper neighborhood."

"Like I said, was."

"Rafe says you got some uptown sweetie pulling weight for you."

"I got all sorts of uptown sweeties pulling weight for me. Damnedest thing. Go figure."

Freddie Boy laughs again. "Cut the crap. I don't want to like you, Wyatt."

"Why not? Maybe you pull a few downtown strings for me some day," Wyatt says with a grin. He makes a two-handed gesture, like someone struggling to pull a thick rope over their shoulder against much resistance.

"Rafe says you moving with the Heartlanders."

"That's a fact."

Freddie Boy shakes her head. She obviously does not want to tell Wyatt anything.

"So what's Rafe got to say for himself?" Wyatt presses. "Do I gotta keep watching him sweep Shakespeare to see him again or what?"

"Maybe it's best if you keep thinking Rafe got disappeared."

"Maybe it is."

Freddie Boy looks away for a moment, then looks back

hard at Wyatt. "You know the Sector Twelve Grille?"

"Been there."

"Be there Monday night. Leave the uptown sweeties home."

Wyatt goes back to his flat, takes a long bath. He has to recycle his clothes to get the tunnel smells out of them.

He calls Rachel on the talkie. There is no answer save the voice saying she is out, leave a short message.

"Hey, Rachel. I'm back. Call me."

Then he lies down on the white leather sofa, falls asleep. He dreams of living in a fine Heartland house beside a lake with Jennie. He is a Committee member, she is just as he remembers her: vibrant, loving, there when he needs her. They watch the sun setting on the lake holding hands. She hands him an ale.

He wakes up to a voice saying he has a visitor.

"Yeah, who?"

"Ms. Void."

"Send her up."

He is waiting outside the lift when it opens. Rachel rushes into his open arms, wraps her hands around his neck, pulling her firm breasts into his chest. Her left leg curls around behind his back as their mouths press together.

"See, I'm still Wyatt," he says when she finally releases him.

He scoops her up and carries her into the bedroom, where their clothes soon decorate all the furnishings. He presses his lips against all of her while she guides his head up and down her torso. Pushing him over, she slips her hands under his shoulders and presses her body hard against him. This time she does not scratch or bite.

125

"I met your grandfather," he says when their lovemaking is over.

"Adolph?"

"Yeah. I don't think he likes me."

"He's half of why I left. He wouldn't keep his hands off me. Nobody can say no to him."

"Yeah, I've seen how it works there."

"Watch out, Wyatt. Adolph can have you killed."

"Victor thinks my loving you might make him and Adolph friends."

"Maybe he'll kill you for Adolph."

"There are a lot of ways to die there, that's for sure. Kinda like the city, only you get to fight back, if you play by the rules."

"The rules change, Wyatt. The biggest killers make them."

"It beats living in Sector Nine, sweeping rats and drossies."

"Does it?"

"Yeah."

Rachel sits up, wraps her arms around the pillow. She pulls it to her chest, hugs it, looking at the blood-colored sunset over the distant plastic dome. Wyatt leans over, begins kissing her bare shoulders.

"Look, Rachel. If Adolph wants me dead, and I'm still sweeping, Curtis will mess with my equipment, or push me off his pod, or just have someone else shoot me by accident—you know that."

Rachel begins to cry softly.

Wyatt massages her shoulders gently.

"Don't do this, Wyatt. Curtis is my friend. He wouldn't kill you for Adolph. He's the one who helped me leave the Heartland. He's the one who brings my friends into the city

126

to visit me. He's good people, Wyatt. Don't take him from me."

"I won't take anyone from you, Rachel."

Wyatt kisses her shoulder blades before working down her back.

"You haven't asked me about the baby," Rachel says.

"What should I ask?"

Rachel laughs and shakes her head. "Maybe you should study anatomy and biology on your screen."

"I will."

"You should ask how I'm feeling. We get a little crazy when we carry."

"So's I'd notice?"

Rachel pulls away until she is sitting on her calves. She smacks him hard with the pillow, then uses it to pushes him back down. She sinks her teeth into the soft flesh of his earlobe, until his blood is running down her chin. Then she rakes his chest with her nails.

He grabs her hands and pins them behind her back.

"I like you better when you're my city girl," Wyatt says.

The tears are running down Rachel's face as she wraps her legs around him, trying to bite his neck. He has to pull her head back by the hair as her hips begin to gyrate.

"Well, I'm a Heartland girl," she spits.

He keeps her arms pinned against the silk sheets with his elbows, picks up the pillow, presses it down over her face, while her hips continue pumping their burning rhythm.

CHAPTER 20

Wyatt is sure he has killed Rachel with the pillow, but she wakes up gasping and choking a few minutes later, his blood dried and flaking on her cheek, on the pillow, under her ivory nails. They make love again after that, tenderly. He asks her to stay, but she insists on going back alone. There is a look in her eye he has never seen before, like a wild beast resigned to captivity.

"Call me next weekend, Wyatt," she whispers to him as they wait for the lift. "I've got a busy week. Better yet, surprise me, but not until late Saturday."

She kisses him long and softly. He does not want to let her go.

Wyatt spends the week practicing for his next inevitable bout with Floyd, when he is not studying genetic engineering and biology on the screen. He is not very good at either subject, so Anastasia drills him mercilessly. He does not recycle the sheets. Rachel's smell lingers faintly in the apartment. Twice he almost forgets his litany, but forces himself to remember, to be who he was as well as who he is becoming. Nothing more disintegrates in the night. Rather than relief, he feels a sense of loss, that another piece of him is forfeited as part of the price of his admittance to the Heartland.

By Monday, he is as edgy as a hungry rat. The martial movements do not flow, he is holding his breath, he cannot concentrate on his lessons. He loses his temper with the recycler when it takes too long to recycle him new togs, smashing his fist ineffectually against its epoxied steel face. Even Anastasia, who usually delights in pushing him past his limits, cuts the lessons short, telling him to go out and have some fun for a day or two before he does himself an unintentional injury.

He spends the afternoon on the balcony, breathing the stale air, watching the thin gray clouds roll in from the north. They begin to billow and darken, heralding the infrequent phenomenon of rain. In their churning sides, he sees the faces of those he is keeping alive in his memory as well as those he has already forgotten. Only Jennie does not appear. Wyatt feels relief at this. Of all his changing moods, this is the only one he would not share with her.

When his stomach's rumblings begin to distract him from his daydreams, he goes back inside and orders a small meal for himself from the tower canteen. It arrives in the kitchen chute moments later. The steak is cooked to perfection, the salad is fresh and crisp, but both taste no differently to him than the nameless gray flakes that have been his staple diet for years.

By nightfall, he begins to understand why some go on sprees, annihilating anyone who crosses their path until the civil guards arrive to annihilate them. Finally he recharges his wand, holsters it beneath the drab synth vest he has selected for the occasion.

He takes the transport chute to the train station. As usual, he spends a moment shaking off his aversion to the chute. The station is crowded. The coming rain always brings people out into the streets, pubs, and gaming houses. The platform rings loud with many voices. Even the commuting day workers seem lighthearted this night. On the train, eight citizens are crammed into compartments designed for six, so he stands in the corridor to avoid the smell he would not have noticed three weeks ago. Disembarking at Sector Ten, he reverses direction, walks slowly back toward Sector Twelve.

The sky is starless, the atmosphere contains a building pressure. A storm is brewing, for certain. Looking up, he cannot see the civil guards hovering above the street lamps' glow, but he feels their eyes. He stops at the first pub he finds, orders an ale.

A driving rhythm, dim lights, citizens packed tightly together, gathered in small groups at the tables and along the bar, are comfortingly familiar. A young woman with short blond hair and nose rings rubs herself against his side. Wyatt smiles for her. Another pair of eyes grip him from a nearby table. He nods knowingly to the young man glaring at him.

Naw, I ain't after your sweetie, citizen.

When the young woman presses her buttocks against his thigh again and turns, looking up into his eyes, Wyatt simply points with his chin at the young man sitting nearby. The woman pouts, moves on. Wyatt finishes his ale, nods his thanks to the barkeep, slips back onto the city street.

No eyes from above following him this time. The driving rhythm from the pub fades quickly behind him. The pressure is still building, but no rain has fallen yet. He moves from the residential portion of Sector Ten into the commercial. A faint humming of machinery from inside the drab buildings finds resonance inside him. A pair of prostitutes leaning against the wall of a brothel eye him. He crosses the street to avoid the prostitutes. One of them heckles something obscene, but her words are garbled. Wyatt laughs softly, moves on.

Four short blocks later, he crosses over into Sector Twelve. Its commercial district abuts that of Sector Ten. A block and a half later, the sultry voice of a young woman, backed up by a pair of twanging guitars and a thumping bass, announces the Sector Twelve Grille. Wyatt steps into the first doorway he finds, looks behind him, then glances upward. If the civil guards are hovering nearby, they have taken no interest in him. He surreptitiously adjusts his vest and trousers, resumes walking, crossing the empty street. A couple stagger out of the Sector Twelve Grille as he tries to enter it. The woman is laughing, the man is keeping her from falling. Wyatt steps aside to let them pass. Inside it is dark. The singer standing on the small illuminated stage announces that the band is about to go on break.

There is just the hint of joystick in the air, heavily masked by the smells of ale, sweat, cooking oil. Wyatt steps to the side to let his eyes adjust to the flickering pink and blue of the iridescent lights, shaped to resemble couples dancing, and stacked kegs of ale. The Sector Twelve Grille is only half-full. Most of the patrons are seated at the tables. Wyatt scans all the dark shapes, but none resemble either Rafe or Freddie Boy.

He goes to the bar, stands patiently waiting for the barkeep to appear from the shadows.

"Buy you an ale, friend," someone says behind him.

He turns to see a lanky young man with a hard face leaning over the bar, resting on both elbows. Wyatt is certain the man was not there a moment before.

"That would make you a friend," he says.

The young man nods to Wyatt, waves toward the shadows. A barmaid appears, bearing two plastic steins, which she sets on the bar before melting back to wherever she came from. He is left with a fleeting image of her pale face, short cropped black hair, thick painted red lips, large polished copper hoop earrings.

"Nice touch," Wyatt says, examining the stein.

"You're not a regular."

"Been a while."

"Looking for someone?"

"Yeah."

"Maybe I help you find them."

"Rafe."

"You Wyatt?"

"Yeah."

"You best have an ale or two. Rafe'll be along."

The young man picks up the other stein, takes a long draught from it. Wyatt does likewise, waiting for the other to initiate conversation. They drink in silence until Wyatt offers to buy the next round. Once again the barmaid appears from the shadows at a wave from the young man. This time she lets Wyatt insert his card into the credit counter.

"This your place?" Wyatt asks after she leaves.

"Yeah."

"The band's another nice touch."

"I like to patronize the arts."

"You got a name?"

"Walter."

"So what's the deal, Walter? Freddie Boy doesn't want to like me; you think maybe I'm poison, or some kinda big trouble."

"You are big trouble, Wyatt."

"Yeah? How so?"

"You hang with a real tough crowd from the Heartland. Anybody draws their eye is disappeared faster than a water ration. Mean bastards, every one. You hang with them, you one of them. You one of them, you kill easy and often. That's poison. That's big trouble."

"Maybe I should go. Rafe's a pal. I wish him well."

"Maybe you should stay. Maybe Rafe needs your friendship."

"Nobody needs poison."

"That's where you're wrong. Everybody's looking for poison."

Wyatt sees Walter's teeth, real teeth, grinning at him, pink and blue by turns in the flashing lights. There is neither camaraderie nor comfort in that smile. Wyatt grins back the same way. The band returns to the stage, Walter waves Wyatt toward a table in the far corner of the Grille. The barmaid follows them, bearing two fresh steins.

CHAPTER 21

"I dunno, Rafe," Wyatt says, "this thing you got for cellars."

Walter scowls but Rafe smiles. He motions for Wyatt to seat himself, shuts the storeroom door behind them. The space is two stories below the Grille, long with a low gray ceiling supported by four columns with two cross-beams. It is illuminated by a single bare bulb in the center, casting deep hard-edged black shadows in all directions. By the stark dim light, Walter looks like a predator to Wyatt, while Rafe looks like a cadaver.

"Hard to hear through concrete walls," Rafe says. "Bug finders say this room is clear."

"The sweep's this Thursday, if you're worried about bugs," Wyatt says, trying to make himself comfortable on the fifty-pound sack of soy meal that is serving him as a chair.

Walter leans against a small square column, shaking his head with disgust.

"Bugs, mikes, long throats, voice boxes . . ." Rafe adds, looking for a sign of understanding from Wyatt.

Wyatt shrugs.

"We don't want to be heard—the civil guards can hear through walls," Walter says dryly. "Don't you know anything?"

"I've specialized," Wyatt says. He smiles easily.

"Doesn't your friend, Victor Crist, listen at doors?" Walter demands.

"Not so's you'd notice."

"He wants to tear down Sectors Eight through Twelve," Walter adds.

"Yeah. He wants to upgrade."

"Is that what he tells you?" Walter asks.

"He's in real estate. Upgrades bring higher rents. What do you think?"

"I think you're having me on, bodyguard."

"Where you get your information, Walter?" Wyatt hisses. "You sound uptown to me. Maybe you're a Heartlander with his own bad plan. Maybe you think Wyatt's gone soft."

"I'm like you, Wyatt, a Heartland boy who got the push. Difference is, I was old enough to remember all of it, fight back. I'll share. I'm twelve. The census figures just in. The Committee enforces the census law. Every house needs to drop one member. My father either kills one of us or sends the youngest to cityschool. Suddenly we're downsized, I'm downtown."

Walter is almost shouting, as he leans toward Wyatt.

"You stay in touch?" Wyatt asks casually.

"Against the law, Wyatt," Rafe says quietly. "Schoolboys make it on their own or get swept. I see you're for real—you still got a lot to learn."

"Hey, Rafe, I just came by to see how you were, not cause a fuss."

"Yeah? That and maybe ask me about a friend gone missing, eh?" Rafe says with a wide-eyed grin.

Wyatt feels a sudden chill. He leans forward. "Yeah," he whispers. "I'm hurting. So I'm asking. What happened to her?"

"I don't know, but she didn't get swept, and she's not a stat."

"You sure?"

"Yeah. Walter's got security clearance—he runs a pub. I looked her up after I saw you. Her record's been disassembled."

"What?"

"Someone took it apart, piece by piece. That means it's rewritten. Saved somewhere else. You get swept, disappeared, or statted, they just erase you."

Wyatt rubs his forearms. His skin is cold. He feels the goose flesh under his palms. "Why, Rafe? Why disassemble?"

"Lots of reasons. All guesses."

"Be a friend, guess for me."

Rafe sighs, looks away.

Wyatt does not take his eyes off Rafe. "So tell me she has another sweetie? Maybe an uptown face?" Wyatt presses.

"If she did, none of us know about it."

"Why didn't Frieda, or Tom, or any of the others remember her?"

"They're not very strong, Wyatt. Y'know how it goes. Something's hot, you drop it. Cold to you and me is red hot to most of them, y'know? It's not for blame, Wyatt. It's for survival. We each do the best we can."

"Yeah. So guess for me, Rafe," Wyatt insists again.

Rafe shakes his head, runs his hand through his thick black hair, slouches his long frame slowly into the pile of sacks beside Wyatt. "I'll tell you the reasons I know, Wyatt. Could be lots more I've never heard of. You move uptown, your files get upgraded. You work in the Heartland, your files get upgraded, like yours. You get collected, your files . . ."

"What's collected?"

"Some faces collect stuff. Y'know? Things, people, situations. She was a real heart-stopper, Wyatt. Love at first sight for you, remember. For just about everyone else, too. Some face could have collected her like nothing. She might be better off with a face than squirting ale, frying soy, growing wrinkles."

Wyatt grinds his teeth, balls his fists, pressing them into the sacks. The sacks hiss back.

"Keep guessing," he presses.

Rafe just shrugs.

"C'mon, Rafe. Don't talk to me like I'm another sack of soy meal. Those were all uptown guesses. That's gotta be half of it. Give me some downtown guesses now."

Rafe looks at Walter. Walter runs a tattooed hand through his dirty blond hair, nods his assent. Rafe looks back at Wyatt. "Downtown's another story," Rafe says quietly. "A pretty girl gets recruited . . ."

"What?"

"For the cribs, Wyatt. You think any of them want to be there?"

Wyatt shudders.

"Civil guards got no accessible files . . ."

"You saying she's flying around, wearing gray body armor, watching me?"

"No, but it's a downtown disassembly."

"Don't stop now."

"She might have left town. To one of the farms. Some folks like that life better. Plants instead of city walls. Records move with her. And then she might have gone underground."

"What's that, Rafe?"

Walter stares at the ceiling.

"Some people want to disappear themselves. They want a better world, and they're willing to fight for it. Some have friends who disassemble their records for them. If that's what happened to her, looking for her might get her killed."

"What do you think happened to her, Rafe?"

"I dunno, Wyatt. I always thought you knew, until I saw you with Rachel Void."

"What's with you and old Adolph's granddaughter, anyway?" Walter asks.

Wyatt shakes his head, buries his face in his hands.

The others wait for him to speak.

"A man's got needs, Walter. Rachel's special, too," he says slowly.

"They're all special, Wyatt," Walter says. His voice is low and steady now. "Every last one of them. So how you gonna keep two special ladies happy? Maybe you gotta let one go. Maybe you gonna hurt them both, you keep pushing your nose into things you don't understand. Maybe you acting like a face, pissing it all away. Maybe you ask yourself who you making mad, who they gonna hurt if they can't hurt you. Maybe you grow up a little now, eh?"

Wyatt wants to draw the wand, incinerate Walter. He stares into the dark shadows beneath Walter's brow, finds sympathy, not ridicule. Walter wishes him well. He nods, says nothing.

Rafe lights up a joystick, hands it to Wyatt. "Laugh a little, Wyatt," Rafe says. "We're still friends. We're neither one of us swept. You're getting too serious about all the wrong stuff."

Wyatt takes a long draw, passes the stick to Walter. He feels like a weight has been removed from his shoulders. He smiles. "What about the others, Rafe? Tell me about them. I remember so many."

"Winston and The Elf joined a band. They're touring. Called *The Sweepers* when they left. Maybe *The Drossies* when they come back."

Everyone laughs.

138

"Crash left town to work on a farm. Don't know about anyone else," Rafe continues after his next draw. "Your guess is as good as mine. Most folks we know just move on. Hope for something better than before. Best to let them go."

Wyatt understands Rafe is asking Wyatt to let him go. He smiles, waves off the joystick. "Long trip back to Sector Thirty-Two," he says, standing up. "Don't want to get stopped by the bug-boys, lose my prospects. Good to see you well, Rafe. Good to meet you, Walter. Maybe we stay friends."

"Stranger things have happened," Walter says, opening the storeroom door for Wyatt.

The rain starts to fall as Wyatt leaves the Sector Twelve Grille. He walks down the dimly-lit street toward the nearest public chute with the sad sounds of the singer and the lonely chords of the guitars trailing off behind him. He trembles as it sucks him toward the Sector Twelve Station. The train is just loading when he arrives. He boards it quickly. It is not as crowded as the earlier ones. Wyatt shares his compartment with two day workers going home and a young couple who are lost in one another's eyes. He no longer finds their smells offensive. By Sector Twenty-Four, the compartment is empty.

Thunder shakes the tube, lightning washes the city in garish shades of green, white, and violet. A driving rain is flooding the empty streets by the time the train reaches Sector Thirty-Two. Wyatt walks home anyway. He is soaking wet long before he reaches his tower. The flat-faced woman security guard stares at him in disbelief. He smiles at her as he makes for the lobby lift, dripping long dark trails of rainwater behind him like blood from an open wound.

CHAPTER 22

There is no sleep. But there are dreams.

Sheets of rain lash at the balcony door, the wide picture windows, distorting the sudden landscape that leaps out of the darkness, throbs to life, disappears with a cold finality that is not wasted on Wyatt. For two hours, he tries to sleep. His bed is a subtle torture chamber. His skin is crawling, his mind is numb. The pieces of his life have become undone.

He gets up. Sitting naked, with his legs crossed, on the blood red carpet in the center of the living room, he peers through the rain into the night, listening to the clamor of the thunder, the cascading of the torrents, feeling the raging wind on his skin, through his hair, in his bones, even though it howls and dances beyond the tower walls.

For a while, he is the storm, raging, singing, dancing. Then he is Wyatt again, sitting quietly on the blood red carpet, waiting. He does not have to wait long. Eagerly they come. The dreams. The faces. The people in his litany. The people no longer in his litany. The people who were never in his litany. They come by ones, twos, threes, fours. They come, unaware he is watching. They come seeking him out. They come surprised to find him here. They come to perform for him. They stay a short while. They go. Behind them the unstoppable storm washes the city clean, plays with the night's shadows, sings its mysterious and mournful song.

Kirsten, his first love, opens the balcony door. The lock

is no obstacle to her. It refuses to deny her entrance. The wind and rain whirl through the living room in a fury of curiosity around her, but she is dry, untouched by the tempest.

Kirsten has never been this far uptown. She touches everything. She touches the smooth walls, tracing the blue designs on the beige paper. She touches the wooden side table, the leather couch, the soft red carpet. In the kitchen, she turns on the tap, squeals with laughter at the clean running water, follows the wind into the bathroom, touching everything. He hears her giggling when she tries the big bed. She comes back into the living room, touching the vases, the dried flowers, the ornate floor lamps. Finally she touches Wyatt. Kneeling before him, she runs her fingertips across his forehead, as if he were carved from a block of wood or stone. She gently runs one finger across his lips, feels his eyes with her open palms.

She is not laughing anymore. Her face is sad. She stands up slowly, backs out into the heart of the storm. The wind and the rain leave with her. Wyatt hears the lock click shut behind her. Tears are streaming down his cheeks. He knows she is only the first of many.

The next ones he barely remembers. Two boys from Sector Nine. For him they have no names. They disappeared shortly after he took his dreary flat. Standing before him, naked, they are covered in bruises. They turn slowly, showing him their scars, their pain. Then, hand in hand, they run to the balcony and jump off. Wyatt sees the pattern on the street he noticed for the first time the day he found Victor Crist sitting in the cafe.

He heaves a sigh, blinks his eyes. He cannot tell if it is the rain or his tears that melt the edges of the flickering shadows around him.

Splash is next. Weaver of words, singer of songs. Splash sits down on a moss-covered stone, oblivious to Wyatt's presence. On his lap, he fingers the small green dulcimer he has made from items missed in the sweeps. Singing songs about the city, about the people he has met, about the dreams he has dreamed, he stays the longest of any, yet never acknowledges Wyatt. When he leaves, he seems to float into the night. Even the storm stops to let him pass.

Suddenly Wiffle runs terrified across the living room. Wyatt watches the papered walls of his flat turning into a twisted city street, elongating before Wiffle, rising too high to climb, pushing him back. Other citizens scramble out of his way, hugging concrete, sheltering in open doorways. Wiffle looks back, dodges, tries a bright red door. It is locked and will not budge.

He scrambles to the next one, pushes buzzers at random, bangs frantically on the dingy blue door. The street empties around him. He turns, his back and hands pressed against the dented steel, his face a mask of resignation and confusion. An arcing red bolt from on high incinerates the young man where he stands. A swarm of civil guards drops like a hailstorm. One turns the charred body with his foot, while another opens a flap on his arm, punching buttons there. From a ramp appearing in the middle of the street, a clean white sweeper truck appears.

Wyatt turns his face away.

The night becomes the night again. His heart keeps time with the wind gusts, the waves of rain breaking against the windows, the balcony door. His labored breathing becomes the wind.

Hans and Effie are in a pub. They turn to Wyatt, hoist their glasses. A young woman with a bright red and green dragon tattooed across her face walks by. Effie hops off his stool to follow her. Hans slaps his knee, turns back to Wyatt, laughs.

Wyatt tries to laugh with him. The sound he makes is the gurgle of a drowning man who has given up on hope. He gasps for breath.

Flicker is on the train with a lady friend. She is thin and pale, with straight black hair that wraps her shoulders like a shawl. Her belly is swollen. Flicker looks worried. Twice he flings his long blond hair back over the top of his head. Someone else enters the compartment, he takes the woman's hand between two of his own. The train rushes off into the night.

Wyatt barely recognizes Rikki, her face has changed so much. Her long straight nose is gone, replaced by a smaller, turned-up variety like those Victor Crist's women wear. She is clad in a fringed white silk scarf with a flamboyant red design, over a deep yellow tight-fitting dress. She looks twenty pounds thinner, smiles brightly as if she had just smoked a joystick. Three men are arguing with great fervor in the next room. One of them turns, calls her name. Rikki turns to face Wyatt, places an emaciated finger to her thin lips, forces a weak smile, then turns back, drifts away like the spiraling smoke from a joystick.

Winston, The Elf, and three others make an awful noise, worse than *The Mimis*, for an appreciative crowd. The Elf beats on a drum as if he were insane. The music is without melody, loud, painful. The crowd is young, they gyrate madly to the cacophony.

All night long, they keep coming.

Sad-faced children from the half-remembered school gather to hear their lesson in his living room. Some disappear in the night, some become obedient, some harden. He watches them age. He sees their faces change. They are sweepers, manufacturing drones, barkeeps, utility tenders, lab techs, day workers, civil guards. They turn away from one another, disappear into the walls.

The thin-faced woman with the potted plants is there. She is his favorite teacher. When no one is looking, she brushes his hair, gives him candied fruit. He sees himself as a young boy, telling her about his dreams. She laughs with him, whispers that his dreams must remain their shared secret. He agrees. Then young Wyatt changes with the others. The thin-faced woman ages, her hands begin to tremble, she develops a cough. The schoolroom is gone. Wyatt remembers her name—Miss Corin. He forms it silently on his lips. Her back is bent as she shuffles down a vacated street. Wyatt hears the warning sirens. Why doesn't Miss Corin take shelter? Wyatt holds his breath. He watches every slow step she is taking. She moves deliberately, as if she knows where she is going, but she is going nowhere, walking slowly down the middle of the empty street. Her face is expressionless, her eyes are blank. Miss Corin is washed away by a churning river of rats and roaches.

Wyatt cries out in the night.

The rain splatters the windows again and again, a driving rhythm. It hammers at the sides of his head. He listens for the thunder, but the thunder is spent. Still he feels the wind. It washes over him, nuzzles him, embraces him, calls out to him to rejoin the storm.

A host of nameless faces keep coming. There is little hope in most of them, little resistance to the forces sweeping them away, little moments of laughter amid a sea of sorrows, little candle flames snuffed out one by one.

Soon Wyatt has no more tears.

The last one is Jennie's look-alike. She comes as a cooing baby, held by a gaunt woman with long blond hair.

The woman soon loses interest, leaves the infant alone. No more than three, she is put on the train for the city. Hardened quickly, she is soon manipulating young men with her subtle charm, the promise of her favors. An older man takes her into his home within a glass tower. He is a supervisor in the civil guards. He teaches her how to defend herself. Her movements are subtle, like a cat. Her benefactor dies. She must leave the tower. Prowling the streets, she takes a series of new benefactors. Some she later kills, some she leaves. Her last benefactor is from the Heartland. He enjoys pain, she enjoys inflicting it. Wyatt watches in disbelief as she cuts long gashes in his back and upper arms with a razor. Benefactor number two is the loser in a personal transport confrontation. The new tenant is a woman, tall, fierce, taloned. The red-haired girl is kept on, first as a lover, then as a bodyguard. It ends with their arriving at the house with the atrium garden and the cellar maze.

The rain is merely pelting the windows now. The dawn is gray, the wind is gone.

Wyatt waits for Jennie.

But the show is over, and Jennie is a no-show.

Exhausted, Wyatt rubs the feeling back into his legs, goes to bed.

CHAPTER 23

The sky remains a dull featureless gray all day. The clock in the wall read five when he fell asleep. It reads five-thirty now. Wyatt wonders if he has slept for half an hour or half a day. He feels drained, lethargic, uninspired. He takes stock of himself, is relieved to find no parts missing. In the tub, he realizes he has neglected his litany. Then he remembers much of the reason for it no longer exists. He does not doubt the veracity of his waking dreams the night before, if truth can be said to have any bearing upon reality. The litany, or most of it, has become redundant. He knows what became of everyone. He can no longer take refuge in his uncertainty.

Only Jennie remains a mystery. Wyatt visualizes her face, fearing that any prying on his part might cause her ruin. He dismisses the notions of Jennie as either a civil guard or a prostitute. He considers it improbable that she would have left the city simply to take another job. What remains are the possibilities of her being collected, an uptown sweetie, a benefactor—such as Victor Crist—or a role in some underground organization. The latter seems most likely to him. It would explain why Walter had permitted Rafe to meet with him. He feels that Walter was holding something else back, something Rafe did not know. Another factor unknown. For now, it is enough for Wyatt to know that she has not been swept or disappeared.

I will find you, Jennie, count on me.

The talkie is flashing on the entry wall. He has two messages.

146

"Wyatt? This is Anna. Victor wants you to meet his train at Heartland Terminal East on Wednesday morning, eight a.m."

Tomorrow is Wednesday.

The second caller leaves no message.

Wyatt replays the blank recording three times, with the volume turned up to maximum.

He tries in vain to hear the breathing on the other end, tries to make it Jennie contacting him. He will not lie to himself, erases both messages, calls the tower canteen. Fresh coffee, dairy cream, a cinnamon bun. He begins his martial dance before breakfast. The movements have never been easier or more fluid. He repeats the steps a second, then a third time. He has lost count of the repetitions when the sky darkens beyond the windows. He now knows for sure he has slept the day away.

His coffee is cold so he orders more, drops the screen down from the ceiling.

"Wyatt Weston?" he asks after going through the security check.

The screen displays a two-paragraph history, listing his schooling, his day jobs, his current employment by Crist Enterprises. There is no mention of his early childhood or of him being arrested twice. There is no mention of any Heartland family connection.

"Weston Enterprises?"

"No such cartel," the screen responds. He is disappointed.

"Weston family/Heartland?"

"Insufficient clearance."

Wyatt smiles. There may be someone who knows or remembers him in the Heartland, even if they have long since disowned him, someone who can tell him about his early childhood.

Anastasia's face suddenly fills the screen.

"Are you just getting in?" she demands.

"I had a long night, Anna. I got your message. What do you want?"

"What were you doing in Sector Twelve last night?"

"Seeing a friend. You said party. I partied. What's it to you?"

"I'm part of Crist Enterprises, Wyatt. Everything you do is something to me. Stay out of Sector Twelve. Just friendly advice, lover."

"I'm not your lover, Anna."

Her face breaks into as wide a grin as her small mouth will form before exploding into tiny granules, leaving the previous screen in its place. He gives up on locating his family, goes back to his studies. Basic physics, matrix algebra, comparative mythology. Anna leaves him alone.

On Wednesday morning, Wyatt feels the world around him coming into and going out of focus in rapid succession. After four hours of sleep, he takes an early train to the Heartland. He is waiting for Victor Crist by seven-thirty. The home guardsman Victor called Charlie greets him as Mr. Weston, offers to contact Mr. Crist for him. Wyatt hopes he does not look as bad as he feels. Charlie acts as if everything were fine.

Victor arrives at eight sharp, just as the outbound train begins taking on passengers. There are several dozen complacent Heartlanders heading into the city. Wyatt counts four bodyguards among their number. Victor says nothing. He looks to Wyatt to be preoccupied. Wyatt stays two steps behind him, looking in all directions. All the bodyguards watch each other carefully as each party boards a separate link in the tube train. Victor leads Wyatt to the first link, then to the first compartment behind the driver. Victor looks into the driver's compartment, exchanges smiles and friendly waves with him before motioning for Wyatt to open the compartment door.

Wyatt pushes the hand panel, the door slides open with a soft hiss.

Once the train is moving, Victor hands Wyatt a small placard reading *Private Compartment*, points at the compartment door. Wyatt places it against the clear plastic door, watches the door become an opaque blue.

Victor opens his jacket pocket, removes a wand. He sets it on *safety*.

"Where did you get that toy you use?" Victor asks.

"Curtis gave it to me. It's what the street sweepers carry."

"Take this one. It's self sighting, packs more kill, holds four times the charge of yours. It can also disintegrate certain forms of inorganic matter."

Wyatt examines the new wand. It is slightly heavier and larger than his old one, but fits into his holster just as easily. He sets the old wand on *lockout*, drops it into his vest pocket. He nods his thanks to Victor, who is once again lost in thought.

The train passes through sector after sector. Twice Victor motions with his head for Wyatt to check the corridor outside their compartment. Cautiously, Wyatt steps into the corridor, remaining there until the next stop. He watches the other passengers exiting, new riders boarding the link. All look self-absorbed, unaware, innocuous. Most are day workers, a few are supervisory staff, one appears to be a young woman with time on her hands. The train starts down the tube again, Wyatt returns to the compartment. Victor looks up at Wyatt, who simply nods—he sees no danger. Victor shuts his eyes and sighs.

For an hour, Wyatt watches the towers with their parks transforming into the uptown, then the spacious uptown turning into the sprawling downtown, with two-minute stops at two-minute intervals as it loops through the maze of streets.

The train passes through Sectors Eight, Four, One. Victor makes no sign of disembarking. Once again he nods for Wyatt to check the corridor. The first link is separating from the rest of the train. Wyatt is unsure if this is normal. He watches carefully, listening for any threatening sound. When the first link keeps traveling eastward, Wyatt walks its entire length, looking into the other passenger compartments. They are all empty.

Wyatt has never left the city, except for his trips to the Heartland. Flat plains filled with brown dust and pale green scrub replace the gray walls of Sector One. In the distance, there is a broken forest of bare blanched tree trunks, twisted boughs, swirling dust clouds close to the ground. Victor begins to relax.

"We're alone, except for the driver," Wyatt tells him.

Victor nods.

"Should I be looking for someone special?" Wyatt asks.

"No. But stay alert. Someone is stalking us. I can feel it."

Wyatt wants to ask more questions. He says nothing, listening to the whoosh of the train, watching the inhospitable landscape flashing by. His body begins to throb from lack of sleep. He forces himself to remain awake, to remain alert, to remain focused.

An hour later, the train begins to slow. Pale blue sky becomes an even paler shade of cerulean. Wyatt realizes they have entered another dome.

"We're here, Mr. Crist," a voice announces.

"Thanks, Harry," Victor replies.

"Where's here?" Wyatt asks.

"Farm One."

Victor motions for Wyatt to go on ahead. Wyatt leads the way, stepping cautiously into the corridor, onto the platform. It is an empty concrete slab with a dozen brown plastic slat benches. Victor follows him. The engineer takes the single train link into a holding bay, turns it around. There is a long mechanical sigh when the link shuts down.

"He work for you?" Wyatt asks, nodding at the link.

"Yes."

The atmosphere within this dome is warm and humid. Wyatt finds it oppressive. Four green-clad home guards appear above them, carrying long barrels. Two descend cautiously. Wyatt notices their eyes are black, their skin is darker than his, their features flat.

"Mr. Crist," one announces. "We didn't expect you."

"Surprise visit, Ray," Victor says and forms a disarming smile. "Will you inform Mr. Han we're here to see him?"

Ray begins speaking in a language Wyatt does not understand. He looks back at Victor, smiles quickly, then speaks into the helmet com again. Another smile. "Mr. Han is in the fields, Mr. Crist. He asks that you join him there. I have summoned a personal transport and a driver for you."

A few moments later an open transport arrives, with a small young woman at the controls. Her short hair is a lustrous black, as are her sparkling almond-shaped eyes. She smiles courteously, opening the rear doors for Victor and Wyatt. They climb in.

The doors shut, the transport soars upward, revealing miles of lush green plants in narrow troughs just above the ground, arranged in neat rows forming a quilted pattern below them. Wyatt counts thirty more home guards hovering in groups of two and four in the vault-shaped dome. Water towers rise at regular intervals, with catch basins in the dome above them. Dozens of white-clad workers move between the troughs, tending the crops. They continue flying over a small complex of interconnected terraced dwellings, then land in a small clearing dotted by smaller dome-shaped huts well past the living units. Two transports are parked near one of them.

A small muscular man with a long sparse salt-and-pepper beard, a practiced smile, flanked by six bodyguards in neat black uniforms, stands in the shade of a bamboo awning at the largest of the huts, watching Wyatt and Victor disembark. Wyatt vaguely remembers him from The Committee meeting.

"Welcome, Victor," their host says. He bows slowly, smiles, never letting his eyes leave Victor.

"Thank you for seeing me, Han," Victor replies, bowing back.

"You are just in time for tea. Afterwards, we can discuss the value of your life and what Crist Enterprises can do for us."

Wyatt feels six pair of eyes glaring at him as Han's bodyguards fan out around them, their thick bare arms folded across their chests.

CHAPTER 24

"Remember why I hired you," Victor says quietly to Wyatt as they follow two of Han's bodyguards into the hut.

For a moment Wyatt is ducking through the low doorway of the adobe hut, listening to the familiar hum of the climate control within. Then he is sitting at the sidewalk cafe, the taste of fried eggs, potatoes, oregano bread lingering on his tongue, gulping down the last of his coffee. *What's in it for you, swami?* he quips at Victor, who smiles, flashing silver teeth. *I need someone to watch my back,* Victor says dryly. The moment passes. Wyatt catches his foot on the reed floor mat, loses his balance.

Han's bodyguards stare in disbelief at Wyatt staggering across the hut. Even with the climate control, the air is still hot and muggy, just less so. They smile, their thin mouths curving up just as their dark mustaches curve downward.

They think it's the heat. He smiles back weakly, feigning embarrassment.

The hut is empty, save for a small black lacquered table, a ceramic tea set, two cane chairs placed in the very middle of the floor.

"Sit," Han says to Victor, nodding toward the table.

Victor smiles graciously, selects the seat farthest from the door. Han sits opposite him. Two of the black-garbed bodyguards stand behind Han watching Victor, two behind Victor facing Han. The last two stand back-to-back with these, facing Wyatt, who remains standing four feet away with his back pressed against the far side of the hut.

The heat from the curved wall radiates into his backside. He feels the perspiration trickling down his neck between his shoulder blades. Wyatt is watching Victor's back as best he can with four large men between them. Without thinking, he eases both his open hands into his vest pockets. The fingertips of his left hand stop when they touch his old wand. He smiles at the two stern faces whose dark eyes peer into his, flicks the safety to *full charge* with his forefinger.

There is a blue and white ceramic tea pot with two delicate matching tea cups in the center of the table, a red lacquered tray bearing six more cups at the edge.

Han nods. One of the bodyguards standing behind him pours steaming yellow tea into the two cups. Han smiles, runs his left hand through his thin black and white beard.

"While your visit is not altogether unexpected, I would have hoped for you to have shown me the courtesy of asking my leave before coming to Farm One uninvited," Han says coldly. "You have no reason to imagine yourself welcome here, Victor."

"I meant no disrespect," Victor replies, "but it was a last-minute decision. I did not wish to alert anyone else to my presence prematurely. We both have enemies, Han. Better we become friends before they unite against us."

"Your logic escapes me, Victor. Most of my enemies are your friends. Many of those you have alienated are my friends."

"Many, but not all."

"What do you want, Victor?"

"Your support, Han. The cities are deteriorating. We must rebuild the slums. We are on the brink of anarchy. You do not see that, here in your private country domain. But I see it every time I journey through them. I know that your opposition to my plan is purely political. You are in-

154

clined to vote with your friends. I am asking you to look past your politics—look past them for the good of all. I am willing to compensate you for this philanthropical perspective, so long as the recompense is reasonable."

Han lifts the smooth round cup before him, sips the tea, shuts his eyes, smiles approvingly. Victor mimics the gesture. Han scowls.

"Since when is Victor Crist the champion of the oppressed?" Han demands. "You were little more than a thieving opportunist when you murdered your father thirty years ago. I have seen no change in you since then. Please do not speak to me as if I were a fool. There is enough bad blood between us already, without your adding insult to the long list of injuries. Have you forgotten? Two of my sons died at your hand. You owe me much already. What if I were to ask you for your sons as recompense, Victor? What then?"

"Han, please do not make this personal. We all play by the same rules."

"Yes, but not all of us have made a religion of them, Victor."

"I do not blaspheme your beliefs, Han. Please show me the same courtesy."

Wyatt sees a change coming over Han. The muscles in his face are tensing, outlining his jaws, making his eyes widen. His patience is nearly spent. He takes a deep breath, calms himself.

"What would you have me tell Chairman Void, Victor? So sorry, Adolph, Victor has had an unexpected attack of conscience that supersedes even our longstanding friendship? Is that how you have foreseen it?"

"Of course not, Han. I will speak privately with Adolph myself. I just want your assurances that you will not oppose me in this matter."

Han laughs, takes another sip of tea. His features disappear in a cloud of water vapor for an instant. When they reappear, his face is relaxed once more. "Indulge me, Victor. What is your idea of just recompense? Three sluts for a week, a complimentary assassination, a penthouse in Sector Eighty-Four?"

"I had the entire tower in mind."

Han seems genuinely surprised. He studies Victor's face, considers the offer. "Why so generous?"

"I would like to see all of us diversify. If we genuinely shared one another's interests, our philanthropical gestures would seem less unbelievable."

"By that, I take it you wish some ownership in Farm One."

"Not right away, Han. But the idea is not necessarily as impossible as you make it sound."

Han laughs again. "You are always audacious, Victor. I'll give you that much."

"I don't believe you are taking me seriously, Han."

"I always take you seriously, Victor. I know that if you are here, you must want far more than you are willing to give. Generosity is not in your nature. I assume you want me dead, that you have come with your new shooter to kill me, that my only alternative is to kill you first. Isn't that the way of your cult? Only the strong survive, they remain strong only by culling the weak; this they call *a celebration of life*."

"You quote us quite well, Han, but you do not understand the nature of the truths you speak. You and I are both the strong. There is no need for us to turn upon one another."

At that, a wand blast rips underneath the small table. Wyatt sees the red swelling between the table legs. Han and his chair disappear in a bright orange fireball. Wyatt drops low, fires his old wand directly through his vest pocket, aiming between the two grim-faced bodyguards, who are momentarily distracted. The front of his silk vest disintegrates in a purple flash as a pair of blue arcing bolts cut across the four-foot space embracing all four men behind Victor. They shake violently, their features darken, disappear, their black cotton jackets and trousers disintegrate, their collection of weapons scatters upon the floor, their bodies harden, crumble.

The wand begins overheating in his left hand. Wyatt lets it fall, drawing the new one from his holster with his right.

Victor has already rolled across the hut to get well clear of Wyatt's blast zone.

One of the two remaining bodyguards stands with his left arm around the chest of the other, holding the limp body upright, a small bloody knife still biting into the soft flesh of the dead man's neck. A stream of deep purple squirts all over the table, onto the reed mat, the hard pack floor. The bodyguard smiles at Wyatt, who looks at Victor before slowly holstering his wand.

Victor drops his wand back into his jacket pocket, brushes the dust off the side of his yellow silk trousers, flicks an imaginary crumb from his lapel.

"How do we get out of here?" Wyatt whispers. "I counted thirty civil guards with long barrels out there."

Victor just raises his left hand for Wyatt to remain calm. "Is Jimmy ready, Roy?" Victor asks Han's remaining bodyguard.

"He's waiting for my call, Mr. Crist."

"Who's Jimmy?" Wyatt asks.

"Jimmy Han," Victor says, "Han's last surviving son and the new proprietor of Farm One."

CHAPTER 25

Victor Crist smiles broadly the entire ride back to the Heartland. His face is as radiant as the summer sun. He even tells Wyatt to remove the *Private Compartment* sign from the door, restoring the plastic to its original transparent state. The link glides down its tube with a soft comforting uninterrupted whoosh, passing through the barren landscape, glowing like Victor's face in the late afternoon sun. The train slows just before it reaches the Sector One station.

Wyatt sees the high walls that resemble a medieval fortress from the outside growing larger as they approach the city. He does not remember this stark unwelcome feature from the trip out. He turns his head to see the factory façade on the other side as they emerge into the bowels of the city, ponders what he has just seen. The walls of the buildings facing it have neither windows or doors. No one would notice these sham factories have no workers.

The link slows to a creep, attaching itself to the waiting westbound train with the slightest of bumps. He feels Victor's inquisitive gaze as he registers the grand deception they have just passed. Those living within the city have no idea they are surrounded by a wasteland. They have no idea they are prisoners.

I guess that's why my history lessons ended with the plagues, the holy wars, and the general disarmament that followed them.

Jimmy Han has agreed to all of Victor's terms, positively ecstatic at obtaining the uptown tower as well as his own fiefdom for doing little more than allowing Victor to assassinate his father, replacing Wyatt's tattered vest with another bearing two imperial dragons, agreeing to Victor's use of Farm One at some future time for a project as yet unspecified, serving his father's assassins lunch. Wyatt wonders what Victor is really about. The elder Han was right about one thing; it would be out of character for Victor to give more than he received in any transaction.

"I need you back in the Heartland for a few days, Wyatt. Have you made any plans?"

"I'd like to get back to the city by Sunday afternoon," Wyatt hears himself saying. He wonders if that is really his voice. The words are strange, the tone is flat, emotionless.

"I'll see that we don't detain you."

"What's next?"

"You humiliated Floyd in your workout, you know."

"Anna told me he felt that way. I think he got the better of it."

"I guess he felt the margin of his victory was too small."

"So what now? He gets to kill me, or just break my face and a few bones lower down?"

Victor breaks into a laugh. "Now you learn to fight without your wand, so he can't bust you up."

"Even Anna busts me up."

Victor laughs again. "For her, you're my surrogate."

"What?"

"She'd rather bust me up, but she's not good enough. Besides, I won't give her the chance. So she kicks the crap out of you instead."

"Part of the job, right?"

"Right. Besides, it looks to me like you get a few licks in."

"Yeah. Few."

Victor laughs out loud. The train pulls into the next station. Two men enter their compartment. Victor stops laughing, looks them over, relaxes, remains silent. Wyatt sees the exhaustion and defeat in their faces. He knows them to be day workers.

The train darts from station to station. Their traveling companions leave, others take their places. Between Sectors Eight and Ten a firefight is taking place in the street below them. Two purple bolts ricochet off the tube. Wyatt winces. Victor barely looks up. Their new traveling companions scramble under the seats. Civil guards descend like locusts just beyond the tube, firing their long barrels as they drop. A moment later, it is all behind them. Those who had hidden sit placidly, as if nothing whatever had happened. Victor is still grinning.

They reach Heartland Terminal East just as the glowing red-orange sunset lights up the three stringy clouds low on the western horizon. They are the only passengers disembarking from this train. Twenty minutes later, they arrive at Victor's house. Armed men wearing the Crist Enterprises silver and yellow watch the sky.

Floyd and Arthur, his younger brother, are waiting for them in the transport park.

"I think you've started something big," Floyd announces.

"What's happened?" Victor asks, leading them to his office.

"You've had fifteen calls, we've been scoped by two transports. I've got men covering every approach. The barricades are ready, should we need them. Any challenges on the way back?"

"The dome was mine."

"Who'd you kill?"

"Bert Han."

"He's got a lot of friends."

"Not anymore. Unless they're stupider than he was, they're chatting with Jimmy right now to make sure they still have a friend on Farm One."

"Adolph isn't going to like it."

"Adolph doesn't like anything I do. Besides, he's getting old, Floyd. The last power play he made, he lost six of his best men for one of Edward's ground crew. He's living on past glories. I doubt his body can take another transplant. He's terminated everyone with any initiative in his own organization, so there's no one left strong enough to take over. Void Enterprises will be lucky to outlast him. He's the last of his line, Floyd, and he's too much of a realist to make another bad move right now. I think it's more likely he's looking for common ground finding a way to profit and save face at the same time. Besides, the other members like him the way he is—a figurehead. There will be a new Chairman as soon as the next real debate takes place, probably within the year."

"You looking for the job?"

"Not this time out. We might be strong enough to take it, but not to hold it. We need a bit more young blood."

"You mean like lover boy here?"

Victor smiles at Floyd disarmingly. "Lover boy just took out four of Bert Han's best—with one shot. Using one of those silly little sweeper toys. It almost blew up in his hand."

A new respect replaces the derision in Floyd's eyes. "Well, I never thought he lacked for guts."

"Wyatt," Victor says, "why don't you get cleaned up, head down to the dojo? Anna will see how far you've progressed. Don't worry, you can have another crack at Floyd before you go back to the city."

"You're too kind."

Victor only smiles. Floyd and Arthur ignore him.

Wyatt leaves them, makes his way to the other side of the house. In the living room he sees Anna, Sonja, and their mother in front of the screen, discussing vitamins with a thin-faced young woman with high cheekbones and thick brown hair who sits before a roaring fireplace.

From the back, the Crist women still look identical to him, but Wyatt is certain that Anna is the one on the left. He wonders how he knows.

"Hello, Wyatt," she says, confirming his suspicion without turning around.

"Hey, Anna."

Thirty minutes later, they are facing one another on the mat.

Twenty minutes of meditation, followed by twenty minutes of warmup exercises, lead to the martial movements together, then practice.

Once again Anastasia moves faster than Wyatt can react. He catches her left heel in the solar plexus, a backhand to the side of his neck, an elbow to the lower back. She flips him over, twists his arm from the wrist until he cries out, then kicks him in the ribs. He feels as if he is moving underwater. His reflexes seem gone.

"Sonja could do better than that, Wyatt. And she's got all the moves of a dead drossie."

Wyatt scrambles to his feet, his head spinning. For a moment he sees two of Anna. Both are laughing at him from across the room. He staggers a step backwards. This time she comes at him rolling head over heels, moving in a straight line. He is sure he can avoid her, knocking her over at the same time, but he is wrong on both counts. She kicks his legs out from under him, catches him around the waist, with her legs coming up on top of him as he falls onto his back. She slams her open hands across his ears, breaking his eardrums.

He screams again, repairing the damage as quickly as he can. But the restoration takes concentration. He cannot repair and defend himself at the same time. The pain is too intense to ignore; he is certain she will not kill him, he will risk it. Closing his eyes to visualize his ears, he feels Anna all over him, opening his shirt, his trousers, slipping her arms around him, rubbing her bare chest against his, pressing her face into his neck. He offers neither help or resistance.

Her breath is hot. She clings lightly, unlike Rachel, who always seems to hold onto him as if her life depends on it. Anna grinds slowly, making no sound, until her heartbeat begins to race with his. She makes a single small noise in the back of her throat. They lie on the mat together, bathed in perspiration, neither one moving or saying anything.

At a creaking sound from the corridor, Anna sits up, pulls on her workout suit.

"You better punch me in the face," she whispers.

Wyatt scrambles to his feet, pulls up his trousers. "What?" he asks, clumsily buttoning his shirt.

"If you don't mess me up, Victor will want me along with the others tonight. He'll know we were together. He'll kill us both for sure."

CHAPTER 26

Anna is grilling him about the reconciliation of the concepts of quantum mechanics and relativity when Wyatt notices the small clock on the screen reading eleven-thirty.

It's Thursday.

Absently, he stops speaking in mid-sentence, walks to the window. The surface of the lake is placid, as always within the windless dome, a blue mirror fringed with houses, trees. There is no alarm sounding for the Heartlanders to take shelter. There are no swarms of rats, roaches, or drossies flowing to the recycling centers. He did not really expect any, but there is a wide gulf between expectation and knowing.

Anastasia laughs.

"There are no sweeps in the Heartland," she jeers. "Did you really think there would be?"

The left side of her face is swollen, lumpy, purple; her words are slightly garbled. Wyatt is certain he did not hit her hard enough to do more than raise a red welt. The sight of her is still disconcerting to him, even after two hours of grilling. He says nothing, walks back to the screen. He knows her haughty attitude, condescending tone of voice are for the benefit of the other members of the household. Someone must be within earshot.

Victor will leave her alone for a couple of weeks now. But Floyd will want to take my head off for bashing her that hard before I leave. She plays everyone. How is she playing me?

"I guess Curtis Void has just figured out I'm not

sweeping for him anymore," he says.

"You make it sound like you miss sweeping."

"I used to hang with some of the guys there. I miss them."

"You still don't get it, do you?"

"Get what?"

"Everything changes. Sooner rather than later. None of your city friendships are ever going to last. Some get swept. Some get disappeared. Some move on. You're moving on. Who's pining for you? Rachel Void? She'll get over you, too, when the time comes. Faster than you'll get over her, from the look of you."

Wyatt feels his face reddening.

"Relax, Wyatt. Nobody at Crist Enterprises is going to do anything to your delicate ladylove, Rachel. She keeps you happy—that keeps us happy. Besides, if anything nasty were to happen to Adolph's granddaughter, it would start a war. I'm just saying that when you tire of her, don't make too much of it. She'll tire of you eventually. The only question is who will get bored first. My guess is Rachel."

"You have it all figured, don't you, Anna?"

"Not all, but more than you."

Wyatt grinds his teeth, takes a deep breath.

Bitch.

"Bow-wow," Anna says, turning off the screen. "Go get something to eat. Daddy wants you to do your job this afternoon. Can't have you at half-steam. You look like you spent yourself on your girlfriend before you came here again."

That's from playing dead for you, Anna.

Anastasia takes a step back from him, sucks in her breath. She looks genuinely pained. She recovers quickly, smiles, blows him a kiss. She brushes past him, runs her hand gently over his cheek as she struts from the room. Against his will, he follows her with his eyes until she turns down the corridor. He hears Anastasia talking with her mother in the foyer.

Can she really hear my thoughts, or is she just slick enough to figure them out?

The sound of measured footsteps in the corridor grows louder. Anna's mother smiles delicately as she comes into the room. Her face is almost identical to that of her daughter, but her eyes are blue bordering on gray, with a fading light she is desperately trying to maintain.

"We've never had a chance to talk," she says in a practiced voice. "My name is Tassy."

Wyatt feels suddenly awkward, forces a smile. "Yeah, I guess you're busy around here."

Tassy smiles back, walks to the window, looks out longingly. "What's it like out there?"

"Out where?"

"The city. I've never been outside the Heartland. I never even leave the house anymore."

Wyatt stops to consider. "It's different. Most people I know are worried about getting swept. They work enough to get by, then party 'til the credits are gone. There's a lot of craziness everybody tries to ignore. You don't get many chances to direct your own life. There's not a lot of good stuff to own. I guess people get by, by lying to themselves. I don't know. It's just different. There's a lot of others who are doing better than my friends. I can't speak for them."

Tassy continues to smile. She leaves the window, stands directly in front of him. It is obvious that half of what he is saying makes no sense to her whatever, while the other half really isn't so different from her life. Wyatt just wants to end the conversation, leave the room.

"Victor says that you're a remarkable young man," Tassy says. "That you forced yourself to remember things . . . that you investigated things on your own, trying to make sense of it all."

"I guess Victor and I are alike that way."

"What way?"

"We both try to figure things out. He's a Committee member and all, so he's got a hold of what's really going on. I just look around myself, do the best I can with it."

"What were you trying to figure out that impressed him so much?"

Wyatt laughs nervously, looks at his feet. "I was . . . looking at patterns in the street."

"Patterns?"

"Yeah. Dark patterns on the pavement that I found in different places. I figured out that jumpers leave them."

"Jumpers?"

"Yeah. They jump off tall buildings. Usually onto someone walking by."

Tassy's eyes grow large, she gapes at Wyatt for a moment. "Why do they do that?" she asks quietly, forcing another smile.

"I guess they've had enough. They want to die. Maybe they don't want to do it alone."

Tassy just stares at Wyatt. She is no longer smiling. "You are a very strange young man."

Wyatt watches her turn, leave the room. He waits until he can no longer hear her footsteps, then leaves the room after her.

He sees the door ajar when he reaches his suite. Cautiously, he pushes it open. One of the women is staring languidly out the window, with her back toward him, her face to one side. It can't be Tassy—he just left her. Tassy surely wouldn't want to speak with him again. It doesn't feel like Anastasia, who knows better than to wait for him in his room.

"Sonja?" he asks, standing in the corridor.

"How did you know?" she asks, turning slowly, her brown eyes sparkling as she cocks her head slightly to the left. She is fingering the drapes, caressing the linen fabric.

"You're not all completely alike," he says.

"We're supposed to be. Daddy likes it that way."

"Maybe when you're with him, but not all the time."

"That's a silly thing to say. He doesn't see us when we're not with him."

"Yeah, right. So what's brought you here?"

"Why are you standing in the hallway? Are you afraid of me?"

"I don't think Victor would approve of us alone in my room."

"You're alone with Anna all the time."

"Yeah, but Victor wants it that way."

Sonja pouts. "Well, Daddy sent me to tell you to meet him in the transport park in twenty minutes."

She brushes past him without touching him, as if he were one of the servants.

I am one of the servants, he suddenly realizes.

Wyatt considers calling Rachel. He drums his fingers on the wall next to the talkie for a moment, picturing her face, tasting the basil on her tongue.

Rachel doesn't want to be reminded about this place. I don't blame her. She really wants to forget all of it. Poor Rachel.

Deciding against calling her, he puts on the silk holster she gave him, the dragon vest Jimmy Han gave him. Wyatt slips the new wand into the charger, leaves it there for thirty seconds, enough to build up a full charge. If Victor needs him inside the dome, there's probably going to be a firefight.

CHAPTER 27

Victor pilots the third transport, well behind the others, keeping it above and to the left of the one directly in front of it, which is behind, above, and to the right of the first. They are not challenged or fired upon, nor do they see any other traffic in the dome as they skirt the treetops. Wyatt rides beside Victor, keeping his eye on the screen. Flat gray translucent images of the trees and the terrain below them drift by, superimposed over a series of blue grids designating longitudinal and vertical distances. Two pink lights glow, moving steadily through the grids.

"Put it on long-range," Victor says. He points at the third of ten black rectangles at the bottom of the screen. "Just touch it," he adds.

Wyatt touches the spot, the screen jumps from a one-mile to a ten-mile radius. The vertical grid remains intact, but the horizontal one becomes more defined. The treetops below them now resemble the tasteless gray mush on which Wyatt used to sustain himself. Small dark blue shapes appear at regular intervals to the right and left of their course. Wyatt realizes these are buildings. A few small deep red dots near one of them must be people. No new glowing pinpoints of light appear anywhere.

"That's not right," Victor announces.

"Why?"

"We should be picking up traffic somewhere in the neighborhood."

"It was like that when we came back from Farm One."

"I know."

"What does that mean?"

"It means one of two things. Either everyone is lying low, making certain what, if anything, will be done in response to the change in the order, or else someone is lying in wait for us and nobody else wants to risk getting in the way. Probably a lot of meetings happening now."

"Never a dull moment when you're around, is there?" Victor laughs.

"What about the house?" Wyatt asks.

"What about it?"

"Anybody left to defend it?"

"Yes, but that's not the way things are done here. Nobody kills family for revenge. Only principals and shooters. If anyone starts something like that, the home guard will respond. Still, we've got enough alarms and weapons there to repel anything short of an all-out invasion by an entire cartel. To the best of my knowledge, that's never happened before."

Victor presses the short-range control. The trees on the screen once again resemble the trees below them. Two more adjustments create a few vibrant reds and oranges darting through the image.

"That's a rabbit, that's a fox," Victor says, pointing. "Those are squirrels and birds. Look for anything moving, or anything that doesn't look like it belongs. This is infrared, but shooters can wear isotherms. Check both short- and long-range."

Wyatt pours over both images. Trees look like trees, with nothing out of the ordinary on short-range. Only wildlife, houses, and the people around them glow on long-range.

"You eliminate a lot of the competition?" Wyatt asks.

"Every now and again."

"Somebody usually come looking to pay their respects afterwards?"

"More often than not."

"Was old Han a popular boy?"

"He thought so."

"You didn't?"

"He took care of his close friends. Grew specialty items for them, kept their larders stocked with fresh produce and meat. That gets you a lot of favors but not a lot of respect. Most of his friends were moderates. Not known for making sudden moves or dramatically expressing their displeasure. There are a few exceptions, however."

"Does that include Chairman Void?"

"You got it."

Wyatt watches the screen silently for a moment. "So you want to see if Adolph has any fire left? No fire, new Chairman."

"Very good."

"Maybe old Han wasn't stocking your larder the way you wanted."

"That, too."

"What's the rest?"

"Wait and see. Once the heat's off, I'll show you—beyond your wildest dreams."

The lead transport cuts sharply to the right, dropping low beyond the trees. The others follow. Victor makes another adjustment to the screen. Wyatt can pick out a fleet of transports parked around a large house, with twenty people scattered in twos and threes around them.

"Where are we?" Wyatt asks.

"Edward's house."

"Who's here?"

"The realty/construction cartel."

Victor parks his transport in advance of his escort, who circle the house twice before landing on either side of Victor. Floyd and his bodyguard follow Victor and Wyatt into the house. Arthur and his bodyguard stay with the transports.

The house is larger than Victor's, rising three stories with high peaked roofs, large Palladian windows, independent turrets front and back, thick ivy clinging to the deep red bricks everywhere. Inside, a large covered atrium filled with lush vegetation, amid dramatic sweeping patios clustered around a large curved inground pool, is visible from the foyer. A servant leads them into the atrium, where a dozen men stand together around a long table chatting amiably while their bodyguards all stand together in a line behind them. Wyatt takes his place among the bodyguards, who quickly make a place for him in their midst.

"It went as planned?" Edward asks.

"Of course," Victor says. "What have you heard?"

"Adolph is not pleased. But that was expected. A lot of the cartels are meeting right now. I don't think anyone is looking to add your head to their trophy case just yet."

"Do you still think everyone will accept the change at Farm One?"

"That depends on whether Jimmy Han can keep his father's seat on The Committee. What do you think?"

"Jimmy and I planned this months ago. He kept it quiet—there were no leaks. No complications, his man did his part. I think Jimmy can look after himself. I'm more interested in what Adolph will do."

"I think I pulled his teeth last month. He won't risk another humiliation just yet. The question is whether or not anyone will do anything for him. There are a lot of people who want to keep him Chairman forever."

"Who's got the most to lose if we pull this off?"

"Manufacturing/recycling. We've got to sweeten the pot for them."

"Agreed," Victor says.

"I'm open to suggestions."

"They get what's left after demo. We can give them a break."

"I'm thinking we just give demo to them outright."

"For concessions."

"Of course."

"A few of the pharm/med boys will probably grouse."

"That's a given. They always grouse. It's got them an empire for almost no risk. I think there isn't much we can offer them."

"New facilities? More bodies?"

"Possibly. I'm not sure they want any just now. They're going to remain an open variable in this thing."

The discussion turns to current projects, rentals, the census. Servants bring refreshments. The members sit down at the table. Bodyguards remain standing. They are served fruit punch, hot coffee, light sandwiches. When it is over, the members leave by ones and twos with their escorts.

The bodyguard next to Wyatt, a young man with olive features, leans over, whispers, "I hear you took out four of Han's men with one shot. That right?"

"Yeah."

"Nice move."

CHAPTER 28

For the first hour, Anastasia takes him through the meditation that relaxes him utterly, the warmups that limber his muscles until he feels like his body moves by itself, the slow measured movements that make his midsection burn, his feet feel as if they are rooted to the earth. For the second, she throws him all over the mat as if he were little more than a sack of bones. Then she begins attacking him in earnest, her blows raining down on him like hailstones. His ribs ache in a dozen places, his arms are bruised, he can feel his upper lip growing large and numb. Her small mouth remains expressionless, her glowing green eyes remain fixed. The swelling on the side of her face has gone down considerably, but it still makes her look like a drossie caught in the sweep.

To his own surprise, Wyatt begins evading her blows after fifteen minutes, occasionally flipping her onto her backside. She is always back on her feet before he can follow up on his advantage, but it is comforting to know that he is beginning to anticipate her attack. For another forty-five minutes, they take turns knocking one another down, until Anastasia sends Wyatt reeling from an unexpected drop-kick to the solar plexus.

"That's enough for today," she says. "Tomorrow it's Floyd's turn. I hope you're ready. There's nothing more I can do for you before then."

Wyatt sits up slowly, gasping for breath. He lets his head hang between his knees until he can stand. He rises gingerly before Anastasia, his body a web of throbbing pain. He tries to gently touch the swelling on her face, but she pulls back.

"Don't," she whispers.

Her eyes meet his with expression for the first time. He sees her determination, patience, strength. He looks deeper, sees what he takes for compassion before she turns away.

She leaves the dojo without another word, her steps still quick, controlled. He follows her at a much slower pace. Victor is waiting for him at the top of the stairs.

"You look beat," Victor says.

"Three hours with Anna—what should I look like?"

Victor laughs. "I thought you might like to know, Edward just called. Somebody paid Farm One a visit last night. Jimmy Han has cemented his hold on his seat, while the opposition lost four more shooters in the process. Still, you better watch yourself going back to the city tomorrow. They may be looking for you. Are you sure you want to return this soon?"

"I have to."

Victor just nods.

Anastasia is waiting for him in the screen room after he has cleaned up, changed, rested.

"Your pleasure," she says.

"If you're asking me what I want to learn today, there's something I'd really like to know," he says.

"Who you are, who your parents are, where they are," Anna says flatly.

"Yeah."

"Let's find out."

"Vector seven, circa minus twenty-three," Anna says.

The screen goes blank, a long list of names appears. Anna keeps issuing coded commands until the list is reduced to one, Wyatt Weston. From that point, the responses are encrypted in odd figures that Wyatt can neither recognize nor read. Anna maintains her dialogue with the screen at a dizzying speed. Eventually the screen goes blank. Anastasia seems lost in thought. She does not even look at Wyatt.

"That was very helpful," Wyatt says. "Any time I can return the favor."

"Your mother was Edna Weston," Anna says.

"Was?"

"She disappeared about the time you were sent to school. Overpopulation in the Heartland. Her people are drones in transportation/distribution. Your father is Mycro Vellum. He heads up transportation/distribution. Odd man. No family members in his enterprise. Never attends Committee meetings. He's very close to Adolph Void."

"So Mycro uses Edna for a tingle, begets me, dumps us both to maintain the census?"

"That's it."

"Wha'd the silly cow get pregnant for?"

"It was her one chance at power, Wyatt. She gambled, lost."

"Yeah." Wyatt heaves a sigh. "How did you learn to do all that with the screen, Anna?"

"Heartland women live off the screen, Wyatt. Most are kept drugged by it. I learned to use it before it used me."

"You're a oner, Anna."

"You'd better remember that."

"So, can anybody in the Heartland do what you just did?"

"Anyone who matters can."

"Teach me about transportation/distribution."

The sun is visible just above the trees when Anastasia shuts off the screen. Wyatt has learned all there is to know about transportation and distribution, from ox-carts to space bullets, from sea lanes to turf lines. He shuts his eyes, rubs them like a baby. "Where's everybody?" he asks absently.

"Victor is with Tassy and Sonja, Floyd and Arthur have their own wing. They don't come into this one unless Victor sends for them."

"What about . . ."

"The servants?"

"Yeah."

"They learn to be there when they're needed, stay away when they're not. Most are keeping watch, just in case someone still feels strongly about Bert Han."

"Bert who?"

Anna smiles at Wyatt's joke.

They eat dinner together without speaking, go their separate ways. Wyatt is tired, turns in early. He dreams he is wandering about an empty house. The rooms are bare, dark, dusty. Thin rays of sunlight pierce thick ratty curtains, he must maneuver by their light. At the top of the house, he finds a large comfortable room with a small bed, an Oriental carpet, an odd-shaped piece of furniture in the center of the floor. There is no dust. Wyatt sniffs the air. It smells of ale and cooking oil.

Jennie? Jennie—are you here?

Wyatt looks around the room, under the bed, then stops before the oddity at its center. It has an hexagonal-shaped end, is long enough to contain a body. The top is flat and smooth, like a table. One long side is divided into two raised panels, each with two brass handles. He tries to turn the top pair, but they do not yield. He pushes, then pulls, on them. A shallow drawer filled with women's clothing opens with a low creak. Wyatt pokes through the stockings, women's undergarments, before closing it. The lower drawer resists his pull. It contains something heavy.

Wyatt must pull with all his strength to open it. It, too, appears filled with clothing. But under the layer of folded blouses, he feels a body.

His heart begins to race. The body is still warm. He brushes the clothes away. The room has darkened, he cannot see anything clearly. His hands touch the long arms, the cleft chin, the thick hair. It is a face he has caressed countless times. He does not need to see the features to know it is Jennie. He puts his hand upon her chest, feels it filling with breath, rising slowly. She is alive. He leans over, kisses her lips. The lips kiss back, but nothing else moves. He kisses them again, as tenderly as he can. Something is tugging at him. He does not want to leave, but he cannot resist the pull.

He awakens to find the entire right side of his body gone.

CHAPTER 29

Wyatt's body is still aching from its regeneration when he reaches the dojo. The rising sun is an orange smear at the edge of the dome, sending tendrils of golden pink spiraling up its sides, across the mirrored surface of the lake. Floyd will not be here for hours. Wyatt does not feel like dealing with Victor Crist or his family just yet. The dojo seems like the closest thing to sanctuary the house has to offer him. Wyatt touches the right side of his face, still not quite certain it is all there. The face feels like wax to his fingers, the fingers feel like ice to his face.

He sits down in the center of the mat facing the door, crosses his legs, shuts his eyes. His breathing is shallow, erratic. Gradually, he takes control of it. His hands are fidgeting in his lap, he makes a point of setting his open right hand upon the left palm. The large room seems even larger in the dark. His thoughts ramble on, like dry leaves spun by a wind gust. He disassociates himself from them.

Jennie needs me. Jennie needs me.

This one thought keeps surfacing through all the rest.

Jennie, where are you? How do I find you? Anastasia could locate you in a heartbeat, but what else would she do?

He waits for her to answer him, knowing full well there will be no response. He tries to visualize Jennie's face, like he has done almost every day since she vanished. He listens, hoping to hear her telling him that she will always be waiting for him in their special place, on that special day. He sees black. He hears his rambling fears lurching off in all directions.

He takes his only comfort from the sound of his own breathing, like slow lapping waves reaching for the shore. He has never seen an ocean, or heard the surf. Still the sound is soothing. He shifts his legs twice as the hours pass. They seem like minutes.

"Waiting for me?" Floyd asks.

"Yeah."

Wyatt opens his eyes to see Floyd standing over him.

"Arthur thought you ran off to hide. Anna knew you were here."

Wyatt stands up, begins his warmups.

"Look, Wyatt," Floyd says. "I know you didn't bust up Anna's face like that. You can kill to defend yourself, lash out when you hurt, but I don't think it's in your nature to inflict pain or make trophies."

Wyatt says nothing.

"I know Anna," Floyd continues. "If she gives you something, she wants something back from you right away. She's teaching you hand-to-hand. What she wants in return is your help keeping her out of Victor's bed. She probably goaded you into smacking her the first time. Maybe she did it again, but I know you didn't do all of it."

Floyd is staring at him.

"She's a good teacher," Wyatt says, not wanting to give Anna away.

Floyd smiles. "Just wanted you to know it's nothing personal."

"Thanks."

Their workout lasts an hour. Floyd's moves are much harder to anticipate than Anna's. Wyatt stays on the defensive, parrying, dodging, occasionally throwing Floyd, who seems to barely touch the mat before he rights himself. Floyd's hands are fast, he punches in hard flurries. He moves suddenly, deftly, leaving Wyatt split seconds to twist out of harm's way, occasionally to even punch back. In the end, Floyd catches him with an elbow, flips him over onto his stomach, pins him by twisting his arm, bending his wrist, shooting a quick kick to his ribs. Wyatt hears bones cracking.

"You can't fight worth a damn, Wyatt," Floyd says. "You make the perfect killer. You'll always have something to prove."

Wyatt listens to Floyd walking up the steps. Everything hurts. Nothing seems even remotely real. He sits up, mends the four cracked ribs.

In the hall, Anna is waiting for him.

"Ready to go?" she demands.

"Yeah."

"Can't keep poor Rachel waiting."

Wyatt frowns.

"No escort?" he asks in the transport park, as they climb into one of the two-seaters. None of the servants are here.

"I'm expendable," she says. "Besides, family is sacrosanct. No one would shoot through me to reach you. Consider me your shield."

Anastasia maneuvers the transport upward, cuts sharply eastward just above the trees. Looking around, Wyatt counts five other transports seemingly oblivious to their presence, moving off in other directions. They ride in silence. Wyatt feels the tension between them like a wedge of cold stone. He is careful not to think of anything. He begins to realize Anna's mental state has nothing whatever to do with him.

"What happened, Anna?" Wyatt asks quietly.

"Nothing ever happens. You know that."

"Something happened last night. Tell me what it was."

Anna's tight-lipped countenance neither changes nor betrays anything. Her green eyes remain fixed forward as she accelerates toward the train station. She drops the transport into a holding bay, agilely turns it around to face the Heartland.

"Bye," she says flatly.

Wyatt does not move. "I'm not leaving until you tell me, Anna."

Anna turns her jade green eyes on him. The whites are bloodshot, the pupils are dilated. He feels the rage and rancor pouring from them. He trembles. An image enters his mind, an image of one of the women, possibly Anna, struggling, fighting, being pinned to the small carpet beside a grand canopied bed. Thin flailing white arms, light blond hair, messy makeup, all in a jumbled blur. Victor's clutching hands, heavy body, leering face falling all over her. Wyatt shakes his head to dispel the terrifying image.

"What did he do to you?" he whispers.

Anastasia begins laughing. She reminds him of Rachel, only there is no hideousness in the sound. Anastasia never loses control. "I thought you could tell us apart, Wyatt."

"Hey, this mindtalk is all new to me."

"You'd better get used to it, if you plan on keeping my company."

She stares at him but no images follow.

"So what happened, Anna? Please tell me."

"She just couldn't do it anymore."

Wyatt says nothing, waiting for the rest of it. Anna leans back in her seat, looks out the windscreen across the green sweep of the Heartland rolling away from them.

"I don't know how she lasted this long. I mean, she always told herself that everything was fine, everything was right, everything was as it should be. Nothing ever penetrated her composure, nothing he wanted was ever too much for her. She kept herself immune to truth, pain, reason, just to please him."

Wyatt wants to reach out, touch Anna, but he is certain she would resent it. He holds himself back. She turns her head, looks at him, smiles.

"She was the only one in that house I loved, Wyatt. And now that sonofabitch has killed her. He's killed my mother, Wyatt. He's killed Tassy."

CHAPTER 30

Standing on the elevated walk, Wyatt watches her speeding away. He knows better than to remain beside the transport when Anna is driving. It glides quickly, easily, veers steeply, vanishes above the trees. He can still taste her on his lips. There's no spice flavor, only Anastasia, and the salt from the one tear that trickled down her cheek into their mouths at the end of it. His heart felt like a furnace, enveloping them both. Not even Jennie ever moved him like that. The kiss lingered until Anna slowly pulled herself away, pushing against his chest with both her small hands. She turned back to the controls, opened his door, practically shoved him out of the transport with one centered thrust.

He neither sees nor hears the two men waiting patiently for him among the trees just beyond the transport park. He feels them. Victor's gift, his new wand, is in his hand when he flings himself off the elevated walk back onto the grass below. The pulsing orange ball that erupts out of the low foliage barely misses him, splashes harmlessly against the side of the dome, onto the walk. He returns fire, shooting at the spot from which the ball originated. At first there is nothing there, but he watches his shot engulf something. It sizzles, crackles, vanishes. Nearby, something else not quite visible darts furtively, but he cannot make out the form. Green on green. More of a vibration than a movement.

Must be isotherms.

He fires again, just as the second assassin shoots at him. Their charges meet head on, erupt into a blinding flash in

184

mid-clearing. The vibration in the foliage ceases. He fires three more times, spreading his shots evenly across the last place he saw any sort of movement. There is a series of flashes. He sees two bushes catch fire, sizzle, burn quickly.

He checks the charge indicator. The wand is on half-charge.

Four of the home guard scramble from the platform, take to the air. Moments later, they extinguish the ground fire from above.

"You can get up now, Mr. Weston."

"Charlie?"

Wyatt rolls over to look at the familiar face within the green ceramic armor standing placidly on the platform behind him.

"You got them both. Spectacular shooting, I might add."

Wyatt stands up, brushes himself off.

"I'm sorry, Mr. Weston, but I'm going to have to fine you five hundred credits each for the shrubs. Nothing personal, but the law is the law."

"Right."

The ride back to Sector Thirty-Two is uneventful.

He does not risk another attack on the street, takes the chute to his tower. Cringing and squinting his eyes, he sees the security guard watching him emerge into the lobby.

"Welcome back, Mr. Weston."

"Thanks. You're . . . ?"

"George."

"Thanks, George."

The air in his flat is stale, he turns up the climate control. He takes off his vest, turns on the talkie.

"Rachel?"

"Wyatt?"

"I just got back. How are you?"

"Fine."

"Wanna come over?"

"Why don't you come here? I'll be ready in an hour."

The talkie goes dead. Wyatt stares at the wall. It was Rachel's voice but it didn't sound like Rachel.

Is she involved in this crazy shit? Does she know about Bert Han? Is the whole I-wanna-get-away-from-the-Heartland-and-get-real a goof? Maybe Anastasia's right. Maybe Rachel's gotten over me. Maybe that's fine. Shit. What about the baby?

He puts the wand into the charger, listens to the humming of the climate control. He slips out of the silk holster straps, hangs the holster on the bed post.

He hears the screen lowering itself in the living room. *Must be Anna.*

"Glad to see you're still with us," Anna says with a smirk. Her pink face fills the screen. "Daddy wants to make sure you're in one piece. His last watchdog checked out at this point. Next time someone takes a shot at you, use the screen to let us know you're all right."

Her father must be in the room with her. She calls him Victor when he can't hear her.

"I miss you, too, Anna," he says dryly.

The screen goes blank just as he realizes he does not know how to use it as a talkie.

The fragrance of the long-stemmed roses fills the train compartment, the transport chute, the lobby, Rachel's flat. Wyatt hands them to her, studying her rigid features. Her black hair is piled high atop her head, wound tightly into a peaked coil.

"I thought we could go to the park, ride around in one of the horse buggies, act like tourists. Just relax, take things

186

slowly. How are you feeling?" he says.

"Not too good."

"I've been using the screen, Rachel, to learn about pregnancy. The first few months are supposed to be kind of uncomfortable."

Rachel breaks into one of her hideous cackling laughs. "Nausea and vomiting is your idea of discomfort?" she asks.

Wyatt says nothing. He barely recognizes the young woman standing in front of him. She seems to have aged. This is not the lover who clings to him like a python, whose violent passion cannot be contained. Her brown eyes glare at him defiantly. Her mouth is clamped shut.

"You got rid of the baby," he says at last.

"Look at me, Wyatt," Rachel snarls. "What kind of mother would I be? What kind of father could you be? Of course I got rid of it. I hated it the first time it made me sick. I wanted to do everything anyone ever did to me to it—and it wasn't even born yet. I hated it! I hate myself! And most of all I hate you!"

She flings his roses back into his face. He catches most of them, but one gets past him. He feels the thorns gashing his cheeks, watches the petals splatter against the ceramic tile floor.

"Get out!" Rachel screams.

"Rachel," Wyatt says, reaching out to her with his free hand.

She steps back, produces something blue black, metallic from her dress pocket. There is a small tube with a fin on top projecting in front of a cylinder with a series of evenly spaced holes in it. Wyatt stares at the object Rachel points at his chest, trying to understand what it is. Then he remembers it from his history lessons: an antique weapon, used for citizen self-protection. It uses an explosive charge to fire lead pellets.

"Rachel, don't," he says, asking her to regain her composure.

He sees at once she misunderstands him. He knows she will defy him whatever he says.

The concussion is deafening. His ears begin ringing. A quick serpentine trail of fire amid a stinking gray smoke cloud reaches out from the barrel into his chest. Wyatt feels his legs wobble, his knees buckle, the floor slamming into his shoulders, the back of his head. Roses flying everywhere, landing on him, covering him. Thorns stabbing him in a dozen places. The blood pumping from the angry wound is hot, there is spittle running down the side of his face. The room reeks from the burning propellant.

"Rachel . . ." he gasps.

She does not move. There is no remorse on her stony features. The weapon is held limply at her side, pointed at the floor, as if it has already done its purpose.

Wyatt shuts his eyes. He must find the bullet, remove it, repair the damage. Cold beads of sweat break out upon his forehead. Desperately he visualizes his lungs, his breastbone, everything else torn or shattered inside him. He has never rebuilt himself this quickly before. It seems like an instant, but he knows it is longer. When he opens his eyes, the flattened lead pellet rolls off his chest onto the floor, disappears into the pile of roses. His shirt is still torn, burned, bloodied, but everything else is restored. He sits up gasping, blinking, gaping at her.

Rachel is still holding the small revolver disinterestedly. She stares at him as if he were some fleeting phenomena barely holding her interest, soon to be forgotten.

Wyatt stands up slowly, careful not to make any threatening moves.

"So that's what this is all about," she whispers. "You're some sort of genetic mutation. They want to study you. I got to play the whore for a freak."

"Rachel . . ." Wyatt stammers again. His ears are still ringing.

"Get out, Weston," she hisses. "Get out of my flat. Get out of my bed. Stay out of my life." She raises the weapon, levels it at his head. "Maybe you can survive one wound in your chest. Want to try four in your brain?"

Wyatt backs up toward the chute.

"Lobby," he says, feels the cylinder drop over him, feels that horrible sucking sensation that always makes him cringe.

His ears are still ringing. He is uncertain whether or not he really hears the weapon discharging again before he is on his way back to the station.

CHAPTER 31

The two security guards in the lobby gape at Wyatt, staring at the scratches on his face, at his torn and bloody shirt. Wyatt notices a nervous hand on one of them. Before he realizes what he is doing, he disarms the man, spins him to his knees, pins him to a potted plant with his face pressed painfully hard into the wall. Wyatt points the first guard's wand at the second while keeping the first helpless by twisting his wrist. This elicits several pathetic whimpers from the face flattened against the wall. Wyatt inspects the wand. It is a new sweeper model, one he hasn't seen before.

"What's it to be?" he asks the second guard, whose hand remains motionless barely inside his jacket.

"Listen . . ." the second guard starts.

"Put the wand on the desk," Wyatt tells him.

The guard complies quickly, taking pains to show Wyatt that he is not going to make any sort of overt movement, that he is neither brave nor stupid.

"I need a shirt," Wyatt says flatly.

"Try the concourse. Thirty credits."

"Let's all go."

"We can't leave our post."

"Wanna bet?"

Wyatt gets a new shirt at a convenience recycling center with the two guards looking on. Both seem genuinely surprised to be alive. No one else is on the concourse. He feeds his old shirt into the machine. After tossing the confiscated wands into the shrubbery just outside the lobby entry, he takes the chute back to the train. He fixes the scratches in transit. No civil guards arrive to detain him. None come hovering over the train. None await him in Sector Thirty-Two.

Rachel must be fine. They'd be all over me if she turned that antique on herself.

The evening air is cool, unusual for the time of year. Wyatt walks the four blocks back to his own tower, almost welcoming another attack on his person. It would give him a way to vent his anger, or else a way to put an end to this spiraling madness. Either would be fine.

Citizens scramble out of his way, as if he were about to go on a spree. He sees his own reflection in the lobby mirrors. He does not recognize himself. He looks older, colder, utterly calculating. George has gone off-duty. The flat-faced woman has taken his place. She looks up disinterestedly as he walks toward the lifts. When she recognizes him, she smiles. He smiles back, as if all is well.

In his room, he wonders about Rachel.

What'd she mean by, "So that's what this is all about—You're some sort of genetic mutation—They want to study you." Was she just playing me like Anna plays Daddy? Maybe we just went too far with that pillow last time. Maybe she just wanted to kill me before I accidentally kill her. Shit—I never hurt a lover before I met Rachel—at least not on purpose. What's with these Heartland women, anyway?

He leaves the lights off, watching the pale blue sky turning golden orange, electric pink, then blue-black beyond the windows. Stars begin winking on by ones and twos. He sits quietly on the couch, his hands clasped together, dangling below his knees. He hears himself breathing against the constant hum of the climate control.

Without giving the matter any thought, he walks over to

the talkie, tries Rachel. There is no answer, not even a message unit. He wants to call Anna, but he knows that is ridiculous. He is not even remotely sure what their relationship is, save that it is layered in pretense. He knows that he is not very good at pretense. The notion to find a pub occurs to him, the notion of lurking assassins from rival cartels lying in wait for him dispels it.

Wyatt takes off his vest, holster, shirt, leaving them on the couch, then kicks off his shoes. He begins practicing his martial movements in the center of the living room. He loses count at twenty-five repetitions, keeps on doing the movements without counting. His mind feels sharp, focused, void of thought. He tries the talkie again. Still no answer from Rachel. He is not tired. He cannot sleep. There is no place for him to go. Louie is the closest thing he has left to a friend in the city, or anywhere else. Their friendship was limited to an ale or two after the sweep. Louie is probably busy with Frieda, anyway.

Wyatt lowers the screen, identifies himself, calls up a biology lesson.

"Genetic mutation," he says.

He reads about cloning, gene splicing, designer genes, gene structuring, gene manipulation, transplantation, stem cell sourcing. His head throbs with the information. When he is done, he suddenly realizes the Heartlanders are looking for immortality. He shivers at the thought of Adolph, Edward, Victor, and his friends living forever.

"You're up late," Anna says, her face breaking through the page of illustrations like a wand blast tearing through a bed sheet.

"Just trying to better myself, Anna."

"What happened?"

"What do you mean?"

"Wyatt, you should be screwing your brains out with the very buxom Ms. Void right now, not stuffing your head full of biology. What did she do? What did she say?"

"What are you—my private civil guard?"

"I'm your friend, Wyatt. Your best friend. Probably your only friend. I've put myself at risk for you more than once. I'm doing it again now. So don't get us both killed. Tell me what happened."

Wyatt doesn't know what to do. He needs a friend, desperately. Anna is growing on him.

She makes him stronger. Everyone else just uses him. So what if she uses him, too? He looks at his bare feet for a moment, looks back into her larger-than-life green eyes on the screen.

"She tried to kill me, Anna. For nothing. Then she told me to get out. You figured it right. But it went down a little more dramatically than *go-away—I'm-bored-with-you*. She said something about genetic mutations. I wanted to know what she meant."

Anna looks genuinely worried. He sees her glancing to the left and right. The swelling on her face has gone down, but is still visible. Probably still enough to offend Victor. Anna gets another night off, courtesy of their workouts.

"Listen, Wyatt. Don't say anything else. Don't talk about this to anyone else. Just give me quick answers. Did you hurt her?"

"No."

"Was she pregnant?"

"Yeah."

"Did she tell you she got rid of the baby?"

"Yeah."

"Damn."

Anna's visage dissolves back into a comparison of two

similar gene diagrams. Wyatt shuts the screen off, watches its black silhouette rising slowly into the ceiling like a civil guard from the street.

"I love you, too, Anna," he says. To his surprise, he wonders if he means it.

What happened to the embryo?

He tries calling Rachel again. This time he gets a message that there is no such listing.

CHAPTER 32

Wyatt is dreaming. He is on a narrow strip of land about five feet above a raging sea. On either side of him, the dark frothy waters churn. To his left Rachel is floundering, shouting his name again and again, begging to be rescued. To his right Jennie is doing her best to remain afloat, struggling against the tide, swimming out to sea. He wants to go after Jennie, but Rachel's voice seems to hold him fast. He cannot move his legs. The thought occurs to him, *I don't know how to swim.* He wakes up with a start, sits bolt upright in his bed. Across the room he sees a familiar form standing quietly, illuminated by the starlight through the window.

"Anna?"

"Don't shoot, Wyatt."

"What are you doing here?"

"Victor sent me."

"How did you get in?"

"We own the tower, remember?"

"I thought you never left the Heartland."

"That's Sonja and Tassy. Victor doesn't trust them to keep out of trouble."

"What are you doing?"

Anna holds a small oblong black box in her left hand, a slender silver-colored rod in her right. She turns around, gradually, facing each wall, pointing the rod at the walls, the floor, the ceiling, the furniture. At one point, a red light flashes on the box. Anna presses a stud on the rod. Something in the next flat goes *poof,* followed by a short whine. Wyatt hears a muffled scream, followed by a soft thud.

"Checking for bugs. Victor doesn't believe in using them. He says that our instincts should be enough to warn us—that bugs make us weak, dependent upon mechanical contrivances. His is a minority opinion. Where's your talkie?"

"In the foyer, by the door."

He watches Anna gliding across the darkness, hears her voice in the foyer.

"Charlie? Anna. Need clean-up at Sector Thirty-Two, tower eight, unit forty-nine. One down, situation unknown. Terminate the living."

Anna glides back into his room.

Wyatt slips into the darkened bathroom, rinses out his mouth, washes the perspiration off his face, neck, and armpits. He is relieved that no parts of him are missing.

"What was that about?" he asks, coming back into the bedroom.

"Eavesdropper next door. Civil guard will clean up the mess."

"Listening to me snore?"

"Maybe."

"Did you come here just for that?"

"We've got about an hour, Wyatt. Let's not waste it."

She is standing in the center of the room when he begins undressing her. He opens her blouse, slips it over her shoulders onto the chair. Leaning over, he kisses her neck lightly.

"Please, Wyatt, don't make any sudden movements," she whispers. "They frighten me. Victor likes me frightened. I'm imprinted to please him. Don't use me that way."

"Imprinted?"

"Why do you think we all look alike?"

"Genetics?"

Anna laughs softly. "Only Tassy ever really looked like this. Sonja and I were surgically altered. Tassy, too, as she got older. We're in the only female form that arouses Victor. That's how we have to stay. We're all imprinted to please him, mind and body."

"I won't use you, Anna. Don't use me," Wyatt whispers back.

He kisses her on the mouth. Their kiss is short. Anna turns her head away. He kisses her neck again, her shoulders, her little button nipples. She pushes him away, finishes undressing by herself. For a long time they lie quietly together, Anna atop Wyatt, her arms under his armpits, her hands lightly on his shoulders. Then they make love slowly, no sudden movements by either one of them.

"How did Rachel try to kill you?" Anna asks.

Wyatt says nothing.

"Wyatt, I know you have some sort of healing factor. I saw Floyd break your nose, thirty seconds later it wasn't even bleeding. Last time he broke your ribs. Now tell me the details."

"She shot me with some sort of antique weapon. It sent a hot lead pellet into my chest."

"She saw you heal yourself?"

"Yeah."

"What did you say?"

"Nothing. She told me to leave before she put four more into my brain."

"Did you try to call her afterwards?"

"Yeah. Twice, no answer. Third time, no such listing. What's it all mean?"

"It means somebody knew about your healing factor.

197

They used Rachel to create an embryo. Now they will try to synthesize the stuff."

"I thought so. What about Rachel?"

"You still care?"

"I'm not in love with her, if that's what you mean. She was good to me, Anna. I don't want her to get hurt."

"Wyatt, she just tried to kill you."

"She didn't try very hard."

"She's a liability to you and me, Wyatt. So long as Adolph is alive, no one will hurt her, unless she hurts herself. Don't worry about her."

Anna gets up, goes into the bathroom. She leaves the light off, puts on the shower. Wyatt listens to the sound of the water splashing against her face, goes in after her. He kisses her shoulders, her spine, her buttocks, her thighs while she lathers herself with Castile soap. He catches some of the lather, washes her back and legs slowly. Anna turns to rinse off. She lets him kiss her but gives him no encouragement. She leaves the shower without touching him. Wyatt stays behind to lather himself.

When he is dry and dressed, Anna is sitting in the darkened dining alcove with two steaming cups of coffee. He sits down beside her, restraining himself from touching her.

"So now that we've done our business," Wyatt says, "what's Victor want from us?"

"He's sent me to pick up his new wife."

"What?"

"He can't leave the house without a heavy guard for a while. I'm a noncombatant, the only one he trusts."

"What's that mean?"

"I can't bear arms. I can't supply arms. I can't be present during preemptive or punitive actions. My field involvement is limited to unarmed search and rescue, reconnoitering, or escort duties. The debugger isn't considered a weapon."

"Tell that to rat bait in the next flat. So you're not a shooter. Why does he want me along? I'm a shooter. I could get you and the new wife killed."

"We're your shields, Wyatt. Victor needs you back in the Heartland. The attempt on your life and this business with Rachel means something's up."

"You told him?"

"It's in the best interest of Crist Enterprises, Wyatt. Maybe ours, too. It got us alone together, didn't it?"

"Anna, I . . ."

She puts her finger over his lips. "Don't say anything silly, Wyatt."

He frowns, says nothing at all.

Four men in tan suits emerge from the next flat while they wait for the lift. Wyatt smells the telltale mixture of ozone and burning flesh. Someone has been incinerated.

"How many?" Anna demands.

"Two. Yours, and a hold-out, both male. You're gonna need a new carpet, a paint job, and a deodorizing."

"See to it. Find out who they were, who they worked for. Leave me a message as soon as you know. Then debug this whole tower."

"Yes, Ms. Crist."

In the lobby, Anna sets the locator on the chute. They emerge in the Sector Thirty-Two Station. Wyatt is cringing. Six civil guards stand about the single link awaiting them on a side track. They board it and it glides down its plastic tube.

"Who and where is the new Mrs. Crist?" Wyatt asks.

"She's the daughter of one of our drones, and Sector Thirty-Eight."

"How are you holding up, Anna?"

She tightens her small mouth, looks at him. He reads the hurt and frustration in her green eyes. He also sees that she will get past it, regardless of the pain.

The link passes a massive structure, consisting of four black towers atop an eight-story common base. Many of the black panels are translucent, revealing lights on within the structure.

"What's that?" Wyatt asks as it disappears behind them.

"The Archives."

"What?"

"It contains all the records of the past, all the antiquities. They also run the screen. It's a conglomerate by itself. Four seats on The Committee. No involvement in any actions. Kind of like the civil guard and the home guard. They keep track of things. It's the safest place to be in this day and age."

Wyatt wonders for a moment. "Just what day and age is it, Anna?"

Anna laughs. "We keep track of time in negatives."

"What?"

"Everything after the historical era is dated from this moment backward. You were born minus twenty-three years ago. Next year it will be minus twenty-four. Get it?"

"Yeah. That's why we celebrate the winter solstice, is it?"

"You got it—we need to know when the year ends."

The link eases to a stop, the compartment door opens.

Waiting for them on the platform is a heavyset tall man seemingly in his forties, with his arm about a small woman seemingly in her twenties. The man smiles when he sees Anna, but his own eyes look pained. Anna quickly steps off the link, embraces the other woman. Wyatt just stands in the corridor, stares. The young woman is the living image of Anna, right down to the green eyes.

CHAPTER 33

Victor stares across the table at him. It is past noon. Wyatt has slept most of the morning away, while Victor joyously celebrated his marriage with his new wife, Melba, and Sonja. Wyatt is looking at the lake from the small glass enclosure surrounding the dinette alcove. A pair of swans have just landed, causing ripples that are reaching out to every shore.

"You look decent for a change," Victor says. "Getting shot by Rachel was better for you than making love with her."

Wyatt says nothing. He looks up at Victor, sips his coffee, feels Victor's eyes probing him, wonders what is next.

"Do you remember what I told you about my women the first time you came to my home, Wyatt?" Victor asks casually.

Wyatt stops drinking, lowers the mug, looks through the steam.

Victor drains the last of his own coffee.

"How can I forget?" Wyatt asks. "You keep reminding me."

Victor scowls. "What did Anna tell you about Tassy?"

"She died."

"Anna is very good with euphemisms. I killed Tassy."

Wyatt sets his cup down on the table. "Why?"

"Don't ever ask me why I do anything!" Victor snarls. Then, in a calmer tone of voice, he asks, "What did you talk about with Tassy, the last time you were here?"

Wyatt has to think. "She asked me about the city. Said she never saw it. I tried to explain it, short and sweet. I guess I botched the explanation. She told me I was a very strange young man."

"Anything else?"

"Yeah—she wanted to know about my *research*. She didn't get the joke. I tried to explain jumpers to her. That didn't go too well, either."

Victor roars, slaps his knee.

"What's so funny?"

"That conversation really upset her, Wyatt. Whatever you said went right into her little pea brain. It turned everything I had arranged so neatly upside-down. That's why I killed her."

Victor stares hard at Wyatt, who just swallows.

"I . . ."

"Don't say anything. I know you didn't mean it. Just don't do it again with Melba or Sonja, all right?"

"Yeah. Whatever you say. What about Anna?"

"She's yours."

"What?"

"I'm giving her to you, Wyatt. All yours. No longer mine. Rachel is gone out of your bed, now. I'm getting too busy for three of them, anyway. Besides, I can't have you wandering around horny, looking for another woman right now. You just took out six of the best the Heartland had to offer. Everybody knows about you. If you go looking for a woman, every enterprise and cartel will have their own candidate ready to hop into my bed—ready to pry into my affairs. Ready to mess us all about. You better get to like Anna. She's really not so bad, once she gets over her resentment. I think she's beat you up enough in the dojo to take care of that anyway. If she isn't to your liking physically, we'll get her changed. Hell, I can have her turned into Rachel Void, if you want."

Wyatt just stares at Victor. "Don't do that," he whispers.

Once again, Victor roars and slaps his knee. "Look, do all three of us a favor. Get her changed. Any way you like."

With that Victor stands up, leaves the room. A thin young woman with nondescript features, wearing a silver and yellow servant's uniform, appears to take away the coffee mug. She does not look at Wyatt. Wyatt remembers what Anastasia told him about the servants knowing when to appear. He watches her leaving.

Now what? Anna will probably tire of me, if Victor sanctions our relationship. She will probably hate me, if I ask her to change herself.

"Wrong on both counts," Anastasia says softly, entering the dinette alcove.

She leans over, puts her arms loosely around his neck, pecks him on the cheek.

That was passionate.

Anna smirks but does not respond to Wyatt's thought.

"What do you want me to be for you, Wyatt?" She assumes an alluring posture, makes her lips look fuller, pouts. The swelling on her cheek makes her stance all the more ludicrous.

He stares at her in disbelief. He does not want any more pretense. He does not want Anastasia playing him like she has played Victor. Wyatt knows for certain what he doesn't want. He has no idea whatever what he does.

"Just be yourself, Anna. I might even fall in love with you."

"You'll do that anyway," she whispers into his ear.

Another peck on the cheek, Anna glides from the room.

"By the way," she says from the archway, "Arthur is waiting for you in the dojo. He's been wanting a crack at you since you got here. Try not to kill him. He's not as reliable as Floyd. Lets his passions get the better of him. Passion will always get you killed, Wyatt. Stick to necessity, tempered by reason. Who knows, we might even grow old together that way."

Yeah, Anna. Two old lovers in the Heartland. Maybe it'll start a trend.

Wyatt goes back to his room to change. Minutes later he saunters into the dojo for his workout. Arthur is sitting in the middle of the mat with his eyes closed, his legs crossed, his hands resting on his knees, palms upward. Wyatt studies the younger brother's face. It is thin, with high cheekbones, a long narrow nose, high forehead, small chin. Wyatt realizes that Victor Crist must have looked very much like that when he came to the Heartland, before he had himself surgically altered.

Wyatt sits down facing Arthur, about twenty feet away, closes his eyes, assumes the same meditative posture. He listens to his own breathing, regulates it, makes it smooth, deep. He has lost all track of time when the sudden urge to fall sideways seizes him. He opens his eyes, falls in time to let Arthur's flying drop kick to his face miss him. The back kick to the side of his head is but a glancing blow.

He is on his feet in a heartbeat. Arthur approaches, arms waving like a pair of cobras. The left hand flicks out toward his face. Wyatt catches it between two crossed arms, spins it around, brings his knee up into Arthur's solar plexus. The youngest Crist staggers backward slowly. A savage right hook sends him flying across the mat. Arthur lands hard, belly down. He does not even try to get back up. His mouth is half open, with streams of blood gushing down his chin onto the white canvas mat, forming shimmering pools under his face.

Wyatt runs back down the hall and up the stairs, right into Victor Crist.

"What's the matter?" Victor demands.

"I think I just broke Arthur's jaw. He's out cold in the dojo."

Victor begins barking names. Servants in various uniforms appear out of nowhere. Two men in short-sleeved white jumpsuits scramble down the steps two at a time.

"How'd it happen?" Victor asks.

"He jumped me during meditation. The whole thing happened in seconds. It was all reflex. First he was all over me, then he was lying still on the mat, a bloody mess."

"Hell, it's my fault," Victor says.

"What?"

"I told him the two of you were going to get Floyd. Arthur wanted you out of it. He wanted to show me he could do it on his own. Now he's out of it and you're on your own."

"Where's Floyd?"

"He's stuck in Sector Ninety-Four, just outside the Heartland. Both his bodyguards are dead. Adolph's men have him surrounded. The civil guards are there to keep it from escalating. It's a stand-off, but Floyd can't get out. I'll give you three of my best men."

"You're not coming?"

"Somebody has to defend the house."

"I thought you said . . ."

"Yeah, well, it's still a little hot for me right now."

"What about Anna?"

"She's in surgery."

"What the hell is Floyd doing in Sector Ninety-Four?"

"He's got your embryo."

CHAPTER 34

Victor and Wyatt sit in front of the screen. Half a dozen of Victor's soldiers sit behind them. Still images, moving footage, floorplans of the Void Research Tower appear. Schematics of all service tunnels, power stations, means of egress.

Victor describes each in detail, using a laser pointer to make certain Wyatt understands.

"How about the people?" Wyatt asks.

"What about them?" Victor demands.

"Show them to me. Their faces, who they are, what they do."

Victor looks hard at Wyatt. "You got a plan?"

"Not yet. Maybe with some more stats, something will come to me."

Victor frowns. He begins calling up faces, names, with pictures, talkies, short bios, titles, their work schedules. From the Void brass, the veeps, through the drones, to the techs. He adds any personal knowledge he has to each personality sketch.

Wyatt studies them all carefully.

Victor ends the briefing, tells the soldiers to assemble at the transport park, calls Wyatt aside, looks at him askance.

"Do you trust me to do this my way?" Wyatt asks.

"I have to."

"Then have some of your intown people grab that last Void drone. He's about my size. Put a mask or something on him, keep him quiet, get him ready to travel to Station

Ninety-Four. I'll let them know when to board your link."

Victor wants to know more, but Wyatt just shakes his head.

He goes back to his room, changes his clothes, selecting a nondescript beige suit that resembles those the Void Enterprise drones wear.

"Look, Wyatt," Victor says to him at the transport park, "it would be a real shame for Anna to become a widow before she's even a wife—I know how much she's been looking forward to getting out of my bed. Don't disappoint her."

"I'll be careful," Wyatt says. "Just keep Herbert out of it."

"It's taken care of. Bring Floyd back in one piece."

Wyatt nods, climbs in beside the driver.

Another transport covers their rear. They are not accosted on the way to the station. Wyatt keeps his eyes glued to the screen, looking for opposition, but none appears. At the station he leans back in the seat, closes his eyes, thinks about his half-conceived plan.

"Mr. Weston?" the man next to him asks.

"Leave two men here with a transport," Wyatt says slowly. "The rest of you wait ten minutes, then spread out along the station platform, wait for me. They're expecting us to come crashing in after Floyd. It's not the way to do it."

The men look worried. Wyatt can see that Victor has told them to protect him at all costs. He smiles, climbs out of the transport. The fewer who know the better.

The usual dozen home guards are milling around the station. No one is waiting for the train. No one pays him any special attention. Victor's link is waiting in the tube with the doors shut. Wyatt raps on the last one. A few moments later it opens. Wyatt climbs in, walks slowly to the front compartment. He raps on the glass. A smiling black face looks up at him.

"You Harry?" he asks.

The man nods.

"Look, Harry, there's been a change of plan. I'm riding alone. I'll wait here until the next train arrives, then we'll link. You find a place to park a few stops away. Someone will call for you when it's time to come back with the next inbound. Got that?"

Harry nods again.

Wyatt walks back to the last compartment to wait.

He is unarmed. It is the first time in months he has left either his flat or Victor's house without a wand. He feels completely naked. He sits with his back to the driver, watching the other passengers enter the station. All of them avoid Victor's link. The next train arrives; five men and three women disembark, ten men climb aboard. The train starts off. Ten minutes later it is in the Sector Ninety-Four Station. Wyatt stays put. At the Sector Ninety-Two Station, he switches links.

He selects an empty compartment in the next link, waits. The train speeds off. He shuts his eyes, visualizes another face. One with a tall forehead, narrow black eyes, a crooked nose, a small chin with a graying goatee. It is the face of one of the night shift drones at Void Enterprises, Herbert Void. Nepotism at its finest.

He feels the change coming over him. The pain of bones realigning, reshaping, skin stretching, hair vanishing, hair growing. It is easier than replacing lost limbs.

Herbert Void seemingly gets off the inbound train at Sector Eighty-Six, boards the outbound train, gets off again at Sector Ninety-Four. Two of the civil guards greet him by name, he nods absently at them. He takes the chute to the Void Tower, making every effort not to cringe. A dozen security guards in padded black uniforms, carrying an assortment of wands, stare at him uncomfortably.

"Yes?" he asks.

"Sir, you know the situation," the closest one exclaims. "You were asked to stay away."

"Precisely."

The guards stare at him without comprehension. One wearing an insignia of command upon his shoulders steps forward.

"He has something of value to us, gentlemen," Wyatt continues. "Something I think I can exchange for his life. Is that a problem?"

"With all due respect, sir, it's his life we want."

"I think you have your priorities backwards."

"Still, we can't let you . . ."

"How are you going to stop me?"

"I need to clear this . . ."

"You need to do what you're told."

For a moment the guard and Wyatt simply stare at one another. Then the guard waves the others off.

"Where is he?"

"He's barricaded himself in Lab 1046. He's disrupted all of the surveillance equipment on the floor. He could be anywhere. There are already five dead. Three of ours, two of them."

"Thank you for your concern and your statistics. Can we look in on him?"

"He's disabled all security scans."

"Can we at least hear him?"

"I can get a long throat up here if you want."

"Don't bother. Just make sure you keep your men away

while I negotiate with him."

"Sir—the order was no negotiations."

"The order has been changed. Give me five minutes. If I'm not back by then, I'm dead."

Reluctantly, the guards lead Wyatt to the corridor outside the lab. Wyatt identifies himself as Herbert Void with a loud voice, announces that he is coming in unarmed, says he has a reasonable alternative to the present stalemate, asks Floyd to let him in. For two minutes, nothing. Then someone unbolts the electric lock from within the lab. Wyatt seemingly hesitates before stepping into a darkened corridor. The door shuts with a hiss, clicks locked behind him.

"Just keep walking forward," Floyd calls from the darkness across the lab.

"Don't do anything stupid, Floyd," Wyatt calls back in his own voice.

"Wyatt?" Floyd whispers from a place of concealment immediately to his right.

"Yeah."

"What the hell are you doing?"

"Getting you out. I hope."

Wyatt walks with his empty hands held above his head. Suddenly Floyd grabs him, pulling him beneath the emergency lights. Floyd's mouth is agape.

"What is this?" Floyd demands, staring at Herbert's face.

"Magic. Where's the embryo?"

Floyd gestures with his thumb at a small silver canister on the floor.

"Open it."

"What? It'll die in seconds."

"Open it."

Floyd punches in a combination unenthusiastically. The lid springs open. A white vapor rises like a ribbon, lingers above the wide mouth. Wyatt picks up a wand next to a large dark smear on the floor. He sets it on low stun, fires it into the container. The embryo disintegrates, leaving nothing behind.

"What'd you do that for?" Floyd demands.

"I like being a one-and-only. Got something else to stuff back in there?"

"We already left a bogus embryo in the lab so's this one wouldn't be noticed missing."

"Get it. And get rid of that container."

Floyd hurries off, returning moments later.

"What was your original plan to get out of here?"

"Walk out the front door with bogus IDs. We were spotted. New codes."

"What about the service tunnels?"

"First place they'd look for us. There's probably an army waiting down there now."

"Can you get a signal to Victor?"

"Yeah."

"Let him know it's now or never. We're just walking out of here. Keep that wand pointed at my head."

Floyd uses his wrist calc to send the signal. "They'll never let us go. They don't give two shits about some Void Drone."

"What if he's a Void?"

"I dunno. Maybe."

"What else is there? Going out, taking a bunch of them with us?"

"Why not?"

"Victor just gave me Anna. I'd hate to miss all the fun we'll have together."

Floyd laughs. "She's gonna have a lotta fun with you, anyway," he says.

"Look nervous," Wyatt says.

"I am nervous, you dumb twat."

They make their way back down the darkened corridor to the security door. Floyd presses a small stud on his wrist calc. The door clicks open. Wyatt exits first, waving the silver container. The ranking guard takes it from him. For a moment, Wyatt expects to be atomized by everyone pointing a wand at him, but the guards just back away.

"Gentlemen, I must accompany Mr. Crist back to the Heartland. Please see that nothing happens to that container. It is worth more than your lives."

The guards allow Wyatt and Floyd to exit using the chute.

No one tries to detain them at the station. They wait for the next train. Floyd recognizes two men in the first compartment, enters with Wyatt. A third man wearing a mask as real as any face sits resignedly between them—his eyes betraying his fear.

"Mr. Void?" Wyatt asks.

"Yes."

"You became a hero tonight. I suggest you bask in the light of your achievement and keep this excursion to yourself. These gentlemen will tell you what to say. Anything else will surely get you killed, by your own people."

The man stares at Wyatt, swallows twice, nods that he understands completely. Both of his captors stare at Wyatt as well. The train stops. Floyd and Wyatt stand up. They wait for everybody else to leave. Wyatt buries his face in his hands in the corridor, remembering his own face. He feels the change coming over him, the bones reshaping, the soft skin realigning itself.

Victor's men are waiting at the Heartland station platform along with the home guard. There is no resistance. No one assaults their transports. Wyatt rides back to the house beside Floyd.

"How'd your men get Herbert so easily?" Wyatt asks.

"We own the building," Floyd says.

Floyd scowls, thinks for a moment. "Where'd you learn to talk like that drone?" he demands of Wyatt.

"I read a lot."

CHAPTER 35

"How'd you change your face?" Victor demands.

"How'd you change your shirt?" Wyatt answers.

Victor scowls. "Since when have you been doing that?"

"Since tonight."

"So what sort of catharsis led to this sudden hidden talent discovery?"

"You wanted Floyd brought back. I knew we couldn't go in there shooting. We were completely outclassed. They were just waiting for us. *Necessity is the mother of invention.* I read that on the screen."

"What else?"

"I was wondering why some face wanted an embryo with my DNA. Then I remembered. I've got this little problem I've never told anyone about. Someone must have seen me deal with it—maybe when I was a kid. It occurred to me that maybe there was an upside to it as well."

"So you had me grab one of the Voids while you strode out of here unarmed, on the hunch that you might be able to rearrange your own face?" Victor shakes his head.

"Yeah."

"You scare me."

Wyatt says nothing.

"How'd you get the drone's features so perfect?" Floyd asks.

"I taught myself how to remember. I remember details."

"At least he's with us," Floyd says. "I saw him fix a broken nose in seconds before he got the drop on me. He's good."

"That's why they want the DNA," Victor says. "Nobody's thought about cosmetic self-surgery yet. Maybe if Herbert loses his nerve or one of ours gets gabby, somebody might put it together. We'll know soon enough."

"How'd you get the wrong security codes at Void?" Wyatt asks Floyd.

"Edward's got a mole in there," Victor says. "He hasn't been able to reach him for a day—security's been tight since Bert Han died. We used the most recent codes he could give us—calculated risk."

"How's Anna?" Wyatt asks.

"Recuperating," Victor says. "She should be ready for the unveiling in a day or two."

"Can I talk with her?"

"Kind of eager, aren't you?" Victor demands.

"I want her to teach me how to use the screen like she does. I can just about get into the educational stuff, none of the archival. It's pretty obvious my screen skills need a lot of work."

"Ask her tomorrow. She's sleeping now."

"Anything else?"

"Yeah. Good job. You rate one of these." Victor hands him a wrist calc.

Wyatt examines the small flexible band with the three black raised squares, each with its own stud. "You gonna show me how to use it?"

"This one's your link to me. That one's for anybody in the Heartland. The other one's for the city. Anna will teach you how. It's a little tricky until you get the feel of it. They're all scrambled if you reach any of our people. You need one of ours to unscramble it. We change the codes daily, so even if an outsider gets one, it's useless the next day."

Wyatt sleeps for ten hours, awakens with nothing missing. He goes to the dojo, works out alone for several hours. He has coffee watching the swans, asks the serving girl where Anna's room is. The girl says she doesn't know, leaves quickly without looking at him.

Anna, where the hell are you?

Third floor, second room on the left at the top of the stairs. But not today. Wait until the bandages come off.

Wyatt sits wide-eyed. He suspected, but never imagined the extent of her ability to hear thoughts.

How many people know you can do this?

You and Floyd. If Victor knew, he'd never have given me to you.

I didn't realize Floyd could keep someone else's secret.

Yours is safe with us, unless someone figures it out like you did. The ones on the train all think you were wearing a mask, like Herbert was. It's a pretty common practice. Sloppy security at Void let Floyd stumble in. It wasn't a high-security facility. Now leave me alone. I'll come see you when I'm ready.

Wyatt spends the afternoon alone with the screen, learning more about antique weapons, security procedures, genetics. He spends the evening practicing in the dojo. He has a light dinner, retires early. After a long soak in the marble tub, he steps back into his bedroom wrapped in a towel. There he finds another of the nondescript Crist maids turning out his bed.

Must be something new, nobody ever did that before.

He tries to look at the woman's face but, like the serving girl, she avoids eye contact, turns her face away, looks down at her feet, scurries away before he can ask her anything. Wyatt cocks his head and watches her short jerky movements.

Glancing across the room, he sees his wand is still in its

silk holster on the wall hook where he left it. Cautiously, he catches the woman by the arm before she can leave the room.

She submits at once, standing still, her head bowed, her eyes lowered, as if anything he might wish to do to her would simply become part of her function in the household, but her willing participation would not.

With his other hand, Wyatt turns her long thin face toward him. She shuts her eyes, stiffens, lets him examine her. The lips are wide and thin, the nose long with a slight bump in the center. The cheeks are high, there is a small cleft in her chin. The woman's hair is hidden beneath her yellow cap, but he can see that her eyebrows are a dark blond.

Wyatt has seen this face before. Then he realizes it is a feminine version of Arthur's face. "Open your eyes," Wyatt says with a sudden smile.

As he suspected, they are a vibrant jade.

"Anna?"

The woman turns her face away once again.

"Look, I know you're a Crist. You'd look like the other Crist women if you were anyone else, so consider yourself discovered."

Anna laughs, takes off her maid's costume. Golden teeth flash behind the thin lips. Dark blond hair falls to her shoulders. Her body is slightly more curvaceous than the last time he saw it, no longer resembling a young man's. The sense of alertness that had intensified all their other trysts is missing.

"What do you think?" she says, turning around so that he can see all of her.

"I think you're beautiful."

"Good answer," she says, pushing him back toward the bed.

CHAPTER 36

It has been five days since he's seen Victor, heard from Anna. Armed with the new rudimentary training of the language of the archival screen Anna has taught him, Wyatt has spent his days researching as much recent history as he can reconstruct. His clearance is still much lower than Anna's, but at least he can track his old friends. Those that live are doing as well as can be expected. So far only two are dead. His vision of them after his evening in Sector Twelve proved correct on all counts.

He feels his heart racing as he encrypts the only name he really cares about, Jennie Height. Wyatt watches the rows of symbols forming, hesitating, surging, until the answer that has driven him into this new life appears. Jennie is still here in the city. Her address and her place of work are one and the same. She is an archivist, fifth class. She lives at The Archives. She has been there all the while. There are no gaps in her record. Further questioning reveals that all archivists are relocated discreetly.

Wyatt sighs, falls back into the leather sofa. He shuts his eyes, sending the screen back into the ceiling with a flick of a switch. His heart is still pounding, his mind aswirl. At least she is alive. At least she is safe. At least she's not in somebody's collection, or worse yet, working in a crib.

Why didn't she come to see me? Why did she just disappear? What happened to her? Does she even want me to find her? Would she welcome me?

He feels lightheaded, dizzy. A myriad possible situations,

actions, reactions begin suggesting themselves to him. He decides he should do nothing in this hyperactive state of mind. He will decide what to do later, when he is calm, when he has collected himself. He smiles. Jennie is alive and well.

Once again he lowers the screen. This time he asks about Rachel Void. His heart is no longer racing, but a sadness takes hold of him. He feels the need to talk with Rachel one last time. To say something kind, to feel something. To let her know he came to care for her. To let her know he does not blame her for shooting him. The dancing rows of symbols begin flickering across the screen. At first they tell him his security clearance is too low. Then they list her two previous places of residence, her address in the Heartland, her tower flat in the city. He approaches Rachel from a different angle, as an employee of Void Enterprises, and finds no such listing. Finally, he inserts his home guard auxiliary code, which is his as a bodyguard to a Committee member. This gets him a swift and curt answer: *DP*—disappeared person.

Now he is angry. Someone has used Rachel, used him; now Rachel is disappeared, whatever that means.

He sees Rachel sitting on his bed, hugging a pillow, watching the sunset over the Heartland dome. *Curtis is my friend,* she says. *He's the one who helped me leave the Heartland. He's the one who brings my friends into the city to visit me. He's good people, Wyatt.*

He remembers Curtis' various threats to him, should he do anything to harm Rachel. But he has done no such thing. Or has he? He almost drowned her, almost smothered her. But that was love play. That was what Rachel wanted. That was a Heartland romance.

Hell, if anyone knows what happened to her, it's Curtis Void.

220

Wyatt steps off the train, glances around. It is mid-afternoon. The usual uptown faces are strutting by. Techs, drones, women with too much time, too many credits to spend, going from market node to market node this time of day. Too early or too late for day workers. No one pays any attention to him. Civil guards hover about, keeping the peace. Except for the new wand, the clothes, the uptown flat, the massive credit balance in his account, it is like old times.

He sets the controls on the chute for the recycling station, the cylinder descends. In a rush of air, he shuts his eyes, grimaces, opens them again. Louie's friend, Bart, is on duty.

"Hey, Bart," Wyatt says.

The lanky man in the white coveralls gawks at him, trying to recollect.

"Wyatt—I used to work here. Remember?"

Bart blinks his watery blue eyes, runs a stained hand across his chin. A slow smile spreads itself across his mouth like a blush. "Yeah. You and Louie were tight. How's?"

"Good, Bart. Real good. How's with you?"

"S'good. What brings you back to Curtis' pleasure house?"

"I need a word with sweet Curtis Void."

"I dunno, Wyatt. I'm not supposed to let anybody who's not a sweeper in here."

"I'm a sweeper, Bart."

"Am or was?"

"Both."

"Yeah?"

"Yeah. Was public, am private. I sweep private now. You know about that, don't you?"

Bart blinks his eyes, runs the dirty hand through his

thinning long brown hair. "Never heard of private sweepers, Wyatt," he says with a nervous laugh.

Wyatt pulls his vest open, showing Bart the new wand. "Take a look at this, Bart."

Bart looks into Wyatt's eyes for any sign of madness, then cautiously draws the wand from its holster. He turns it over, examines the buttons, makes like he's about to direct a fusillade at Curtis Void's office, then puts it back in Wyatt's holster.

"It's a beauty, Wyatt. Looks like it packs a wallop."

"Oh, yeah. Little orange balls that grow big as train compartments, make a man disappear before you can blink or fart. A real wallop, Bart. A real beauty."

"So, you're a private sweeper now."

"Yeah."

"I guess it's legal for you to be here, then."

"Thanks, Bart."

Boldly, Wyatt saunters across the epoxy floor, watching the other men in white coveralls, helmets with mirrors for faces, work the machines that line the far end of the great hall. He scans the rows of parked vehicles, remembering the sweeps that kept him fed, clothed, housed, almost since he left school. The memory is bittersweet.

He pauses before the black door below the clock, decides not to knock, lets himself into the private office. The dour-faced clerk looks up from her screens, scowls, blinks at him.

"Curtis here?" he asks.

"You're not on the payroll," the clerk says stiffly.

Wyatt stares into her narrow gray eyes, scowls back at her. "Tell my friend Curtis I'd really like a short word, if you please."

The clerk leans back in her chair, a look of unaccustomed terror stamped across her gray face, her fingers

222

inching toward an alarm button.

"Don't do that," Wyatt says. "Cause a fuss, might just get your nasty skinny ass canned. Bad reference. A month or two from now, you're a drossie. Last trip back here will be the next sweep. Tough old bird like you might just find herself gone all soft and fluffy inside a box or four of food flakes. Know what I'm saying, sweetness?"

Wyatt nods slowly, smiling disarmingly. The clerk nods back, a weak smile on her tight thin lips, her hand slowly recoiling from the alarm.

The door behind her opens. Curtis Void steps into the outer office.

"Wyatt," he says flatly.

"Good day to you, Curtis. Hope you're well."

"Very well, Wyatt. What brings you back here? You don't look in need of honest work."

"Actually, Curtis, I'm here to ask about Rachel. We had a bit of a misunderstanding the last time I saw her. Maybe you heard something about it. I'm very concerned about Rachel. Really I am. I'd like to see her again. At least make sure she's all right, even if she doesn't want to see me. She was someone very special to me, Curtis. I'm sure you understand."

Wyatt watches for signs of anger in Curtis' face. He expects to see the small mustache twitching, the thick purple lips pouting. Maybe hear an eruption of threats or demands for him to leave at once. Instead he sees a blank stare, as if Curtis cannot understand a word he is saying. The eerie calm is completely out of character for Curtis Void.

"Did she ask you not to say anything?" Wyatt presses.

"What are you talking about?" Curtis demands.

"Rachel. Remember?"

"Who's Rachel?"

CHAPTER 37

The encrypted language of The Archives fills the screen one moment, Anna's new face fills it the next, dissolving the black letters like dust before a wind gust. There is an eagerness about her that reaches down to Wyatt's loins. Anna's green eyes sparkle.

"Victor wants you to meet him at Heartland Station East at ten o'clock sharp, lover."

Wyatt remembers telling her that she was not his lover the last time she used that turn of phrase. Now she is his wife. Her iced jade eyes shimmer again.

"I'll be there," he says.

I miss you, Anna, even though you are a manipulative little bitch.

"I know," she says.

The screen returns to its encryption of the structure of Void Enterprises, the most extensive holding company in the city. Crist Enterprises is barely a vendor's pushcart in comparison, in spite of its extensive real estate empire.

Why was Victor so eager to give away a tower for Jimmy Han's good will? He's not stupid, but the deal smacks of stupidity. What's at Farm One Victor wants?

At nine fifty-five, Wyatt steps out of the train, looks around, eyes each of the assembled Heartlanders on the platform. Most barely return his gaze, those that do are all bodyguards. Wyatt counts forty faces, an even assortment of veeps, drones, shooters, all men. As always, six of the home guard hover above the platform.

Victor Crist appears at the entry after the others have boarded the train. He walks over to Wyatt, smiling.

"Is that grin from Melba, or is some poor face about to get got?" Wyatt asks.

Victor scowls. "Watch your mouth. We're going back to the country, boy. Back to claim our part of the bargain. So smile, Wyatt, any lingering doubts you might harbor about leaving Void Enterprises will be gone before we get back. Anna sends her love. I think she's fallen hard for you. I've got to admit you have some way with the women."

"Yeah."

Right. The love of my life leaves me without a word, the next one puts a lead pellet in my chest, and your daughter would just as soon make a meal of me as kiss me. Worse yet, I never know what she's about. I got some way with them all right.

They find an empty compartment near the front of the train in Victor's link. Victor hands Wyatt the *Private Compartment* placard. Wyatt presses it against the glass, watching the transparent surface turn an opaque sky blue.

Victor seems unusually jovial as the train passes the lake, the first towers surrounded by their parks, the stations set at regular intervals. Wyatt listens to the hiss of the compartment doors opening on either side of them, the footfalls in the corridor, the bustle of the crowds in the stations. Summer is fading fast beyond the tube, the hot muggy air has given way to a warm crispness that harbors many small winds spinning across the landscape, down the city streets, grabbing loose-fitting caps, small items from the push carts, bits of scrap, sending them all rolling, spinning, stopping, then rolling on again as the train hurtles past in its colorless tube.

Twice Wyatt draws his wand as someone seemingly pauses before the blued-out glass. Victor smirks both times, his hands clasped loosely across his belly, no sign of worry on his face.

By eleven-thirty, Victor's link is unhitched from the rest of the train. It passes through the unobtrusive-looking factory wall, out into the wasteland surrounding the city. Wyatt removes the placard from the glass, exchanging it with Victor for the debugger. He gets up to make sure the rest of the link is empty, save for Harry, who looks at him, grins. The debugger notes two bugs, one beneath the train, one in the next compartment, both of which Wyatt dissolves. It occurs to him that someone could have left a bomb just as easily.

Whatever Victor's about, there must be a good deal of profit in it—for him and for anyone else involved. Everybody's afraid. Afraid of what Victor will do next. Afraid for their lives. Afraid they will get left out of the deal. He keeps them guessing, just like Anna. Nobody wants him dead before the deal, just after it. Clever bastard.

"How many?" Victor asks when he returns.

"Two."

"Where?"

"Two compartments down, and close to the back under-carriage."

"You want to know why there's no bomb."

"As a matter of fact."

"Destruction of public property, especially anything to do with utilities, transportation, or distribution, is a capital offense. Anyone remotely connected with the act will be immediately terminated. These items are too difficult to replace. Any major destruction to our ability to supply, transport, feed, or provide amenities might lead to civil unrest. No one wants anarchy. No one will tolerate having any less than they already have. People are expendable. We can always make lots more of them. Our other resources are not."

"Suppose somebody just doesn't care anymore?"

"That's the real trick, now, isn't it? Keeping everybody caring. Toys and trinkets for the uptowners. Tattoos and tingles for the downtowners. Visions of power for the Heartlanders."

"And a shiny new tower for Jimmy Han."

"That's right."

"So tell me something, Victor."

"What's that?"

"How much is really left? How long do we really have?"

Victor slaps his knee, lets out a belly laugh. "It's that kind of thinking that makes for drossies, brain-dead drones, topples Heartland enterprises, Wyatt. There's always enough for those who rule, those who serve them, trust me. Like you said, necessity is the mother of invention."

Wyatt sighs, hands the debugger to Victor, who puts it back into his briefcase. Mile after mile of wasteland flash by. Barren ground, without grass or shrub, showing the stone bones of the earth thrusting through. Distant forests, blanched white tree trunks, shattered boughs, without branches, twigs, leaves, birds flying above, land animals scurrying below. Dust clouds billow behind them, churning on the horizon, noting the change of season. The sky is streaked with thin straggling clouds, like the scratches Rachel Void used to leave upon his back.

"You gonna tell me about it?" he asks Victor at last.

"Not yet. More fun just to watch your eyes every time the world gets bigger. You think you've seen most of it now, don't you? You figure a few weeks on the screen will fill in all the missing details. That's why you're getting all pissy about what's left, isn't it?"

"I dunno. Maybe. The stuff I saw that used to scare me doesn't anymore. But now I'm wondering about everything I don't see."

Victor laughs again. "Yeah. I remember going through all that. You wanna know something, Wyatt?"

"What's that?"

"I'm still discovering new things. This trip will be as new for me as it is for you. The difference is, I figure it out, you let it happen. Your edge is your reflexes—you know you're fast enough to deal with anything that might go wrong. The wonder of youth. Mine is I make things happen, all sorts of things. I know what will work, who will play what part in it. The wonder of maturity. We make a good team, Wyatt. Don't go getting ambitious on me."

Wyatt cocks his head, stares hard at Victor. "You worried about me turning on you?"

"No. Not now. Hopefully not ever."

Wyatt just shakes his head.

The link begins to slow when they reach the outskirts of Farm One. The pale blue sky lightens as the train enters the dome. The featureless clouds become three-dimensional above them. Harry brings the train to a dead stop at the platform. Wyatt sees Jimmy Han, flanked by a dozen bodyguards. Another dozen home guards hover over the link. Jimmy looks worried.

"Jimmy, good to see you," Victor says, stepping onto the platform behind Wyatt.

Jimmy Han looks to either side before stepping forward. "For God's sake, Victor, what's this all about?" he whispers.

"A better world, Jimmy. It's about a better world for all of us."

The two men just stare at one another, Victor smiling

easily, Jimmy working his jaws nervously, wiping at his forehead with a bright yellow silk handkerchief.

"What's up, Jimmy? You look like you've seen a ghost."

"Adolph Void left here an hour ago, Victor. He shows up
uninvited with a small army of shooters. You know he
hasn't left the Heartland in ten years. He wants to know
what sort of deal I made with you. He wants to know what
you were up to. He wants to know who you are going to kill
next. He wants to know what's in it for me."

"What did you tell him, Jimmy?"

"I didn't tell him anything, Victor. I don't know anything. I don't have any idea what you're up to. I stalled him
as best I could. I think he believed me. But he was very
angry. I don't like it, Victor. I don't think he's even worried
about the law anymore. I wasn't sure that you would come.
He stopped just short of threatening me. He stopped just
short of saying you and your new shooter were already as
good as dead."

CHAPTER 38

"Would it put you at ease, Jimmy, if I told you I expected Adolph to come here—to make some sort of hollow show of his waning power?" Victor asks. "Would it make you feel any better if I told you it's Adolph who's already as good as dead?"

"Don't say things like that, Victor," Jimmy protests. He shoots quick glances to the right and left, looking for signs that any of his own people might secretly owe their allegiance to Adolph Void. "Nobody is as powerful as Adolph. No ten people are. Void Enterprises . . ."

"Void Enterprises is top-heavy, Jimmy." Victor dismisses his concerns. "There's a big toothsome dinosaur sitting atop a pile of bones, surrounded by lots of snotty little bone pickers. You know what a dinosaur is, don't you?"

Jimmy scowls. He nods his head. He knows what a dinosaur is.

"Adolph never groomed a successor," Victor continues. "He disappeared anybody who showed any initiative. Everybody left is too frightened to fart without first asking. Who's going to replace him? Do you really think he is going to live forever? The man's a hundred and sixty-seven years old. Did you know that? No? I'm not planning to kill him, Jimmy, if that's what you're worried about. He's already outlived himself. He's on borrowed time. I don't care how big he is. I don't care how big Void Enterprises is either. As soon as Adolph realizes he can't survive another new heart, another artery transplant, another gene implant, another set of eyes, another whatever, Void Enterprises is going to fall apart. The bone pickers can't abide one another because that's the way he wants it. Without Adolph, it's just a bunch of bickering idiots fighting over table scraps. The whole damn conglomerate will be up for sale to the highest bidder within two weeks, Jimmy. Piece by little piece."

"That may be, Victor, but Adolph's still among the living. He's frantic, angry, frightened—call it what you will. So if he's still of a mind to kill you when he finds you, he'll kill you."

"Really?"

Jimmy does not answer.

"He tried to kill Edward, the head of my cartel, three months ago. Edward is doing fine, Jimmy. He isn't afraid to leave the Heartland. Do you know why? I'll tell you. Edward is alive. He can feel which way the wind is blowing. It's Adolph who's dead. All he feels is his time running out. Yeah, he might have a try at me—but that's life, Jimmy. A couple of my men shot up one of his research facilities last week. He stole something from one of mine, I wanted it back. It bruised his ego. Only a fool would go around making threats. The rest of us know that what I did is just part and parcel of being in business. You let these things get to you, Jimmy, you'll wind up like Adolph—spent. Better to relax, enjoy life's bounty."

Jimmy nods.

Victor puts his arm around Jimmy's shoulder. "So tell me, Jimmy, just what exactly did you tell Adolph?"

Jimmy is clearly uncomfortable by this physical contact. He seems to shrink in Victor's embrace. His voice falters. "I told him that you had an interest in Sector Twelve. I had to. Besides, everybody already knows that, Victor."

"Good man, Jimmy. Good man. You did exactly right. I

won't forget that. Have our other guests arrived yet?"

Jimmy nods.

"Did Adolph ask about them?"

"No, he didn't. They come here once a month anyway."

"Yeah. I know. Isn't dependability wonderful?"

Jimmy and three of his bodyguards climb aboard one transport. Victor and Wyatt ride with two more of the bodyguards, with the rest flanking them on three sides.

Jimmy thinks he is taking no chances with Victor. Jimmy remembers how easily Victor dispatched his father. Jimmy is very afraid.

Rows of elevated troughs filled with all manner of plants stretch out for miles below them. Wyatt sees three small settlements of interconnected terraced buildings, several large bulky transports ferrying workers to other parts of the farm. A herd of cattle graze within the fenced confines of a lush green field near the horizon. The transports land near them. The cattle do not even look up.

A group of six men wearing spotless white linen suits stand with their hands clasped before them near the landing spot. Victor beams at them. One of the men looks up, flashes a quick insincere smile.

"Morris, good to see you again."

"Victor."

"Have you found it?"

"Yes, Victor. It was exactly where you said it would be."

"Is it operational?"

"As far as we can determine."

"And the pilots?"

"They're prepping the ship now."

"Who'll see us take off?"

"It's radar-shielded, but anyone with a long-range scanner will register something. I'm taking a rather large risk. No one else has pilots capable of this."

"Keeps the adrenaline flowing, Morris. The rewards will justify it, I assure you."

"So you keep telling me."

"You wouldn't be here if you didn't believe it."

"It's a calculated risk, Victor. Nothing more. Everyone knows you're capable of anything. If something goes wrong, you'll be on your own."

"Where is it?"

"This way."

Two of the men in white lead Victor and Wyatt to what appears to be a small outcropping of stone. One removes a small wand from his pocket. Victor's hand is on Wyatt's arm before he can reach for his weapon. The front end of the stones rises up slowly on two large stainless steel pistons, revealing a narrow set of concrete steps leading into the earth. Victor follows the men down the stairs with Wyatt bringing up the rear. Jimmy and Morris remain behind.

The concealed stone door closes behind them. It takes Wyatt a moment or two to acclimate himself to the dim lights near the floor. Many of the fixtures do not function. It reminds him of the maze where he earned the right to remain in the Heartland. Their shoes pop against the hard concrete, the sounds echoing against the concrete walls. The corridor is long, sloping downward toward a larger space lit by soft blue light. Five minutes later they arrive at a large underground hangar, ablaze in white light.

Near the center two dozen techs in gray and green coveralls swarm about a black wedge-shaped craft. One handles a hose from a cylindrical tanker truck, fueling it, while another inspects the landing wheels. Two are going over the entire surface with handheld scanners, while two others perform routine maintenance at the rear. The rest man terminals at the perimeter of the hangar.

Wyatt wonders what Victor is starting. "What is it?" he asks.

"A gift from the past," Victor says. He quickens his pace.

The men in white stop, turn, block their path.

Once again Victor places his hand on Wyatt's arm.

"Your boy is a little jumpy there," one of the men says.

"Yeah. I like it that way. He's fast, hits whatever he aims at, whether or not he can see it. So just you keep it slow, friendly, sincere. You'll be all right."

The man swallows, stares hard at Wyatt for a moment.

"Morris wants everything understood from the onset, Victor. No surprises, no changing the rules later, no loss of memory. That's all I want to say."

"Nothing's changed, Spark. Morris gets all, I repeat *all*, the transportation involved in the renovations. Demo, reconstruct, manpower, materials, even food to and from the site. Anything else he can think of, so long as it's necessary. Just don't hold me up for more than we agreed."

"What if this little brainstorm of yours turns out to be a flop?"

"We still share ownership of the craft. What else do you expect?"

"What about Adolph?"

"What about him?"

"Who takes care of Adolph, Victor?"

"I do, Spark. Nothing from your end."

That seems to satisfy the men in white linen. They stand back to let Victor pass. Wyatt stares hard at the one called Spark. Spark takes a respectful step back, keeping his hands clasped tightly in front of him.

As they approach the black wedge, Wyatt notices the open hatch near the base, with the gangplank lowered. Victor waves Wyatt on. He ducks his head, climbs inside. Victor is right behind him. The black walls are thick, padded white inside. The vehicle seats eight. Two pilots are already in the forward section. Victor motions for Wyatt to seat himself, strap himself in. There is a small slit beside him. Through it, he watches the men in white walking back toward the tunnel while the techs complete their work, call out to each other through their helmet coms, fall back. The gangplank closes with a soft thud, a series of muffled clicks. Wyatt hears a humming, feels the wedge turning ninety degrees, then rolling smooth as silk down the center of the long hangar. It comes to a stop at an elevator marked by a ring of red lights.

Daylight pours down upon them as the iris door above opens. The elevator rises easily until the craft sits purring on the hard surface of the wasteland just beyond the dome of Farm One.

Victor can barely contain himself.

Wyatt feels the craft moving. The desolation surrounding them becomes a dusty red blur through the slit. The nose points up. Wyatt feels as if he will fall through the seat or be swallowed up by it. Something behind them is whining. Moments later they are surrounded by a white haze. Victor is laughing softly.

Wyatt can barely believe the incredible brightness surrounding them. The craft vibrates for thirty seconds. Wyatt is certain he is being crushed. His skin feels as if it is disintegrating against his skull, his lips roll back painfully. When next he looks out the slit, they are surrounded by millions of stars floating in a soft black sea reaching out toward infinity. He is weightless. Only his harness keeps him from floating around the cabin. Below them the earth is a giant blue opal, all aglow beneath the black ocean of space.

"I should have studied astronomy instead of history last night," Wyatt mutters.

Victor breaks into another bout of laughter.

CHAPTER 39

"Can you tell us what we're looking for now?" the pilot asks over the talkie.

Wyatt is still adjusting his pressure suit.

Victor answers with a series of numbers, tells the pilot to take up orbit there. The pilot does not understand. Victor describes a portion of the control panel, explains how to set the coordinates. The pilot signifies he understands.

Wyatt's breath fogs his faceplate. The copilot turns on the suit's internal climate control, the image of Victor and the copilot wearing their own pressurized suits returns.

"This is the pressure control, this one is the temperature, this is your head lamp, this one regulates the air. A twist to the right is more, to the left is less. Got that?" the copilot asks.

"Yeah."

The copilot closes the cover on Wyatt's left forearm. He makes his way back to the elevated cockpit using the grab bars along the right wall. Victor follows him. Wyatt returns to his seat, peers through the slit into space. He does not like this feeling of weightlessness. The black wedge floats above the glowing blue opal like a feather floating on the still waters of Heartland Lake for two boring hours before Victor begins shouting to the pilot.

"There it is! Dock with it!"

The pilot protests the difficulty of the maneuver, the questionable state of the station's docking hatches.

"We're not here for the view, boy! Dock with it! On the

237

cylinder, below the wheel, at the end opposite the tubes."

Wyatt floats to the cockpit, keeping his arms outstretched. There, through the four narrow windows, he sees what looks like a slowly orbiting wheel with eight spokes, linked to a long cylinder surmounted by a series of broad solar panels and an array of cones and spikes.

"What is it?" he asks Victor.

"Sweet Sally M," Victor replies. "The best kept secret in this world."

Wyatt knows better than to ask again until they're alone.

Neither the pilot nor the copilot show any sign of knowing what the space station is about.

The pilot flies the wedge within a hundred feet of the station. He shines a floodlight on the cylinder, begins circling it.

"There," Victor shouts.

"I see it," the pilot growls.

"It was designed for this ship," Victor assures him.

"Yeah, well, I've never flown anything like this ship before."

"Just get our roof hatch aligned with it, about four feet away. I'll work the docking apparatus from here."

Victor moves to the rear of the cockpit, directly above where he and Wyatt were sitting. He places his palm in the center of a large panel, which suddenly becomes a screen lit with blue and red lights. Wyatt follows him. When the pilot signals he is as close as he can get, Victor touches one of the lights, creating an image of the station's hatch in the center of the screen. Deftly he activates an accordion-like attachment from the station which reaches out to the hatch atop the wedge. Wyatt hears a series of clicks, then a hiss as the wedge's hatch opens slowly inward.

"We'll be awhile, so don't get edgy," Victor tells the pilots. "Wait for us."

"Morris said to go with you," the copilot protests.

"Wait here."

There is no more argument.

Victor and Wyatt climb up into the bridge. Victor places a small box-like device on the station's hatch, stands back. A moment later, the hatch opens with a groan. Victor laughs again. He removes his box, steps inside, motioning for Wyatt to hurry. When Wyatt is in, they both turn on their head lamps before Victor shuts the hatch behind them.

"Without this box, any attempt to open the security hatches will set off a detonator," Victor says. "Goodbye Sally, goodbye wedge. A short one-way trip to nowhere."

"Swell," Wyatt says. "What's Sweet Sally M, anyway?"

"The end of history, boy. The beginning of the world as we know it."

Victor makes his way down the corridor, staring at the walls until he finds another panel. A few well-placed touches, and the darkness within the station gives way to a diffuse light that emanates from twin lines that follow the length of the tube. Victor keeps pressing but nothing else happens.

"No more air. We'll have to make do with what's in our suits."

They shut down the head lamps. Victor leads Wyatt to a shaft at the very center of the cylinder. They both float upward until they reach another hatch. Victor uses his box to open it. They enter a large room with round walls. Four ancient pressure suits—torn, ragged, filled with bones—float about the room. More white bones litter the space.

"Poor bastards were left behind," Victor says. "The original flight crews were probably killed off in the plagues. Nobody left to bring them back. Either the food, the water, or the air ran out and that was that. Probably no worse off than those below."

Victor holds on to the hand grips, pulls himself toward the main control. He begins laughing and rubbing his gloved hands together again.

"The Archives make no mention of this place, Wyatt, but I found some ancient texts that described it in great detail. Along with this little key box."

"Where?"

"In The Archives. I used to work there. Half the stuff in that place is beyond anybody's ken. I was cataloguing it. Once I knew what this place was, I made certain there was no further mention of Sweet Sally M anywhere. I've been dreaming about this moment for thirty years. I wasn't sure what I would do with her when I first found out about her, but I've had a chance to figure all that out. It's so perfect. In a few minutes I'll accomplish what Edward has spent a lifetime trying to do. I really must savor the moment."

"What are you doing?"

Victor does not answer. Once again he begins activating the ancient equipment. There is a hum as more lights illuminate more displays. Wyatt comes closer to get a better look. On a screen in the center, an image of the wasteland appears. Victor adjusts the coordinates, and different images float by until much of the city and part of the Heartland appear. More adjustments and twenty city blocks full of buildings fill the screen, along with their web of interconnecting streets. Victor keeps adjusting, the blocks and streets change. Wyatt does not recognize the sector from above, but he is certain it is Sector Twelve.

"What's the M stand for?" he asks.

"Maser."

"What's maser?"

"Power."

Victor keeps manipulating the controls until a new display forms itself to the right of the imaging screen. It is a series of illuminated touch pads with a word display above. Victor presses six of the pads in unison. Words—*activating,* followed by *powering up*—appear. There is no change in the image. *Powering up* becomes *maximum.* Victor presses a sequence of the illuminated touch pads. *Discharging* appears, then *sweeping.* This word gives Wyatt a chill. He holds his breath, watching the image of the city, yet there is still no change to any of the buildings. *Completed* begins flashing in orange. Victor shuts the entire panel down.

"So what happened?" Wyatt asks.

"Maybe nothing. Maybe the conclusion of one era and the onset of the next—the end of stagnation, despair—the rebirth of progress, I hope."

"You hope?"

"I assume it worked. We'll have to get back to find out."

The flight back is anticlimactic.

The blue pearl disappears in a rush of fire and light that unnerves Wyatt. He is sure he sees some part of the black wedge dislodge itself, burn off. The heaviness of being returns. He sinks back into his padded seat, certain that he will pass through the back of it again. The minutes drift away until the pilot lands the wedge deftly just beyond Farm One, taxis to the elevator. The earth swallows up the ship again, the iris door closes above her. The techs swarm over her as Victor and Wyatt disembark.

Morris and Jimmy are not there to greet them.

Two of Jimmy's bodyguards fly them back to Victor's link, with three other transports flanking them. Victor is beaming all the while. Bodyguards and home guards see them off without a word.

Everybody wants in on whatever it is Victor's about, but nobody wants any part of either one of us. What the hell did we just do?

Victor begins laughing again as the link leaves Farm One.

"The beauty of it," Victor says, "is we use the bane of the past to usher in the future."

"You mean that station?"

"That, too."

CHAPTER 40

Victor pulls back his sleeve, presses one of the studs on his wrist calc.

"Daddy? Are you all right?"

Wyatt notes the subtle hint of anxiety in Anna's voice.

You're good, Anna. Whatever else you are, you're good.

"I'm fine, Anna," Victor says. "What's happened?"

"Is Wyatt with you?"

"He's right here. What's happened?"

"It's still a little sketchy, but it's big, whatever it is."

The wasteland slips by slowly as the link hurtles northward. For a moment Wyatt thinks he sees a large black bird circling above the distant dead forest. But when he looks again, it is gone. Soon the spot is beyond his perspective. He turns back to Victor, who is still smiling.

"Tell me what you know for certain," Victor presses Anna.

"All of Sector Twelve is cordoned off. Nearly every available tech and day worker at Void Recycling is sealing it up. Anyone who has gone into Sector Twelve in the past half-hour is under quarantine. Autopsy information will be available by morning, once the survivors are all removed to Void Labs in isolation tanks."

"What's Void looking for?"

"Evidence of plague."

"Which one?"

"Omega. Apparently everyone in the sector was afflicted

about an hour ago. The symptoms are identical to those in the historical records."

"Anything else?"

"If you're east of Sector Twelve, you'll have to route yourself around it. The direct line from Farm One is down from Sectors Ten to Fourteen. The rest of it is only rumor, from encrypted transmissions. Everybody has a theory. Everybody has a plan. Most of it is controlled hysteria. It's hard to say what's real, what's not."

"Such as?"

"Adolph Void might have been in Sector Twelve when the plague broke out. His people are trying to locate him frantically. On secure as well as open channels. There has been no response. He got off the train at Sector Twelve Station this morning."

"Anything else?"

"They're talking about you and Wyatt. It seems Adolph went looking for both of you. He seemed to think you would be heading somewhere in Sector Twelve after your meeting with Jimmy Han. He wanted to be there waiting. No one is sure why."

Wyatt feels a knot in the pit of his stomach. He suspects he was followed to the Sector Twelve Grille when he went to speak with Rafe. It must have been someone from Void Enterprises. Adolph went to the Grille looking for his hopes and fears. Wyatt knows it was Victor and Sweet Sally M that annihilated everyone. He suspects that the Omega Plague, the last plague at the end of recorded history, was anything but a plague—it was the name given to the effects of a secret weapon which was too awesome for anyone to accept. Like the wands, its effects were largely limited to the disruption of organic matter. He feels his arms and legs going weak. He wonders if all of him will melt away before Victor's eyes.

"Daddy?"

"Yes, Anna."

"Is this your doing?"

Victor does not answer her. He locks his fingers behind his head, leans back into the seat, smiles at the ceiling. Wyatt can see that Victor's plan has worked beyond his own expectations. Not only will Sector Twelve be razed for fear of this mythical plague spreading, his cartel will have to renovate the site, while the power structure dominated by Adolph Void crumbles in the wake. Victor obviously imagines that he will have a dominant place in the new order. Maybe he will even own many of the new buildings.

"Tell Harry to reroute the link," Victor says. "Keep us out of sight."

Wyatt gets up to speak with the driver. Harry has already heard the news from Transportation Central. He will take the tube within the walls that conceal the wasteland from the city. It connects with the main line at Sector Ninety-Four. Wyatt goes back to the compartment. Victor is sleeping peacefully.

The tube within the wall is blacker than night. The only illumination is from the dim strip lights at the floor, and above their heads. Wyatt sees his own face peering pack at him from the curved lexan surface. It is a hard face, empty of compassion, humor, life. He shuts his eyes, tries to convince himself he had no idea what Victor was about to do.

Wyatt?

Jennie is sitting on the seat beside the sleeping Victor. Her knees are wide apart, hands are folded easily between her legs, her arms rest lightly on her thighs. She leans toward him. He can feel her breath on his face, smell her sweet scent. She is wearing a long black dress that hides most of her body. Her face and hands seem pale as death.

What are you doing here? he thinks.

You know where I am, Wyatt. Why don't you find me? I was certain you would have come by now. If you truly love me, you will not keep me waiting.

Until today, I didn't have any idea where you were, Jennie. Please wait for me. I'm dying without you. Every day I lose another piece of myself.

I was sure you could have found me by now. But since you didn't, I'm not so sure you really love me. Everything in this world leads back to the same place, Wyatt. That's where I went. To the one place you have to go if you want to understand. Isn't that what you always told me? You wanted to understand more than anything. Was that so hard for you to figure out?

The image of the lithe young woman with sky blue eyes, deep red hair, high freckled cheeks begins to fade.

Jennie, don't go. Don't scold me. Talk to me. Please . . .

"Who are you talking to?" Victor demands.

Wyatt blinks his eyes. Victor is awake, staring at him.

"You were moving your lips, whispering something inaudible, staring at the empty seat. Do you talk with ghosts, boy?"

"All the time, Victor."

"That'll get you killed. You busy yourself in their world, this one will sneak up on you. I know. I used to talk with them, too. Everyone I knew who disappeared. Losers. Take some well-intentioned advice, boy. Give them up before you join them."

"They're leaving me anyway. Only one left."

Victor nods sympathetically. He raises the wrist calc again, presses one of the studs.

"Victor?" Floyd asks.

"Go ahead."

"There's an emergency meeting of The Committee

called. It's been in session for less than an hour. I'm here, as your second. Only about half the delegates are in the Heartland now. Things are getting a little out of hand. Everybody is running scared. So far, the city's still calm. Rumors of the plague have been contained. You may want to stay there tonight. Void Enterprises is trying to get the home guard to detain you."

"What's their charge?"

"They haven't got one. They're trying to get martial law declared."

"What's Edward doing?"

"He's stopping them for now. He's demanding to know if Adolph is still alive."

"What are they saying?"

"Not much about that. I don't think anyone really knows where he is. But it's not like Adolph to let his presence go unfelt. Everyone is speculating that he's been stricken with the plague or else he's already dead. Edward is demanding that Adolph be present or another Chairman be elected at once."

"And?"

"Not enough votes either way. There's a call for all Committee members to come back to the Heartland. As soon as there is a quorum, Edward will get his vote. But I wouldn't be in any hurry to get back for it if I were you. I'm sure the Voids are waiting for you somewhere along the way."

"You think they'd risk the penalty?"

"They've got nothing to lose if Adolph's dead. It's going to be open season on all of them. They think you're at the bottom of it, whatever it is anyway. There's at least a hundred pairs of eyes looking for you."

"Thanks, Floyd. Harry?"

"Yes, Mr. Crist?"

"Where are we?"

"Sector Twenty-Four."

"Let us off at Sector Thirty-Two."

"Yes, Mr. Crist."

"My flat?" Wyatt asks.

"No, mine," Victor says. "If we're in a shooting war, I want it on home ground."

CHAPTER 41

Victor and Wyatt both turn, draw, fire their wands in unison. The lobby erupts into exploding orange fireballs. Two would-be assassins standing in front of the lifts posing as tenants' visitors turn to raise their own wands. They are vaporized before they can fire a shot. A third emerges from behind the large potted plant, fires his weapon in their general direction without taking the time to aim. The flat-faced woman security guard disappears behind the desk just as an arcing purple bolt scars the wall behind her with a dark black streak. Victor fires again. The lush fern fronds evaporate. Someone Wyatt half-recognizes pokes their head and arm from the steel door leading to the service corridor, fires at them. Victor and Wyatt both leap to the side as the purple bolt lashes out at anything organic in its path. The security guard has the misfortune of appearing behind the desk, her own weapon drawn, just as the purple ripple reaches her. She lets out a short scream just before it finds, incinerates her.

Wyatt recognizes the shooter. It is Freddie Boy. Once again he and Victor fire in unison. His shot misses, bathing the steel door in an orange glow as Freddie Boy ducks back into the service corridor. Victor's finds its mark, shattering the urn, obliterating the last remaining shooter behind it. A belt buckle and a sweeper's wand clatter to the carpet. The rosewood panels have his silhouette, arms raised, burned into them.

Victor and Wyatt remain crouching, their wands leveled at the closed door beyond the lifts. Nothing happens.

249

Freddie Boy has had enough. Not even the sound of her footfalls remain.

"Amateurs. They weren't Void shooters," Victor growls. "Who were they?"

"Resistance," Wyatt mutters.

"Who?"

"City people tired of Heartland manipulation, Victor. People like us, who don't want to wind up on the autopsy tables at Void Labs because they were in the wrong place at the wrong time. Y'know?"

"Yeah, I know. How come you know them?"

"I have friends there—if you didn't kill them all this afternoon."

"Don't get soft on me, Wyatt."

"Which way was I shooting, Victor?"

Victor doesn't answer. He lifts his hands to his face, pressing the stud on his wrist calc. "Get men into the service corridors," he screams. "Terminate anybody you find there. Send down eight more guards to the lobby. Ones who aren't completely brain dead. Nobody comes in or out of this building who doesn't live here."

"Right away, Mr. Crist."

"Is this the new order you were talking about, Victor?"

"I'm sorry about your friends, Wyatt. But this is the just the beginning of the end for the old order. It's going to go kicking and screaming. A lot of citizens are going to go out with it. No fault of theirs. The luck of the draw. That's the nature of revolution, remember? I thought you were a comer—four with one shot and all. I better be right or we're both going to miss the new beginning. I brought you in because I need you watching my back. You've got nowhere left to go except with me. Now stop your grousing. It isn't going to get any better than this for a while. Void's people are still out there somewhere, just waiting for us to turn on each other."

"Yeah. I know. I'm not turning on you, Victor. I just think my friends deserved a lot better than they got."

"They did. But nobody gets what they deserve unless they work for it. You've got to make your own luck, Wyatt. Make it all the time."

All the lift doors open. A dozen men in Crist security silver and yellow uniforms stream into the lobby brandishing an assortment of weapons. Most continue into the service corridor, two more take up positions at the front desk. Others step into the small garden outside, disappearing like shadows into the night.

"Get this place cleaned up," Victor snaps at the one who stands at attention before him. "I don't want the other tenants alarmed."

"Yes, sir."

The guard begins barking orders into his own wrist calc as Victor makes for his private lift with Wyatt in his wake. Victor presses the lift control in his wrist calc. The door concealed within the rosewood paneling glides open soundlessly. They ride up to the penthouse together in silence. Wyatt swallows to unblock his ears.

They step into a large teak- and ash-paneled room filled with opulent furniture and an ornate curved agate bar. Victor heads behind it, takes two tumblers from the glass rack, pours an inch and a half of a golden brown liquid into both of them from a cut crystal decanter. He takes one, hands the other to Wyatt.

They drink. Wyatt feels the smooth warmth flowing down his throat. He takes a deep breath, then finishes the glass. Victor does the same. The liquor is calming, soothing, reassuring.

"Why here?" Wyatt asks. "Why not further uptown?"

Victor laughs. "This is my first building, Wyatt. I fixed it up to show Edward what I could do. He was very impressed. I decided to keep a place here to remind myself where I started. Pride cometh before the fall, and all that. No snooty neighbors around here. No veeps, or first-rank drones. Just mid-range drones, chief techs, security captains, contract workers. Nobody too rich to think theirs don't stink."

"Nobody worried about becoming a drossie, either," Wyatt observes.

"That, too," Victor concedes. "Hungry folks, not starving ones."

"Yeah."

"We better sleep in shifts, Wyatt. You want to go first?"

"I'm wide awake, Victor. You better go first. Any of your men on this floor?"

"There are a few just below us. I don't want them up here. They'd probably shoot us by accident if things got a little tense."

Victor glances at the old-fashioned grandfather clock across the room. It has a wide gold face with large black Roman numerals that read nine o'clock. "Keep the drapes drawn. Give me four hours, then wake me," he says.

Victor goes back to the bar, opens a panel. He presses a series of buttons. Wyatt feels something warm to his left, as if someone were sitting beside him.

"What's that?" he asks Victor.

"Just a little something to confuse the boys from Void, should they drop in uninvited."

He smiles at Wyatt, then disappears into the room to the right of the bar, shutting the door with a soft click behind him.

The hours crawl by. Wyatt tries to visualize Jennie. He thinks about the things she said on the train, remembers their time together, their walks, their touching, their love-making. But no images form to breathe life into the memories. Only bittersweet pangs crisscrossing his chest.

Twice the building creaks; twice Wyatt is on his belly on the carpet, wand in hand, heart pounding. He glances at the clock at fifteen-minute intervals, then ten, until he refuses to look at it again. He takes his vest off, begins his martial workout. It makes him relax, but it does not make the time pass any faster. After an hour and a half of practice, he sits in the center of the room with his legs crossed, letting his mind go blank.

Wyatt awakens with a start. The clock reads three o'clock. He draws his wand, crawls as quickly as he can across the floor, slithering behind the bar. He pushes open the door.

"Victor," he whispers. "Are you awake?"

"Yeah. What time is it?" Victor whispers back.

Wyatt tells him.

He hears the sound of Victor scrambling into his clothes. It is followed by the sound of an explosion from the living room. Everything is suddenly bathed in an orange flickering light, accompanied by the whooshing sound of wand fire. Thick gray smoke begins to billow into the bedroom. Victor bellies across the floor, a large weapon vaguely resembling a long barrel in his hands. He rests it on the rubble of the agate bar, the stock pressed against his right shoulder, aims it at the nearest transport hovering beyond the gaping hole in the wall and roof, fires. The transport explodes, careening downward. Victor rolls across the floor as the next transport appears.

Wyatt rolls into the bedroom door opening, sights his

wand on the shooters bunched in the open side of the transport, fires twice. The second transport flashes orange, wobbles, follows the first one plunging down to the street. Wyatt hears one crash, then a second. Lights fill darkened windows in the nearest towers visible through the shattered wall.

Wyatt follows Victor into the burning living room, just as another blast tears open the bedroom wall. Wyatt turns, still on his back, then fires, watching the orange ball bathe the closed craft ineffectually. He dives across the floor to avoid the next shot from the transport, which destroys the remnants of the bar, most of the floor. Pieces of burning wood, shards of metal have raked his left arm, back, the left side of his face. He pauses to eject them, repair the damage. Victor is on his left knee and right foot beside him, firing his weapon into the hole in the bedroom wall. The third transport explodes in a fireball. Two screaming men tumble from the wreckage, their clothes aflame.

There is one more distant explosion from below before the morning silence is restored.

Wyatt is coughing when Victor grabs him.

"This way," Victor screams.

They scramble across the devastated living room toward the grandfather clock. Victor pushes it aside, revealing a stainless steel hatch, bathed in firelight. He punches in the access code. It opens. He jumps in feet-first, clutching his briefcase, the handheld artillery.

"Come on," he yells back to Wyatt.

Wyatt follows him, feels the cool metal of the slide beneath him as it spirals downward, hears the sound of Victor laughing.

CHAPTER 42

The rapping at the front door grows louder, faster, more insistent. Wyatt draws his wand, tiptoes to the peephole. Four men with utterly humorless faces wearing gray ceramic helmets, body armor, stand grouped together behind three nervous men wearing the silver and yellow security uniforms of Crist Enterprises. Wyatt turns to look over his shoulder. Outside, just above the terrace, two more civil guards hover. Wyatt holsters the wand, opens the door.

"Mr. Weston, you're alive!" Victor's chief of security says.

"Last time I looked, George."

"Where is Mr. Crist?"

"Upstairs."

"Uh, didn't you hear the commotion this morning?"

"Commotion? No, I guess not. I took something to help me sleep. I would have slept through a thunderstorm. Is something wrong with Mr. Crist?"

"I thought you were his bodyguard . . ."

"I am, when I'm with him. He wanted to be alone last night. What happened?"

"Ah, someone attacked the building. Very illegally. I'm surprised you slept through it. Everyone else on the block was woken by the commotion. Two of the bodies have been identified as Void Enterprise employees. Martial law has been declared."

"Am I under arrest?"

"No. Nothing like that. We're just looking for Mr. Crist."

"I'll go with you. Let me finish getting dressed."

"It would be better if you stayed in your flat."

"What?"

"There is reason to believe your life is in danger, Mr. Weston. We should leave a few men with you just in case."

"Just in case what?"

"Ah, just in case you need help."

"I'm like Victor. I help myself."

Wyatt shuts the door, watches the men talk among themselves, disperse. The civil guards board the lift. The security chief goes with them. The other two security guards remain in the elevator lobby. Wyatt walks over to the terrace door, draws the drapes shut. He wonders if the flat has already been scanned, if the civil guards know he is not alone.

"They gone?" Victor asks from the darkened bedroom.

"Not quite. Two of yours are still out there."

"Let them all think I'm dead for now. Makes it easier to move. Floyd and Anna have been trying to raise me all morning. I can't risk being monitored, even if no one can understand what we're saying."

"What about the guards out there? You think they're listening to us?"

Victor looks at the debugger in his hand. "No scanners, no long throats."

"What now?"

"Now Void Enterprises is on its own. They're big, but not big enough to take on all the rest of The Committee combined. It'll take a few days for the feeding frenzy to begin."

"How's it play?"

"Last night's shooters have been identified. At least one Void veep will have to be sacrificed for that botched operation, maybe more. If I know my friend, Edward, he's already taken out what's left of Adolph's small personal army in the Heartland, if only to keep another Void from commanding it. Morris has a grudge, as well. He probably figures he's in this as deep as we are. He's taken the initiative as far as transportation is concerned. A few well-placed shooters will give him control of the recycling vehicles in any event. There are quite a few others who never backed Adolph wholeheartedly. Most likely they are settling old scores, now that Void Enterprises is disintegrating into two dozen or more uncooperative individual cartels. I think you should weather the storm right here, unless someone wants to make sure you're out of it. I don't think that's too likely. No one thinks you have any initiative."

"What about the Omega Plague?"

"What about it?"

"By now, Void labs must realize there's no such thing."

"Who's going to believe them?"

"What if they figure it out? A lot of people saw us go out there."

"So what? The maser uses microwaves. Unless you're scanning the heavens, you don't see or hear a thing. If that was the case, they'd be here arresting us, not taking a head count."

"But that thing's still out there."

"So what? I've got the only key. If Morris or one of his gets jumpy, tries it alone, he'll just blow up the wedge trying to get in. There's just one wedge left. It's the only way out there. We don't have the raw materials to build another. So Sweet Sally M's mine or nobody's."

Victor holds up his briefcase, salvaged from the morning's carnage, to show Wyatt he still has the key.

"Besides," he adds, "Morris isn't the sort to take a broad

initiative. He likes small precise actions that expand his holdings securely. He's more likely to demand something he wants from me the next time I want to go out there again—which I don't plan on for now."

Victor goes into the kitchen, calls up a big breakfast for one. He and Wyatt share it at the small table next to the food lift.

"What about Floyd and Anna?" Wyatt asks.

"What about them?"

"You think they're safe without us?"

"I'm the only Crist anyone wants dead, Wyatt. They're safer than they've ever been."

"How you figure it ends?"

"Back to business in a week or two. Tear down the old Sector Twelve stone by stone. Start building the pretty new one. A lot of misinformation about the plague. By week five, nobody remembers anything except the new construction. Void Enterprises gets chopped up, sold off. A lot of Voids turn drossie. A lot of new blood joins The Committee. Life improves downtown. Folks in Sector Ten move into Sector Twelve. We rebuild Sector Ten. Et cetera. Your friends in the resistance get a lot less to be pissy about."

"So who's the new Chairman?"

"There are several possibilities. Edward is one of them."

"Where you going to get the material to rebuild the buildings?"

"We've got stockpiles of that sort of stuff. Enough to reconstruct the whole damn city five times. Besides, if I have my way, we'll be back in the wasteland for new resources in a decade or so. We pretty much know where everything is."

"You learn all that working in The Archives?"

"That's right. Everything in this world leads back to The Archives, Wyatt. Sooner or later it would do you good to go

258

there, just for a look-see. Maybe while we're waiting for things to cool down."

Wyatt nods, leaves the small kitchen table. He sees Jennie, sitting on the train beside the sleeping Victor. *Everything in this world leads back to the same place, Wyatt. That's where I am. At the one place you will have to go if you want to understand. Isn't that what you always told me? You wanted to understand more than anything.*

Wyatt sits down in the leather overstuffed chair. He feels his insides shaking. Watching his hands, he sees no visible tremors. Jennie is still sitting across the room from him. She looks like she is about to cry, staring at him. Wyatt opens his mouth as if to speak, remembers Victor, his advice about ghosts, closes his mouth, closes his eyes.

For you, Jennie. For you, your touch, your love. I did everything I've done to learn how to find you. I've become everything I've become to be with you. Don't give me ultimatums. Please don't judge me. Come back to me, or tell me why and go your own way if you must, but don't condemn me, Jennie. That would kill me for sure.

Wyatt falls asleep in the chair. He dreams about Anastasia. They are flying together above the wasteland, above the Heartland, above the city. The air is cold. The sky is filled with lashing winds that lift them higher. They do not touch one another for warmth or love. They fly like two great carrion birds above a dying world. Wyatt knows he belongs here. Anastasia looks over, smiles at him. He suddenly knows there will be no other woman in his life.

The sun is setting when he awakens, a blood red smear right through the dome on the horizon. He hears the stuttering sounds of demolition, construction, above him. Pulling back the drapes to look, he sees a swarm of civil guards surrounding the tower. Large transports are flying back and forth. Those leaving are filled with jagged piles of debris. Those arriving are filled with neat piles of framing, paneling, crates containing new finishes. On the street below, the repairs to the damage to the pavement are almost complete. Ten men in gray coveralls are spraying the new surface so it will blend in with the old. Wyatt watches them complete their task, load their equipment into the fixall, climb aboard, disappear via elevator-ramp into the maze of tunnels beneath the street.

Wyatt pulls back the drapes, smacks his lips. He turns, looks into Victor Crist's glowing cat's eyes in the falling darkness. Victor is sitting quietly on the couch, his open briefcase upon his lap. Wyatt goes into the bathroom to rinse out his mouth. When he returns, Victor is still sitting silently in the unlit room.

"There's one more thing," Victor says softly.

"What's that?" Wyatt asks.

"I'm going to need your face."

CHAPTER 43

The sensation of warmth, the smell of ectomold. Once to get the under impression of Victor's features, once to get the over impression of Wyatt's, again to meld the two into a perfectly-fitting mask for Victor to wear out of the tower.

"If you're me leaving, what are the lobby guards going to think when they see me later?" Wyatt asks.

"Sloppy work on their part, as usual, if they even notice. Not much memory there, if you recall. Not much of anything, when you get down to it."

Wyatt nods.

"There's a problem," Victor adds, "only if somebody is hunting you. Anything you want to tell me before I go?"

"Give my love to Anna."

Victor laughs. "Stay inside for a day or two. Anna will let you know when to come back to the Heartland."

Wyatt sits in the dark, listening to the steel door open, click softly shut behind Victor. The work on the penthouse continues all night, most of the next day. Wyatt sleeps for twelve hours straight, waking up to watch the last load of materials arriving by transport. The workers leave at sunset, their transport skirting the glowing orange edge of the horizon until it is swallowed up by the night.

Wyatt orders himself a light snack. It is delivered without question. He spends the evening in front of the screen, reading *Macbeth*, then watching a dramatic adaptation of the play.

He meditates, practices his martial movements, spends the next two hours soaking in a hot tub. One question keeps repeating itself.

What did we do to Sector Twelve?

One answer keeps following the question.

We killed everybody there.

Wyatt sees Victor smiling, *We can always make more people,* he says.

You're poison, Wyatt, Walter says.

Maybe I should go. Rafe's a pal. I wish him well.

Maybe you should stay. Maybe Rafe needs your friendship.

Nobody needs poison.

That's where you're wrong. Everybody's looking for poison.

Wyatt shakes his head, gets out of the tub, listens to the water gurgling in the drain, dries himself, decides to see Sector Twelve for himself. He checks his wand, to make certain it is on full charge, dresses himself in gray synths, slips into the elevator lobby. The guards outside his flat are gone. He has the lift to himself. George sits behind the main lobby desk; two other guards stand at either side of the street door, one watching the chute. Expressionless faces above silver and yellow uniforms, staring dumbly as he walks across the lobby. Wyatt sets the chute controls for the Sector Thirty-Two station.

He arrives with a wince. The station is filled with hovering civil guards, watching everyone come and go. They outnumber waiting passengers three to one. Wyatt waits five minutes for the inbound train, watching everyone around him. Three young women in loud clothing, flashy jewelry, garish makeup, enter the platform from the street, laughing, talking loudly, jostling one another. They walk up to him, give him the eye. Wyatt smiles.

The evening train is short, four links. Wyatt walks

through two cars until he finds an empty compartment. The door gasps as it opens, hisses as it shuts. Wyatt closes his eyes. He sees the face of the man with the cleft chin. The man he had forgotten about until the night he had to kill for Victor's friends. The man is leering at him, touching his hair, stroking his head, towering above him. Large, controlling, intimidating. The door hisses again. Wyatt looks up. The three young women from the platform enter his compartment. One sits next to him, the others sit opposite him. Their eyes are wild, the smell of joystick is everywhere.

"Hey, pretty boy," one says, leaning toward him. Her eyelids are painted orange, her cheeks a light blue. A black line outlines her glossy lips. She blows him a kiss.

"I saw him first," the one next to her says, reaching out and touching Wyatt's knee.

"M-m-m-m," the third says, leaning into his lap.

Wyatt is twisting the wrists of the one holding his legs when he feels the teeth sinking into his neck, the poison rushing into his bloodstream. All three of them are on him as he rips himself free. Blood splatters the compartment, runs hot down his neck, over his synths—his blood. He is on his feet, his knee crashing into someone's face, his hands twisting someone else's neck. He is on his back on the floor, a body on top of him, a river of blood rising around them; the man with the cleft chin is standing back at a safe distance, leering at him.

Must stop the blood flow.

Wyatt's legs are rubber, his arms are ribbons of smoke. He puts all his attention on his neck wound. He visualizes the flesh whole. He feels only his neck. The rest of his body is a dream. The man with the cleft chin is there, squeezing his neck, stroking his head, putting his fat sour fingers into Wyatt's mouth, telling him to be a good boy.

The door hisses again. Distant voices curse down twisted hollow tubes.

"He broke my nose."

"Damn your nose—Marcie's dead."

"Did you see him close that wound? What the hell is he?"

"Hurry up. We've got to get him out of here at the next stop."

"What about the guards?"

"Shoot him full of this—get him on his feet."

Wyatt feels nothing. Wyatt feels pain, a very localized pain, but he cannot tell where. He tries to cry out. He cannot find his voice. The body atop him is lifted off. Someone picks him up by the armpits, puts a broad-brimmed hat on his head. A hand reaches into his vest to remove his wand. A jacket goes over his arms, a scarf around his neck. He knows it is to hide the blood. Somehow his legs are working, as if by themselves. His right arm is over a big man's shoulder, his left one around the young woman with the orange eyelids, blue cheeks. The door hisses again. Wyatt sees the glass turning blue as they walk him into the corridor.

On the platform the man with the cleft chin stays in front of them, leering at Wyatt. Two others are with him, flashing something at the questioning civil guards. A door opens in the wall.

Wyatt feels the floor dropping below them. It is a lift to the service tunnels. The woman holding him up turns, faces him, slams her knee into his groin. The man lets go. Wyatt sinks to the cold steel floor. He knows it should hurt, but he still feels nothing.

If you're a good boy, I can make things nice for you, the man with the cleft chin is saying. *If you're a bad boy, I can make bad things happen to you.*

"That's enough," the man says.

"He killed Marcie," the woman growls.

"Get a hold of yourself."

Wyatt smells lubricants, stale air, something rotting. The man lifts him by the armpits to his feet. Once again they point him. His legs just start walking. The space is long, dimly lit.

Walls of black rough hewn stone, floor of smooth black pavers beside a single thick rail. They walk him a short distance, lay him face down on a flatbed tram. Wyatt cannot tell how many there are. Sometimes it looks like five, then only two. The tram moves slowly down the service corridor, clinging to its single rail. The woman strokes his neck, cheek, ear with her wand. The man with the cleft chin is floating above them, leering, reaching out to Wyatt, touching him, taking Wyatt's small hands, placing them where Wyatt does not want them.

The lights keep coming on, going out. The smells change, but they are always bad—human excrement, urine, rotten meat, something burning, something acutely acidic. The tram ride is smooth. Wyatt tries to move his head, finds he can't.

The tram finally comes to a stop in another long, dimly-lit black hall. He is marched into a small well-lit room just off it, dropped face-up onto a canvas cot. This time he counts four faces. Three men, one woman. The man with the cleft chin is gone. They peel the hat, scarf, jacket off him, cast them aside. Their faces seem too large for their bodies, their eyes are the eyes of death. Their teeth are sapphire, ruby, ebony, silver.

One of the men opens a bag, removes a small black object, pushes it into Wyatt's arm. A new sensation, one of floating, drifting, tumbling. Wyatt watches the faces break up into shards of color. A bit of orange eyelid, a speck of black silk, glitter from a stud earring, a smear of brown mustache. They are speaking, but their words are shards of sound. Overlapping syllables, clashing consonants, reverberating vowels. Somewhere in the midst of all of it, he realizes he is taking part in the conversation, or rather his voice is adding to the din.

It goes on and on like this. Smears of color. Specks of noise. Long pauses. The sensation of floating, tumbling, plunging into a bottomless void.

In the void the man with the cleft chin is waiting, putting Wyatt's small hands into his pants. *No!* Wyatt screams. *I won't!* A large hand slams into his face. He feels himself flying across the room. Large hands scoop him up by the armpits, hurl him into the chute. The chute sucks him up, sends him sprawling onto the floor of the school. Other children are there. They are laughing. Wyatt hears their voices, fractured, high-pitched, gibbering.

The first voice that makes sense is that of the young woman.

"You know all of it, Spiff. You have a nice big piece of him in that jar for the damn lab. So, can I kill him now?" she demands.

CHAPTER 44

The door swings into the dingy little room with such force it knocks one of the men onto his face, sends another reeling into the woman, who stumbles into Spiff. All four of Wyatt's captors are bunched together beyond the cot, two of them struggling to rise, two struggling to aim their wands at the open doorway. The sound of crackling wand fire fills the air. Wyatt lies still, watching the arcing purple bolts engulf those beyond him. He is unsure how he escapes the blasts. The room reeks of charred flesh, he finds himself gulping down mouthfuls of foul-tasting air. Someone leans over him. The face is only a maze of pink dots with odd colored splotches here and there, the smell of sweat. It seems vaguely familiar. A second face appears beside it. Gradually the features form, grotesque, exaggerated.

"Looky what we got here. It's Poison Wyatt."

"What's wrong with him?"

"He's been sipping truth-soup from the look of him. Hey—don't do that!"

Wyatt sees a brown arm lift a gray one. He knows without seeing it that there is a wand in the hand at the end of the gray arm.

"Why not? He just . . ."

The speaker stops in mid-sentence. Wyatt recognizes both voices. He tries to talk, but the sounds he makes are hardly words. He tries again, forcing his tongue to enunciate the words slowly. "Walter? Freddie Boy?"

"Hey Wyatt—you look like shit," Walter observes.

"Day old," Wyatt struggles.

"What's happened to you? First you disappear everybody in my sector, then you kill three of my best shooters. Not the way to stay friends."

"Didn't know about the sector until after," Wyatt whispers. "Shooters get disappeared. Goes with the game."

Walter's hand grips his throat, lifting Wyatt's head above the cot. "I'd cut you up slowly into lots of little pieces, Wyatt, only you wouldn't feel a thing right now, would you?"

Wyatt just stares into Walter's squinting brown eyes, tries to locate the poison in his body, isolate it, remove it.

"What'cha doin' here?" Walter asks.

"I came to see the sector for myself."

"What about the plague?"

"No such thing."

"What then?"

"A nasty weapon, left over from the past."

"Victor find out about it?"

"Yeah."

"Anybody else have access to it?"

"No."

"How'd you figure to get past the quarantine?"

"Dunno. Just wanted to see if what I heard was true."

"It's true, all right. Everybody above second-level underground got turned to bones and stew. What's Adolph want with you? Those were his people sucking out your brains."

"Adolph's dead. He was in Sector Twelve when it happened. Maybe even at the Grille."

"We have you to thank for that, too, don't we?"

"Yeah. Someone must have followed me to your place. I took precautions . . ."

Walter releases his grip on Wyatt's throat, lets him fall

back onto the cot. "Find your girlfriend yet?"

"Yeah."

"What's she got to say for herself?"

"I haven't made it there yet. Too many citizens trying to kill me."

"You gonna wait a week—give us all time to forget?"

"Don't feel like I got a week, Walter."

Walter laughs.

"What's the big plan?" Freddie Boy demands. "What was worth doing that?"

"Dunno. New order, maybe. Truth and beauty. New flats for the downtowners, new toys for everyone else. Better deal for the living. Better deal for realty/construction, anyway. Downsizing of Void manufacturing/recycling. Maybe no more drossies for a while. Why you asking me? I'm just a private sweeper. Nobody tells me about plans."

"Don't much care who you kill, do you?" Freddie Boy growls.

"I took the best deal I got. Adolph made me a sweeper. Victor got me uptown. Rafe just disappears, Walter calls me poison, you don't want to like me. Not much of an offer there. What d'ya expect, Freddie Boy? We all do what we have to, while the crazies run the show."

"Maybe you're one of the crazies, Wyatt," she growls.

"Maybe we all are."

"What's in the pot?" Walter asks, pointing at the stainless steel lab cylinder.

"Me."

"Why?"

"I heal fast. Adolph wanted to live forever. Now somebody else does. Figures I'm the answer. Beat that. Poison to make you immortal."

Walter picks up the container, stuffs it into his inside

jacket pocket. "Y'know why we're not going to kill you, Wyatt?"

"Do tell."

"Because as big a shit as you are, you're still the best the Heartland has to offer. Don't push your luck, sweeper boy. Things change."

"Does that mean Freddie Boy likes me now?"

Walter steps back. Freddie Boy snarls. A fist cracks four of Wyatt's ribs. He still feels nothing. Freddie Boy spits on him. Walter leans over to pick over the remains of the Void crew, looks carefully at the wands, selects two, pockets them, tosses the others back onto the floor, stands back up, smiles.

"We can't leave him here," Walter says.

"Why not?" Freddie Boy demands.

"The Voids will be back before he can move."

"What do you want do with him?"

"He came to see the sector. Let's leave him there."

"How's he gonna get back out without winding up in the meat wagon?"

"That's his problem. Grab his feet."

Walter and Freddie Boy carry Wyatt back out to the tram. They toss him on. Walter climbs aboard. Freddie Boy walks back into the tunnel where a second tram awaits— one with a light mounted onto the front. Walter inches forward until the two cars connect with a loud click.

Once again the cool dark tunnel surrounds them to the sound of steel wheels grinding.

"Can you walk?" Walter asks.

"Not without a lot of help."

Freddie Boy stops the trams in the middle of the tunnel. Walter stands up. Wyatt hears the sound of rusty metal hinges opening. Walter lifts him by the armpits, drags him off the flatbed into a confined black space just inside the tunnel wall, sits him on the floor propped against the metal mesh below the railing. He hears something landing on his stomach.

"What's that?" he asks.

"Torch. I'm locking you in. When you're ambulatory, go to the bottom of the stairs, turn right, walk until you can't walk any farther. That will put you under the Sector Twelve Grille. Take the stairs up. The door will lock behind you. How you get out is your problem. Let me know what you think of Victor's handiwork if we ever meet again."

"You got a spare wand?"

"I told you not to push your luck."

"I never killed anyone who wasn't trying to kill me, Walter. I gave Freddie Boy a chance to get out, when I could have shot her. Besides, who's left in there—Void techs?"

There is a prolonged silence. Wyatt hears Walter breathing. Something else lands on his stomach, clicks against the torch.

"It's been in a blast. Usually we have one of our techs check them out before we put them in the field. Might blow up if you try to use it. Your choice," Walter says.

Wyatt hears the metal door clanging behind him, the locking mechanism clicking shut. He hears Freddie Boy tell Walter it is a mistake to let him live. The trams grind on down the tunnel into silence.

It is a night that never ends. No dawn, no weather, no lights from the nearest towers, no citizens in the street. Stale air, blackness, ringing ears, nausea. Wyatt loses all sense of time. He feels his ribs smarting as the drug wears off. He tries three times to heal them before he feels the bones reforming. He tries to stand, stumbles. The torch and the wand clatter onto the floor. He slides back down the metal mesh. His head is spinning as he gropes for the torch, the wand. In the dark, they feel the same. Wyatt decides to put the wand in *active* mode, to see the small blue lights. It is the torch. By its crisp white light, he examines the wand. It does not look any worse for wear. He holsters it, stands a second time by clinging to the railing. He descends four flights into a dank square tunnel. Red eyes peer at him, blink. He hears the sounds of skittering rat feet.

Wyatt stops to rest, end the spinning, catch his breath, sitting on the bottom step in the dark. His stomach begins to lurch. He turns his head, vomits twice. The smell is so foul, he forces himself to rise, staggers down the endless corridor. Waving the torch back and forth, he counts four large rats watching him from the front. They stand their ground as he draws near. He kicks the first one hard. It screams, bolts. The rest scamper beyond the beam.

He feels faint, but he dare not stop, lest the rats think him too helpless to defend himself. The sweat beads up on his brow, clammy, cold. The air is so thick Wyatt is certain he can wrap it about himself like a blanket. Again he tries to locate the poison. It is everywhere.

His feet are aching before he arrives at the next stairway. The rats are hiding. Wyatt sits down again, listens to his own gasping, the thunder of his heartbeat.

In the distance he sees the man with the cleft chin.

You should have been a good boy, Wyatt, the man says. *You should have let me touch you. Then you would have been a tech. You and Jennie could have gone to The Archives together.*

I should have bit your damn hand off, you perv.

The man vanishes abruptly.

Once more Wyatt focuses his attention within, on all that does not belong there, drawing it together, sending it through his system, up to his skin, out his pores. He feels as if he is afire. He screams in the dark. He stinks worse than the vomit. The dizziness is gone, the ringing in his ears stops. He wants a bath.

Grimly, Wyatt draws the wand, activates it, begins climbing the concrete stairs into Sector Twelve.

CHAPTER 45

Wyatt stops to catch his breath at the top landing. He shines the fading torch around to make certain the rats are not nearby. Setting it on the floor, he struggles with the cold steel wheel that opens the door, but lacks the strength to turn it. His ordeal and the long walk have drained him. Once more he slides down the metal retaining wall to regroup his strength in the dark. He shuts the torch off to conserve what is left of the power cell. Once more time flows by like a rushing river. He is a stone in midstream.

Wyatt awakens with a start. A screeching voice just beyond his feet sends him fumbling madly for the torch. By its sickly yellow light he sees a rat bunching itself up, preparing to leap. The wand is in his hand, the safety off, the orange fireball on its way before he remembers Walter's warning. The rat is gone in an instant. The darkness is blacker than before. The smell of ozone permeates the air.

Wand works fine. Silly shit knew it, or he wouldn't have taken it. Nice try, Walter.

He is back on his feet, turning the wheel with both hands. It is a struggle the wheel eventually loses. It takes nearly all his weight to push the door open. For a moment Wyatt looks around for something to wedge into the opening to keep it from locking shut—then he remembers the door on the other end of the tunnel is locked from the outside. He slips through, lets it go, hears it click softly. He is on his own in a quarantined sector.

The first one he sees is a dead rat. One level above the storeroom where he, Walter, and Rafe chatted. He knows it's a rat by the skeleton, turned onto its side. The rest of the body is a putrid black smear on the concrete floor. A little farther on he finds a citizen. He recognizes the copper hoop earrings. It is what is left of the barmaid who served him ale in a stein. Bent copper hoops, bones, a reeking black slick filled with crawling maggots.

Wyatt's stomach starts to heave, but there is nothing left to vomit. He takes off his vest, his holster, the bloody torn shirt, filled with whatever the Voids put into him. Wrapping the shirt around his face like a mask to keep out the cloying reek, he slips back into the holster and vest. He stops to listen. There is nothing, yet he is certain he is not alone. Cautiously, Wyatt makes his way to the next flight of stairs, on his way up to the Grille.

By the daylight streaming through the street level windows, he counts forty stinking corpses, sprawled on the floor, draped over charred furniture, huddled behind the bar. He wonders if Adolph Void is among them. All of the ale barrels have exploded, leaving twisted jagged metal shards everywhere. The few glass bottles on display against the mirror have all blown out their stoppers. Some are tipped over, their volatile wares splattering the reflecting glass. The power is shut off, so the neon lights that resemble dancing couples and stacked kegs of ale that line the walls do not flicker. They look like ghosts.

Slowly Wyatt makes his way through the mess toward the filthy window. The glass is smeared with something dark and translucent. Looking out, he sees the shadow of a glider pod moving down the street. Recycling is here. He pulls back quickly.

Wyatt hears the sound of a sweeper van at the other end

of the street. He will have to wait for nightfall to make his move.

He walks back to the lower basement, looking for air that does not gag, food, something to drink. He takes the soiled shirt off his face. Walter's office is at the end of the hall. Rummaging through the old oak desk by the waning light of the torch, Wyatt finds tins of sardines, crackers, a bottle of scotch left over from another era. It is a feast he savors in the dark. He also finds another wand, a sweeper model, which he drops into his vest pocket.

Muffled voices from above give him a jolt.

Wyatt jumps up, takes another swig of scotch, draws the wand from his holster. For a while, the noise stops. Then a racket begins in earnest when the sweepers start cleaning up the mess in the Grille, scraping the remains from the floor, turning the antiseptic hoses on everything. Once again there is silence. This is broken by the sounds of two voices coming nearer. Wyatt pushes the remnants of his feast into the desk drawer, shuts it quietly, ducks down into the knee well. Twin beams of crisp white light crisscross the room. Wyatt squeezes deeper into the well when the beams reach around behind the desk.

"Someone's been here, look at that."

"Well, they're not here now."

"Might be one of ours. Nobody survived this plague."

Wyatt sees white toes less than a foot away. There are cracker crumbs all over the floor, glistening by torchlight. He clutches his wand in one hand, the bottle of scotch in the other.

"Call it in. We got the rest of the block before we go home."

"I call it in, we stay half the night looking for whoever."

"Right."

They leave without calling anything in. Wyatt hears them searching the other storerooms.

Footfalls on the stairs, in the corridors above. They find what is left of the barmaid and the rat. More sweepers, more scraping, more hoses. Then nothing. Wyatt listens to the silence until his ears ring. He guesses it has been hours. He cannot risk anyone finding him here.

He crawls out of the desk well, takes one last shot of scotch, holsters the wand, makes his way back upstairs. The reek of antiseptic is everywhere, making his nostrils burn. It is no worse than the smell of his shirt. He peers out the open door. The sun is setting, painting the sky with broad strokes of orange and crimson. The street is empty, no white sweeper trucks looming, no pods hovering above. Wyatt darts along the street, hugging the side of the buildings. He ducks back into the next open storefront he finds. The antiseptic odor is not as bad here. He waits, listens, looks into the deepening twilight, makes his way westward.

At the intersection, he sees searchlights. Transports hover a block away, shining their lights on the sweeper crews below. Two small pods drift back and forth through the beams like insects drawn to the light. Wyatt takes a deep breath, darts across the street, turns northwest, hugs the cool stone wall, jogs away from the activity.

There is no smell of rotting flesh, so he enters an open doorway. Up one flight he finds a corridor filled with open doors. The torchlight is barely a glow he hides by cupping his hand over the lens. He tries four flats, looking for a shirt, but there is nothing left. Bodies, furniture, clothes, food—everything is either burned or swept.

Again Wyatt finds himself in the dark street. Taking his time, he walks to the next intersection. Here, the reek of death is everywhere. He cuts due north. The smell abates.

Another short block, he is moving westward again, through the commercial district. He stops to listen. The machines are not humming this night. Not even the drossies are rummaging. He slows his pace, expecting to see the lights from Sector Fourteen beyond, but there is only the dark shapeless form of the night everywhere.

He comes to the last Sector Twelve intersection. Once again he sees bright downlights with pods weaving in and out of them, but at a three-block distance, everything hovering well above the low walls of the commercial buildings. Still no light from Sector Fourteen.

The last block in the web maze is a short one. Every step Wyatt takes is slower than the one before.

Did we cook more than one sector?

The black plastic containment wall stops him short. He walks right into it, loses his balance, slides down it, landing on his buttocks in the street. The entire sector is wrapped in flexible plastic. Wyatt feels his face. It stings from the impact. He hears the sounds of voices on the other side. People walk by, speaking as if the barrier is not even there, as if it was always there, as if there is no plague.

In one of the manufacturing facilities Wyatt finds a knife. The torch burns itself out illuminating the stainless steel edge. Wyatt picks the knife up carefully, drops the torch, returns to the barrier, groping at the air lest he walk into the plastic sheet again. Following the barrier to the stone wall, he sits down to wait, listening to the sounds of life in the next sector. In the distance, the transports inch closer, the sweepers disappear Victor Crist's handiwork.

Eventually the voices beyond become fewer, more infrequent, silent. Wyatt listens, straining to hear anything. He knows the civil guards make no sound as they hover. It is a calculated risk.

Pushing with all his might, he forces the knife tip into the plastic, about a foot from the stone wall. The barrier expands, rather than tears, but Wyatt is persistent. It takes nearly half an hour to cut a two-foot-high slit about a foot above the street. The knife is hot in his hands. He wipes his fingerprints from it, leaves it on the ground.

Pulling the plastic apart, Wyatt looks up, then down, the street. The manufacturing facilities are dark. No work tonight. Pubs and brothels closed until tomorrow. No one else is moving about the dimly-lit street. He will have to risk the presence of the civil guards.

Like a thief, he squeezes himself through the narrow opening. He is reborn into the light, darting from shadow to shadow, avoiding the chutes, making his way to the Sector Fourteen Station, the image of the microwaved bodies decorating the Sector Twelve Grille superimposed over every wall, window, darkened doorway he passes along the way.

CHAPTER 46

Outside the Sector Fourteen Station, two civil guards drop noiselessly onto the street about fifteen feet in front of Wyatt. Their gray ceramic body armor makes them look like giant beetles. They move in slow motion, advertising their intentions long before they can act upon them. He can see that they mean to approach him from two sides at once. Wyatt turns to face the men, stepping backward until his backside is no more than three feet away from the nearest city wall—far enough away so that he cannot be pinned, close enough so that neither guard can get behind him. He has also moved sideways, keeping the two men in a straight line in front of him, preventing them from splitting his attention.

It has been too long since he entered this sector for anyone to have seen him emerging from the black plastic containment. The civil guards would have come en masse, incinerating him on the spot as a potential plague carrier had he been seen.

He is the only citizen on the street, at a time when all should be sleeping. That, along with his filthy vest worn over a torn bloodstained shirt, has summoned them. From their ponderous nervous eye movements, he can see that they both know he is carrying two wands. Cocking his head to one side, he stares into the eyes of the closest guard, who stops approaching immediately.

By the lamplight he watches the limpid pools of blue seemingly recoil from him, as if the image of the skeletal remains in the Sector Twelve Grille have been transferred straight from his memory to them. Slightly to his right, the second guard now uses the first for cover. Without looking directly at the man, Wyatt sees the second guard reaching cautiously for his wand. A soft *thwip* marks the release of the safety strap that keeps the wand from falling out of its holster. In the heavy silence of the night, it sounds like a sudden thunderclap. The jarring sound echoes off the hard surfaces of the city.

"Don't do that, friend," Wyatt hears himself saying. "It's been a long night for all of us already." His eyes remain locked upon the eyes of the first guard. He makes no overt movement of any sort toward either one of them.

The second guard hesitates, his hand poised upon the wand still nestled in its holster upon his hip. The moment seems to last forever. Gradually the second guard refastens the holster strap. Both civil guards nod to him, signifying their recognition of a Heartlander traveling incognito. They rise effortlessly into the darkness above the streetlights without saying a word.

Wyatt makes his way into the covered stairs that take him into the elevated station. He knows there is no need to look up. The confrontation is over.

Inside, two more civil guards hover immediately above the platform. They land directly in front of him.

"No trains until six a.m., citizen," one says flatly.

"Unless you got a private," the second adds.

Wyatt pulls back his sleeve, looks at his left wrist. The calc is still there. He had not even noticed it amid the horror of the Sector Twelve Grille. He selects the correct button, presses the code for Harry, and waits.

"Who's that?" a nervous voice demands.

"Mr. Weston. I'm at the Sector Fourteen Station. How

soon can you get over here?"

"Be there in ten minutes. Going uptown?"

"Yeah."

The two civil guards take a respectful step backwards before rising silently like a pair of guardian angels. Wyatt watches to see if they are alerting anyone to his presence. They do not speak or activate their own helmet coms.

Harry is there in eight minutes, all smiles. Fifteen minutes later, Wyatt disembarks at the Sector Thirty-Two Station, after thanking Harry and wishing him a good night. Wyatt feels his innards shaking. He wants to walk, to touch the night, to smell the air. But he is not up to another showdown with either the Voids, the civil guards, the resistance, or anyone else, so he takes the chute back to his tower. Three Crist security guards watch nervously as he appears, smiles at them, makes his way to the lift.

Back in his flat, he checks the talkie for messages. There are none. He checks the water gauge, then fills the tub. Leaving the sweeper wand within easy reach of the tub, he stuffs all his clothes into the recycler, steps in, sinks down into the hot water.

The water is cold, dingy, covered with a thin oily film when he awakens. He releases the stopper, watches the water level drop, pushes the grit from the bottom toward the drain with his hand, refills the tub. His body aches in a dozen places. There are pains in his kidneys, lungs, heart, liver, behind his eyes, at the sides of his head. With a sigh, he focuses inward. There are many complex things wrong here. Thought patterns have been altered, barriers erected, reflexes are off, toxins have accumulated in various organs, in spite of his ejecting most of them through his pores.

Carefully, Wyatt makes each adjustment, until things are back to normal. He feels the rest of the toxins oozing from his skin into the bath water. He opens his eyes, watches the vapor billowing into thin clouds above the tub, shuts his eyes, goes back inside. He hones his reflexes sharper than they have ever been, rids himself of emotional defense mechanisms of his own making that no longer serve him, frees himself of the subtle suggestions planted by the Voids. It is an aspect of his self-healing ability he has never considered before. He knows there is much more to it than this, but for now, doing away with the pain, the commands, the restraints will suffice.

He lathers himself all over, rinses, lets the water out again, dries himself with a thick towel, calls up a new silk wardrobe, a comfortable pair of shoes from the recycler. Wearing only the pants, he begins his martial movements in the living room. For the first time, he finds the movements are making themselves—he no longer has to think any part of them. Like riding the wind in a dream, the process is ethereal, rejuvenating, exhilarating. Once again, time passes him by, only this time he is the river while it is the stone caught in the effortless torrent.

The clock in the bedroom reads eleven thirty-six. His stomach reminds him he has not eaten since breakfast the day before. He orders a vegetable salad, fresh bread, soft cheese, white wine. He thinks of Anastasia, wonders what she is doing, if he dare love her.

From the wide picture window, he looks down into the street. Three clusters of rats and a wide band of roaches scramble into the heart of the sector toward the summoning sounds of the recycling station. It must be Thursday. The sweeps are every other Thursday. There are no more drossies in Sector Thirty-Two. He watches the white-clad sweepers pick up the few pieces of litter, toss them into the lumbering truck. The all-clear sounds. It is as safe as it gets for citizens to be on the city streets again.

Wyatt finishes dressing, calls down the screen. He spends the rest of the morning into the early afternoon reading about the Victorian era and the British Empire. He marvels at how utterly real and unreal all of it was simultaneously, without any apparent contradictions. This leads him to the *Tao Teh Ching*. It is dark by the time he has reread it for the fourth time, as well as two dozen commentaries on the work.

He orders stir-fried vegetables, white rice, green tea for dinner.

Closing the drapes, he lowers the screen again, calls the Crist household.

Anna is waiting for him in the living room.

"Good to see you, Anna," he says. "I've missed you."

Anna smiles, signaling that she is not alone, even though he can see no one else with her.

"Did Victor make it home?" he asks.

"Daddy's here."

"How are things in the Heartland?"

"Tense. There have been several small wars. Four enterprises have been wiped out. We've not been attacked. The Committee can't meet again under the circumstances. No one wants the home guard to patrol the Heartland. That will happen if any Committee members are assaulted en route. Edward appears to have enough backing to become Chairman at the next meeting, but who knows when that will be. Even food deliveries have been suspended—everyone is living on their stores. You had better stay put for a while, Wyatt. I'll let you know when to come back."

The screen goes blank.

He waits for her voice inside his head. There is only silence. A surging wave of doubt swells within his mind. Has he been used? Does Victor know about his trip to Sector Twelve? Does Victor know that Void Enterprises has picked his mind for all its contents, even if the information never left the underground? Does Victor know that he told Walter the truth? Is there any place for him within the new order? Wyatt does not let his hesitation form even a single concrete thought—he will not give voice to his uncertainty—he will not let Anna hear any of it. Leaving it all as turbulent feeling, he pushes the wave back, diminishing it, leveling it until all that is left is clear still waters, reflecting the unseen stars high above his tower.

Wyatt sits silently in the dark.

CHAPTER 47

Wyatt is up before dawn—meditates, limbers up, practices his martial movements by the time the sun rises. He looks at his wands, selects the sweeper model as the more reliable of the two under the circumstances, charges it, holsters it, takes the lift to the lobby.

The walk uptown to Sector Thirty-Eight takes just over an hour. It is the first time he has walked his new neighborhood. Unlike downtown with its ever-present stone walls hemming him within the web maze of narrow streets, the boulevards are tree-lined, the trees are filled with birds, the birds are filled with song this crisp autumn morning as they greet the rising sun. Here and there, uptown faces leisurely walk their dogs, occasionally stopping to chat with one another as the dogs wander about sniffing at everything, doing their business with a ritualistic frenzy that makes Wyatt smile. The towers are not yet surrounded by wide parks like they are further uptown, but they are staggered to give the tenants a feeling of spaciousness, with small gardens on all sides.

The ghosts of his past leave him alone. He takes in everything around him as he walks purposefully beneath the broad-limbed beeches, elms, oaks, ashes. It occurs to him that the sweep has no effect on the birds, that it is tuned into the specific animals it means to recycle. A woodpecker begins thumping rhythmically above his head. Wyatt stops, peers up at it. The bird stops its thumping, cocks its head long enough to look back down at him with one eye. Wyatt

286

is delighted. He passes a woman clearly in her forties, feeding sunflower seeds to a group of appreciative cardinals, nuthatches, titmice, doves, chickadees, all of whom converge about her without fear. For awhile he forgets Sector Twelve.

There are no civil guards hovering about here, yet Wyatt is certain they must be nearby.

Civil guards are everywhere in the city. Then it occurs to him that perhaps something is happening elsewhere to draw them away from this placid neighborhood. He wonders who controls the civil guards, the home guard. With that many shooters, do they have ambitions like Adolph Void, Edward, Victor Crist?

The sun clears the horizon as he enters Sector Thirty-Four. The dog people are going back inside, faceless black silhouettes surrounded by shimmering orange coronas. Drones and techs that opt not to take the chute are walking purposefully toward the station. No one takes any special notice of him, now that he is wearing fresh silk, now that he has contained the horror of Sweet Sally M within himself. He wonders if he has become just another face.

Shooters are never faces, he tells himself. Yet Victor Crist is a face. *Maybe I'm one, too.*

By Sector Thirty-Six, the sun is a full gold. He shades his eyes from its light. He notices the broad-brimmed hats on those he passes, decides to begin wearing one of these. He moves westward at the next intersection, toward the train tube. There are no manufacturing districts this far west, he passes only one school. It is easily recognizable by the twelve-foot-tall black metal pikes linked together surrounding the playground equipment, the two-story complex of dark-windowed red brick structures comprising the dormitories, classrooms, auditorium, outbuildings. He wants to stop, to watch the children come outside, to see if he is still one of them. He slows his pace until the next intersection, hoping. No one comes out for supervised exercise or play.

He reaches the tube two blocks later, changes direction again, following it northward. A downtown train passes an uptown train above him, making a sound like a flush toilet. Wyatt laughs to himself.

Flush the faces to their jobs, while Victor shapes the future.

It becomes a singsong that he repeats like a litany until it is no longer amusing.

On the next block Wyatt finds an odeum, surrounded by cafes, shops, services. He stops at a shop, buys a broad-brimmed felt hat that matches his tan trousers. The proprietor is gracious.

He stops at a cafe for a coffee and a pastry. Open umbrellas shade small white wrought-iron tables with cushioned matching chairs. It reminds him of the time he sat with Rachel Void after *The Mimis'* concert, making small-talk until the jumper landed across the street. He scans the nearest tower. No sign of jumpers here.

He sips the coffee, watching the other patrons surreptitiously. Less than half the seats are taken. The patrons are mostly grouped in twos, threes, fours. There are only two other tables with one seat taken. No one here looks tired. No one looks worried. No one appears to be in a hurry to do anything. Conversations are quiet, gestures are few, staid. The waiter smiles as Wyatt inserts his card into the credit counter. He sees his balance is in the tens of thousands. The coffee, the pastry bring it down by five. Three months ago this would have been beyond his dreams. Three months ago he would have had to save his credits for a trip to a cafe. Three months ago he would have thought Sweet

Sally M was a prostitute or a singer with a band.

What now? What will I say to her? What will she say to me?

Wyatt gets up, leaves the umbrellaed sanctuary, goes back onto the tree-lined boulevard.

This is what I wanted. Access to the Heartland. Credits to spare. Jennie free of the ale house. Knowing what was really happening. Real prospects. A comfortable flat. Yeah. Only not like this, not a shooter for Victor Crist. Like what?

Wyatt wonders what else he could have been. *A tech?* His school rating had been adequate. Only the exceptional were made techs. *A drone?* He had no connections there. He had always been a day worker. Sweeping had paid better than anything else he had done. It had had some small status as well. Although in retrospect he no longer understands why.

Maybe the wand. The right to kill. The reflexes, the skill to use it. That's what I had. That was my way out. Jennie knows that.

How do I explain Anna? Other lovers never bothered Jennie. I was the one who wanted her to myself. She said that I was the only one at the end—that she did that for me. I believed her. I still do.

Why did she leave? Was it something I did? Something I said? Something I was?

Something I still am? Something I could never be?

Two main avenues intersect at the start of Sector Thirty-Eight. Wyatt follows the train tube, looking for the four black towers of The Archives, but they are still beyond his field of vision. He follows his train of thought, giving silent voice to all his fears.

What if she's not working today? What if she's moved on? What if . . . ?

Wyatt suddenly brushes aside his doubts. He knows

nothing has changed in one regard. He is still looking for Jennie. This is the only clearly-marked trail he has followed throughout. He will follow it through to the end.

A small breeze ruffles his hair, seemingly lingers around him, then moves down the avenue. He breathes deeply from it, letting it fill his lungs. It is soothing, calming, hopeful.

Looking up, he sees a group of six civil guards. These take no special notice of him. A block later, he sees another group. He wonders if they are here to protect The Archives. It makes sense. They house the only real record there is, they dispense the only real knowledge to be had beyond the limited teaching of the schools. If someone like Victor Crist took a notion to destroy The Archives, to rewrite history, to further limit the available knowledge, the result for the future could be devastating.

Two blocks further north, Wyatt catches his first glimpse of the black towers. He stops, notes his accelerated heartbeat, calms himself. He feels his eyes growing moist.

Jennie . . .

A block away, he finds another cafe, orders another coffee, uses the toilet. There he combs his hair, examines his face, restructures his jaw line, softening it, changes it back the way it was. He barely touches the coffee. The waiter asks him if there is something wrong, sending him into a spasm of laughter. He asks the time. It is not yet eight o'clock.

I wonder what time The Archives open—what time she comes to work.

He asks the waiter.

"The Archives are always open," is the curt answer.

The waiter leaves. Wyatt drinks the coffee slowly, stalling, making the moment last, bracing himself for disappointment, fortifying himself for the only thing he ever really wanted, to be with Jennie without the oppressive weight of poverty.

He does not remember walking the last block. He does not hear the trains whooshing overhead. The bird songs, a welcome novelty an hour ago, are barely noticeable now. Wyatt moves like a man adream, bouncing through a fluid world with limited gravity, free of harsh edges, without danger, until he is standing before the block-long black glass building below the four imposing towers.

An awning reaching through a narrow rock garden marks the main entrance halfway up the street. He sees his double in the reflective surface of the glass, remembers himself, slows his pace, cocks his hat, straightens his vest, rubs his palms together to dry them.

Wyatt feels the embrace of the awning's shadow, walks the twenty paces to the revolving door, lets The Archives swallow him whole like he hopes it has swallowed his Jennie.

CHAPTER 48

From the bright morning without to the smoked glass muted interior, the revolving door glides effortlessly for the first quarter-turn. It comes to a dead stop, leaving Wyatt pressed against its glossy black surface, trapped between the street and the building. A small stainless steel drawer opens quickly just below his waist, touching his right thigh.

"Please deposit your wand in the drawer," a soft feminine voice states. "No weapons of any sort are permitted inside The Archives."

Wyatt unholsters the wand, sets it in the drawer, watches the drawer close. Nothing more is said, so he presses lightly against the push bar. Once again the door glides easily on its track.

A short thin young woman with pale gray skin, large brown eyes, shoulder-length straight black hair is waiting for him in a large open room with a deep red glazed tile floor. She hands him a hexagonal green disc.

"This will allow you to claim your weapon on the way out," she says in the same soft voice. "Is this your first visit to The Archives?"

"Yeah."

"I am your guide, Wanda. How should I address you?"

"Wyatt."

"Is there something in particular you came to see, Wyatt? Or would you rather a general tour of the museum? I can, if you prefer, give you a specialized tour of any area of interest you may have, or take you about until you find something of interest."

Wyatt is not ready to tell her he came to find Jennie Height. Not until he learns more about the workings of The Archives.

"A general tour sounds like a good beginning," he says.

"There is an entry fee of ten credits, Wyatt. Would you be so kind?"

Wanda gestures toward the credit counter behind him next to the revolving door. He smiles, inserts his card, watches his balance drop by ten credits.

"This way, Wyatt."

Wanda leads him through the well-lit atrium to a stainless steel portal. He watches the other citizens moving about their atrium workplace as she presses her hand softly against the lock plate. The door slides open, admitting them both into a small darkened room. Purple lights glow to the familiar sound of soft humming.

"Bioscan . . ." Wanda starts.

"I know," Wyatt cuts her short.

"Did you know that the device was developed by Archival engineers?"

"No."

"Well, it was. We are quite proud of the fact that we not only house, maintain, analyze, categorize, and protect the legacy of mankind, but we also continue to make many significant contributions to it as well. These include the transport chute, the antigrav, and the recycler."

She looks up at Wyatt, expecting some sort of response.

He smiles, raises his eyebrows, nods his head.

The lights go off, the next door clicks open.

"May I ask why you carry a wand?"

"I'm a bodyguard."

"Where is your patron?"

"At home."

"You have the day off?"

"Yeah."

"Then why do you still wear the wand?"

"It's become part of me. I feel naked without it."

It is Wanda's turn to smile weakly and nod.

Wyatt laughs.

Wanda leads him into a vast chamber lit exclusively by floor lights. A diorama to their right is suddenly illuminated as they stand before it. Inside are lifelike replicas of humans wearing crude leather garments, fashioning tools, hunting, taming wild animals, tending domesticated ones, gathering wild plants, harvesting grains. The image seems to go on forever, the figures diminishing, the background becoming a realistic painting. An actual body of a man with torn leather skin, dried up muscles, missing eyes, lips curled back in death's final sneer is on display next to the diorama. Laid out neatly below him are his tools: knives, sewing needles, arrowheads, spear tips, an ax, hammer, awl, wedge.

Wanda explains the origin of modern man after the probable catastrophe which obliterated the historical record of the times before it—how he came back from the brink of extinction all over the world, following much the same pattern of development. Once again she mentions the significance of The Archives in saving the record after the most recent series of catastrophes. Wyatt suspects he will be expected to make some sort of donation before he leaves.

"If this is of interest to you," she says, "I can show you a complete collection of Stone Age tools, more bodies retrieved from glaciers, a large variety of treatises by men who devoted their lives to studying such things."

"You're doing just fine."

"I beg your pardon?"

"I like the tour. Keep doing what you're doing."

Once again Wanda smiles weakly. They pass fourteen-foot-high stacks with motorized ladders. All are contained within glass-enclosed rooms, climate-controlled, temperature-controlled, sanitized, free of insects, mold, mildew. Wanda explains the significance of each stack, the manner of research one would conduct if one were interested in each subject.

"Have you done any research, Wyatt?" she asks, pausing before the next stainless steel portal.

"Yeah, a little."

"What sort?"

Wyatt grins. "All sorts."

"Such as?"

"Jumpers. Memory. Genetics. Shakespeare. Antique weapons. Whatever arouses my curiosity, I guess."

Wanda stares blankly at him. He can see that she is unsure if he is serious or having some sort of joke at her expense.

"I am serious," he assures her. "I research whatever impacts my life. I want to understand it all, piece by piece. It's just that the pieces seem to come at me in a totally random order."

"I see." Wanda looks definitely uncomfortable. "So what brought you to The Archives today?" she presses.

"I've heard a lot about them lately. I came to see for myself. Once I know what's here, I'll know where to go the next time I need to research something."

"Your research—it's done with the screen?"

"Sometimes. Sometimes it's field work."

"Field work?"

"Yeah. Hands-on. See for myself, never mind some

face's opinion. You ever do any field work, Wanda?"

"No, not really. There's not much field left, Wyatt."

"Oh, but there is. Everything outside this complex is the field."

"I suppose so."

Wanda places her palm against the door plate, it slides open. Wyatt follows her into another large dimly-lit gallery. Once again a diorama lights up as they approach. This time it is a composite of early Egyptian life, complete with looming pyramids, a battle with charioteers at the forefront of an infantry charge, a magnificent city filled with painted stone buildings, sculptures, peasants harvesting grain along the banks of the Nile River. Wanda drones on for half an hour about the uniting of the Upper and Lower Kingdoms, the three kingdoms which followed, the countless dynasties, the high and low points of three thousand years under the watchful eye of Ra.

"That's quite a feat," Wyatt says, when she pauses for breath.

"What is?"

"Three millennia under the same order."

"Yes, I suppose you're right."

The room is filled with artifacts of gold, wood, cloth. With bright tomb paintings, rings, necklaces, fly whisks, idols, statues, dehydrated bodies swathed in cloth left centuries ago to walk among their gods in places far from the lands of the living.

Wyatt asks questions about everything, Wanda answers. Her explanations begin as long-winded discussions embracing religion, philosophy, economics, history, geography, magic, medicine, diet—degenerate into terse sentences no longer than the questions he asks.

She leads him to the next stainless steel portal, presses

her palm against the plate, brings him into a small room with two bright red upholstered benches facing each other on a polished maple floor. Wanda gestures for Wyatt to sit down. He complies. She sits opposite him.

"What's next?" he asks, after an awkward silence.

"That depends."

"On what?"

"On whether you're going to tell me what you really came here for, or if you're just going to give me a sore throat and tired feet making me lecture you on everything else."

Wyatt laughs aloud. "All right. I really do want to know about The Archives, Wanda. But you're right, that's not why I came here today. I came to find someone."

"You can do that with your screen, Wyatt. Your security clearance is no higher here than it is at home."

"What if the person I came to find is here, Wanda—right here in The Archives. I've heard that you people keep to yourselves—that once you come here, your records are disassembled, so that those that knew you . . . those that loved you . . . can never find you again. Is that true, Wanda?"

Wanda's face grows rigid. Her jaw tightens, her mouth puckers, her eyes narrow. She folds her arms across her chest, crosses her legs at the ankles. She does not answer Wyatt.

"Let me ask you something else, then. If I were to ask to see someone here, would that endanger them? . . . Compromise them? . . . Ruin their prospects?"

"We are not," Wanda says slowly, "encouraged to fraternize with those outside The Archives. Ours is a scholarly life—one difficult for those without to appreciate."

"I appreciate it, Wanda. If I had known about The Archives before I became a bodyguard, I might have come here instead. My patron was the one who told me about it. Now I have reason to believe the woman I love is here, Wanda. I'd like to find her. I'd like to ask her why she just disappeared. I'd like to know if there is still any place for me in her life. I'd like to know that she's happy, in good health, doing well, doing what she wants. That she's not unhappy doing what someone else wants. Can you appreciate that, Wanda?"

Wanda looks like Wyatt has just wrung every drop of life out of her. Her eyes are wild, afraid. Her hands are clasped together tightly, knuckles turning white. Wyatt thinks she will melt all over the seat if he keeps staring at her, talking to her, asking her questions she cannot answer.

The door behind Wanda opens with a whisper. From the shadows beyond, a pale face with cinnamon freckles, high cheekbones, bluer-than-blue eyes, thick red hair tied back emerges.

"It's all right, Wanda," Jennie says. "I knew he'd find me eventually. I'll be fine with him. You can go now."

It is Wyatt's turn to melt into his seat. He barely notices Wanda slipping out of the room with a heavy sigh.

Jennie sits down easily opposite Wyatt, says nothing. He sees none of the love he remembers in those blue eyes. But there is a sense of urgency. She folds her hands lightly in her lap, looks at him. The metal door slides shut. Jennie smiles the smile that has kept him going.

CHAPTER 49

They stare into one another's eyes, each looking for something different. Wyatt looks to Jennie for passion rekindled, she looks to him for understanding. Jennie is even more radiantly beautiful than he remembers her, sadder, too.

They do not speak, they do not touch, they do not express their pent-up emotions. Wyatt wants to jump up, take Jennie in his arms, shower her with kisses, make love to her on the bench. He wants to give up everything he has gained these past months, join her here. He wants to hurl away the life he has made for himself to become part of hers. He knows it is not to be.

He can see that she will deny him nothing, that she has not changed in that respect. But he can also see that this Jennie is not the Jennie on the train, asking him to find her. She is not the Jennie in his memory, waiting for him in their lasting embrace somewhere down the endless spiral corridors of time. Nor is she the Jennie of his half-formed waking dreams, the one who stands by him regardless of the circumstances.

"How are you, Jennie?" he says at last.

It sounds like his voice, but did he really speak the words?

"I'm well, Wyatt. How are you feeling?"

"I'm not sure. It's been a little crazy lately."

"You're lucky to be alive, especially after your trip to Sector Twelve. Did you go there to see for yourself what really happened after Victor's last maneuver?"

"Yeah. I had no idea. Please believe me."

"I do, Wyatt. I know you wouldn't have knowingly done that. I admire you for going. I've been following your career. It's a dangerous path you've chosen. Your patron, Victor Crist, is a very volatile individual. Many people die around him. Nobody leaves him of their own volition."

"Many people die all over this crazy world, Jennie. Is Victor worse than the other Committee members?"

"He's far more dangerous than most."

"You know he used to work here."

"Most of them did—Adolph Void, Victor Crist, Edward Coyle . . . We seem to cultivate—in spite of our best efforts—a breed of ambitious, sometimes ruthless, individuals. I suppose that's why most of them continue to encourage us after they've left."

"Listen to you," Wyatt exclaims. "I can hardly believe that's you I'm hearing. You've changed so much. You've come a long way since the pub, Jennie. You're a brand new woman."

"I've been studying hard, Wyatt. I've been given a chance to make a difference, to create something of myself. I'm taking it all very seriously."

"How'd you come to get this chance, Jennie?"

She unclasps her hands, looks down at her feet, forces a smile, looks back into his eyes.

Wyatt reads a strange blend of pain, shame, sorrow, relief there.

"I was pregnant, Wyatt. I didn't want to tell you. I didn't want you to feel you had to take care of me. You have no idea how difficult it is for a pregnant woman living in this era. Once motherhood was considered the crowning achievement of womanhood. Now everyone on The Committee is worried about the census. Can't have babies pop-

ping out faster than we can kill each other off, you know.
You expect understanding, caring, medical attention—you
get drones lecturing on overpopulation, the lack of available
resources, the lack of opportunity. Only the bravest women
bear children anymore, Wyatt. I wasn't very brave.
Someone made me an unusual offer to end the pregnancy. I
took it."

"Who, Jennie? Who made you this offer?"

"It doesn't matter. It's better for everyone involved if
you don't know. My silence was part of the deal, anyway. It
really is for the best, even if it was motivated by the basest
self-interest."

"Someone wanted the embryo, didn't they?" Wyatt
whispers.

"I know that now, but I didn't then. I knew only that I
had a chance to leave the pub, come to the safest place in
the city, have a chance to make a difference, to learn, to
take pride in myself, what I'm doing. I took it without much
hesitation."

"Why didn't you tell me?"

"I never got the opportunity, Wyatt. I had to make my
choice the moment the offer was made. It was part of the
deal. I gave up everything I had, everyone I knew, to come
here. All of us do. I'm sorry. I never meant to hurt you. I
loved you, Wyatt. I hope you believe me."

"I believe you, Jennie. I never loved anyone like I loved
you. I still do. What about you? Could you love me again?"

"You've changed, Wyatt. You've become part of the
Heartland. You're part of everything wrong with our society. You've grown cold. You kill without thinking. Besides, you're married, remember?"

"How do you know all these things?"

"This is The Archives, Wyatt. Knowing is what we're

301

about. Studying is what we do. We study everything, all of the time, especially anybody making a name for themselves."

"When you disappeared I almost went insane, Jennie. Nobody could remember you. I made it a point to hold you in my mind, to remember you, to find you, no matter what."

Jennie's eyes grow moist. A single tear runs down each pale cheek. "At first I wanted you to find me. I knew you would, one day. I thought about you day and night. Then, when you learned to use the screen, I watched you calling out to me. I wanted to answer, but it isn't allowed. So I began following you. Every trip you took, I was there. But every trip you took, more people died. Bert Han was a good man, Wyatt. He didn't deserve what you and Victor Crist did to him. I already told you I know it was something the two of you did that killed everyone in Sector Twelve, too. I don't know how. I'm not sure I want to know. I haven't said a word, but I'm not the only one who knows. Many people are watching Victor. You seem to live a charmed life, Wyatt. I'm glad. I don't want anything bad happening to you. I was happiest when I was with you. I will always remember you the way you were."

He reaches out to take her hand. As expected, she offers no resistance. But there is no encouragement, either. It is cold to his touch. He trembles, lets it fall back into her lap. He drops to one knee before her, gently brushes away her tears instead.

"Please let me hold you for a few minutes, Jennie. Just to say goodbye. I never had a chance to do that before. I won't ask anything else of you. I won't ever bother you again. I'm glad you have this place. I'm glad you got out of the pub. I'm glad you have prospects. We neither of us had any before. We used to talk about going to the Heartland together, remember? I figured you went first, waiting for me to follow. I went there hoping to find you. I got there the only way I could. I wish it was different, but I know I'm poison to those I'm near. I won't spoil it for you. Just let me hold you once more."

Jennie puts her arms around his neck. He sits down next to her, pulls her close without squeezing her. The smell of ale and cooking oil is long gone from her hair, but the good smell of her is still there. He runs his hands over her back, feels her shoulders, her neck. She feels so good to touch. He feels her convulsions as she cries, he cries with her.

"I will always love you, Jennie," he says at last. "I hope you find happiness here."

"Don't go yet."

Wyatt takes a deep breath. He is ready to spend the rest of his life on the bench. He pulls her closer, she hugs him tightly. Eventually his back muscles cramp. Jennie pulls away. They both stand up. They hold each other's hands, peer into one another's eyes one last time.

"I'm glad you came, Wyatt. Stay away from the Heartland for a little while longer, if you can. Things have gotten pretty unstable the past few days. No one knows how it will sort itself out. The violence isn't over yet."

"I know. It was good to see you, Jennie. Good to know you're doing well."

"Wanda will have to take you back out the way you came in. You have to leave with your guide. We live by rules here, Wyatt."

She kisses him on the cheek, lets go of his hands, turns away, without looking back.

He watches her press the pad on the portal. She seems to glide over the surface of the maple floor without touching any of it, glides into the waiting shadow beyond the stainless steel doorway, glides out of his life forever.

CHAPTER 50

Wyatt does not bother to reclaim the sweeper wand he left in the security drawer. He sees the relief on Wanda's face when he enters the revolving door without stopping, without looking at her, without speaking to her. Wanda wants him gone. Gone from The Archives, gone from her life, gone from Jennie's. Once outside, he tosses the green hexagonal disk onto the ground, walks off without purpose or direction, wandering down the center of the street, his attention largely on his own dark brooding thoughts.

It is mid-morning. The avenue is beginning to fill with pedestrians. Faces out for a stroll, for a visit to the cafes, the shops. Faces with credits to spend, toys to buy, pleasures to indulge. Wyatt has no use for toys or pleasures this afternoon.

It was all for nothing. I went along with anything, waiting for my chance at happiness, throwing everything away. Blind Wyatt, trying so hard to open his eyes. Poison Wyatt, carrying his own plague, spreading it wherever he went. At least one of us got what she wanted, Jennie. At least one of us did it right. Please be happy for us both.

He wonders if he could have done any of it differently.

I was a sweeper when we met. You knew what I did, you loved me anyway. What else was there? I'm no actor, I'm no musician, all my friends disappeared, nobody said, "Hey, Wyatt, come along with us; we got us a really good gig we want to share with you. Hey, Wyatt, come disappear with us." What else could I have done, Jennie? What else was there?

Wyatt tries to relive his life from the moment Jennie disappeared. He is surprised at how much of it he cannot remember. He looks for places he might have let opportunity slip away, people whose friendship he might have cultivated, times where he might have simply sat out the storm. He could have remained a sweeper, forgotten about Victor Crist, waited for Rachel Void to snap, gone looking for another job—if he survived Rachel's inevitable outburst—keeping Jennie's memory alive through it all.

Would Rachel have lost it if I hadn't gone to work for Victor? Would she have let Adolph have our embryo if I had stayed at the Recycling Center? Would I have forgotten Jennie and been happy with Rachel?

He admits to himself he has no way of knowing.

He wonders who disappeared Jennie. *Curtis Void for Rachel? Rachel—for a taste of city real? Adolph Void—through Rachel, or anyone else—for the embryo? Victor Crist—for what? Walter—or one of his people—why? For Jennie? Someone inside The Archives—for Jennie herself? Someone I haven't met yet?*

Maybe Jennie's right. Maybe it's better I don't know. Maybe it's time I remember how to forget. I've already forgotten more than I remember.

He takes the chute outside the odeum to the Sector Thirty-Eight Station. He feels an emptiness in the center of his solar plexus, a hollowness from his bowels to his brain. He wants to beat on his chest like a gorilla, just to hear the thunder within the cavity. He knows he has lost something so large he cannot begin to perceive it. He knows he hurts from a wound he cannot heal.

Is this what makes a jumper jump? A spreer spree? Is this why nobody wants to remember? Is this why the pushers push all the way to the Heartland, to The Committee, while the rest disappear themselves, or run away to the farms, or live behind the

305

invisible walls of the city until they get disappeared?

He rides the train uptown and downtown for hours, half-wishing the Voids would find him, end it once and for all. No one pays him any mind. No one seems to notice the Crist shooter sitting quietly next to the window, ravished by his own inner torment. No one comes looking for him. He watches the city degenerate from uptown to downtown, then prosper again the other way. He takes side trips, to the sectors adjacent to the ones he usually sees. There is very little difference in the view. His thoughts run rampant all the while, revisiting the same old mental cul-de-sacs again and again.

If I believe that bastard, Victor, I got poor Tassy Crist killed. For what? So she could play Ms. Victor while I stayed Mr. Stupid? So nobody would suspect that Anna and I were sharing spit? So nobody would notice I can regenerate myself?

Jennie, why didn't you tell me you were pregnant? Was I that asleep? Would I have gone to pieces? What did I do when Rachel got pregnant? Nothing. But Jennie's not Rachel. Jennie was my life. I would have managed for Jennie. Rachel was just there.

Did you really want to get away from me, Jennie? Did I just take that easy way you have for love? Were you too afraid to tell me no? Were you too afraid to tell anybody no? Was I lying to myself all the time? Was I as blind to you while you were there as Rachel was to that jumper once the mess was gone? Was it one and the same? Was it me holding on tight to whatever I needed, while you were wondering how to get away?

Maybe love was just for fun with you back then. Maybe you just needed some real fun after a hard day at the pub. Maybe you did need me for a little while. Maybe everything was as good as it gets. Maybe I should be happy I had something nobody else gets. Maybe I should just let you go, wish you well, remember you until the memory fades. Maybe, maybe, maybe.

What could I have done different? How could I have kept you there?

His stomach begins to grumble so he returns to Sector Thirty-Two. Physically and emotionally drained, he takes the chute back to his Tower. His thoughts continue to ramble on, but he begins to ignore them.

There are no assassins waiting for him in the lobby. There are no messages for him on the talkie. He calls down for a steak, a potato, a salad, an ale. He eats slowly, knowing the food is delicious. He tastes nothing. He fills the tub, soaks for an hour, recycles his clothes, goes to sleep. For most of the night he does not dream.

Before dawn his dreams begin. He meanders from one impossible pointless situation to another. Nothing remains what it is, everything blends into everything else in a nonsensical unending hodgepodge. In his last dream Anastasia finds him beside the reservoir. She is wearing a deep yellow one-piece dress, the color of the late afternoon sun. She smiles at him, draws a wand from the wide orange sash she is wearing around her waist. Suddenly everything in the dream is crystal clear, hard edged, realer than real. Suddenly Wyatt's whole attention is there.

I loved you, Wyatt, Anastasia says, *but you loved Jennie Height. I've listened to you think about her all day. I've felt your fierce desire for this woman. You never desired me like that, you never will. Now what's left for me? I betrayed my father for you, Wyatt. What's worse, you know I hear your thoughts. Usually you make an effort to control them. You made no effort at all today. You indulged yourself as if I didn't exist.*

You had it all, Wyatt, every bit of it. You let it slip away—not with Jennie, who left you—with me!

She levels the wand at his head. Tears are streaming

down her cheeks. She shoots him without hesitation. He feels his skin burning, his face evaporating, his body disintegrating. He tries to scream. He has no mouth or vocal cords to do so. Everything is black.

Wyatt wakes up suddenly in a cold sweat.

He rises slowly, pushing his hands into the mattress, gets up, staggers into the bathroom, splashes cold water on his face, neck, chest, arms. Lets it air dry. Rinses out his mouth with antiseptic. Splashes more water on his face. To his surprise, nothing has disintegrated.

"Wyatt?"

It is Anastasia's voice.

He staggers into the living room. The screen is down. Anastasia's face is framed by the still waters of the lake behind it. The swans are gone, the water is obscured by a fine haze. Wyatt is not certain what he is seeing, but he knows something is not right. Anna's green eyes watch him. They betray nothing.

"Are you all right?" she asks. Her voice expresses a genuine concern.

"Just woke up," he says, forces a smile. "Had a very strange dream. I'll be fine in a minute or two."

"You had better come back to the Heartland."

"The war is over then?" he asks.

Anastasia shakes her head. For just a moment he sees the worry in her eyes. "I need you here with me, Wyatt. Will you come?"

"I'll be there in an hour and a half."

"I'll be waiting for you."

Anastasia smiles, blows him a quick kiss before the screen goes blank.

CHAPTER 51

There are dozens of home guards standing alert on the platform or hovering above it at the Heartland East Station. Most appear nervous to Wyatt.

Fifty or so women, with their children huddled around them, are waiting anxiously for the inbound, maybe two dozen veeps and drones. The platform is filled to capacity, with no one expecting or waiting for anyone to disembark. They all surge forward as soon as the doors open. Wyatt has to fight his way through the crowd. He is the only passenger for the Heartland.

"Mr. Weston."

Wyatt looks into Charlie's surprised face. "How are you, Charlie?"

"Very well, thank you. We weren't expecting you. Does Mr. Crist know you're here?"

"Anastasia should be waiting for me."

Charlie checks the vidcom on his face shield. "She's in parking bay number eleven."

"Thanks, Charlie. Take care of yourself."

"You, too, Mr. Weston."

Wyatt finds Anna in the two-seater. She is wearing a one-piece yellow dress with an orange sash. Wyatt sucks in his breath when he sees it. The air stinks inside the dome, a faint smell of something burning, something rotting. There is a fine haze near the ground, seemingly clinging to every blade of grass. Another dozen home guards patrol the transport park in the air, on the platform, scanning the foliage, the air, the ground.

Inside the transport, the smell is good, it is all Anna. Against the backdrop of the bioscan and filter, she turns, embraces Wyatt, presses her lips softly against his. He leans into her, his arms around her. Their kiss is long, gentle, mutually reassuring.

"Wyatt, do you believe I love you?" she asks him. Her green eyes bore into his.

"Yeah, I do," he says without thinking. He is surprised at his own conviction.

"Then hold that thought, no matter what else happens."

"What's this about, Anna?"

"Don't ask. If you knew, you'd give it away. Just remember what I said. It isn't likely to get better than this for a while. It's probably going to get much worse. Love me like you once loved Jennie. You won't be disappointed with me. I won't desert you, ever."

Wyatt feels the blood rushing to his face. Anna presses her forefinger against his lips, turns around, begins driving back to the house.

"Anna?" The voice is Victor's.

"Yes, Daddy."

"Where are you?"

"Picking up Wyatt."

"Good. Edward is sending some of his men over to augment mine. Things should come to a head in a day or so. We need every available shooter."

Anastasia keeps the transport low to the ground, close to the trees, away from open fields. Wyatt watches the screen. He sees other transports hurrying about their own business, no one paying any mind to anyone else. He places his hands easily on her shoulders, massages her back. Anna leans forward, lets him work his thumbs into the soft places between

310

her shoulder blades. He feels her tension in his hands.

In the front yard, Wyatt counts twelve men in Crist silver and yellow, two others in black and red. All are carrying long barrels, or small shoulder-mounted artillery. A number of barricades have been set up on the perimeter, each with multiple viewscreens and several weapon holes. Anastasia takes him around the house. The scene is the same on all sides.

They enter the house through a basement bulkhead facing the lake. Anna takes Wyatt past two sterile labs where men and women in white coveralls are working—seemingly oblivious to the preparations taking place around the house—down another corridor where emergency dormitory accommodations have been prepared in several large open rooms across from others filled with crates of food, twenty-liter carboys of water, cases of wine, medical supplies. They go up one flight of stairs, down another corridor, into familiar territory.

Anna stops to listen. She looks past Wyatt at nothing in particular, cocks her head to one side, then the other, smiles, apparently satisfied for the moment. She takes Wyatt into the dojo. No one is working out; it is cool, quiet, dark. By the dim light of the corridor, Wyatt begins peeling off the top of her dress. The look on her face is an avid blend of agony, expectation, pleasure.

She turns her face away from him. He kisses her neck, her shoulders, her hands—always slowly, always without any sudden movements. The tears are trickling down her face when she pulls off his vest, holster, shirt. Wyatt kicks off his shoes, takes off his trousers while Anna removes the sash, kicks off her own shoes, steps out of the yellow dress. She sits, straddling him. They embrace one another lightly, rocking back and forth slowly, listening to the silence from the corridor. Wyatt doesn't want the moment to end.

Anna is right. It won't get any better than this, ever.

He is kissing her neck again when he feels her tense.

It's starting, he hears her voice inside his head. *Follow my lead, Wyatt. No matter what. It's the only chance either one of us has. Hold on to that love, Wyatt. Use your instincts, your reflexes; don't let go.*

I'm right here with you, Anna, he thinks.

They dress quickly without speaking. Wyatt draws his wand. Anna opens a small wall cabinet beside the dojo door, selects a wand from the cache, makes certain it is on full charge.

Wyatt watches her wince. She scowls, motions for Wyatt to take the lead. They are both sprinting when they reach the main floor. The ozone scent of wand blast is there. Anna overtakes him, jumping the stairs two at a time.

On the third-floor landing, two of Edward's men turn quickly to face them. Wyatt and Anna fire simultaneously, incinerating both of them before they can react further. A naked Victor, his face a mask of rage, meets them in the corridor.

"That bastard," he growls. "He sent his men here to kill us, not defend us. After everything I did for him. Now he's Chairman, he decides I'm a liability. I'll show him what a liability is."

"Where's Sonja?" Wyatt whispers.

"She's dead. Melba, too. While I was in the toilet, the cowards. How many of them did you get?"

"Two," Anna says.

"I got two in there. There are six more around. He's probably got a small army waiting to join them somewhere close by. I've already alerted Floyd and Arthur. They'll secure the grounds. We've got to secure the house."

"You might want to put your trousers on first," Wyatt suggests.

Victor looks down, heads back into his bedroom, emerges a minute later wearing only pants and shoes, carrying a wand in each hand.

There are two heading for the labs, Anna tells Wyatt.

"We'll take the lower levels," Wyatt offers, taking the stairs three at a time.

"I'll take the main floors, and meet you out front," Victor responds.

The house seems twice as big as it was a moment ago. Every step seems to take forever. But Edward Coyle's men do not realize they've been found out when Wyatt and Anna reach them in the basement corridor. Wyatt vaporizes them both with a single shot, to the surprise of the terrified techs behind the glass.

What now? Wyatt asks.

He stands, staring at Anna's blank face. Her eyes look past him.

They've killed Arthur. Floyd's just finished the last of them. Three transports are coming at us from the front, another is skimming the lake. I've alerted Floyd. The house is secure. We've got the back. Let's go.

Anna puts the wand on *safety,* stuffs it into her sash. In a weapons cabinet in the wall below the bulkhead, she removes a small cannon. Motioning with her head for Wyatt to get the bulkhead door, she raises it to her shoulder. She has it primed and aimed before either of them see the large transport coming up fast below them, churning the mists clinging to the surface of the water. Anna fires. Wyatt recoils at the *wah-wah-wah* sound. The plastic bubble on the transport shatters. It flips over, spilling eight men into the lake before it crashes into the steep embankment below the house.

Wyatt can just make out eight bobbing heads through the haze. He fires eight times in rapid session. The lake erupts with orange bursts that shimmer across the entire surface.

The Crist men around him stand and gape. They have never seen anyone move that fast.

"We're under attack by Coyle Enterprises!" Wyatt shouts at them. "Kill anyone wearing black and red. Somebody get me a fresh wand."

The nearest man quickly hands Wyatt his holstered weapon. Wyatt tosses the other to the ground.

What now? he thinks to Anna as he activates the wand.

We've got to get to the front. She winces again.

Floyd? he asks, seeing the sudden sadness come over her.

Anna only nods.

They scramble around the side of the house. Anna throws herself against Wyatt, knocking him to the ground. A moment later the flawless fieldstone wall erupts, showering them with shards of burning rock. Wyatt leaps over Anna, just as the glowing bits of stone shred his backside. He heals himself with a reflex, looks at Anna, who appears unharmed. She has already sighted the transport with the cannon. She fires once, sending it careening, twice, sending it plunging into the ground, and again, into the shattered bubble, incinerating all those inside. She tosses the spent cannon aside. There are tears in her eyes. Wyatt still hears the *wah-wah-wah* inside his head as he pulls himself off her.

A loud series of explosions from the front have them back on their feet, running.

All four transports are down, Wyatt hears her mindvoice. *No survivors. Edward is sending reinforcements. He knows his first wave is finished. We've got about three minutes before the next one arrives.*

314

Wyatt marvels at her ability to discern so much accurate information at a distance. Anna turns to smile at him.

"Hurry," she says aloud. "There are two things I've got to do before they get here."

She sprints ahead of him.

Victor is barking orders, repositioning his men, calling for more artillery, shouting into his wrist band at those at the back and sides of the house. He knows the battle has just begun. He turns, stares at Wyatt and Anna. "Well?" he demands.

"I took out two shooters in the cellar before they did any damage," Wyatt responds. "Anna dropped two of their transports. No survivors. The house has been hit. I don't think we lost anybody in the back."

"That bastard's not finished with me," Victor snarls. "He won't rest until I'm dead or he is. I know him. Anna, what are you doing?"

Wyatt looks over his shoulder to see Anna discharge her wand at Victor. Victor is already vaporized before Wyatt turns his head back to look at him.

"I love you, Wyatt. Please remember that," Anna says calmly.

Wyatt spins around just in time to see the orange ball from Anna's wand expanding before it engulfs him.

CHAPTER 52

Wyatt feels the blast shredding every iota of his flesh. He knows it is an instant, but he feels it as a lifetime. He has seen so many men disintegrated by wand blasts that the notion of blast lapse time has never occurred to him. Yet he experiences it as the vaporization of his clothing, the burning off of his skin, layer by layer, the incineration of his muscle, the electrification of his nerves, the melting of his bones, the chaos of a painful, violent death.

She's killed me, he thinks. *She's killed me and I still love her.*

The battlefield becomes a disjointed montage of irreconcilable images, seen from too many perspectives at once. Edward's second wave appears above the trees. Wyatt counts six transports. Five drop down while the sixth fires at the house. It is hit by three cannons at once, shatters, crashes, spilling screaming men into the woods.

All is still for a moment. Edward's men begin moving on foot through the trees. Wyatt sees each and every one of them, notes their positions, notes their shields, notes the image distorters some of them carry, to make themselves appear elsewhere.

Crist shooters brought in from the rear are lying belly-down in the side yard. Wand fire fills the space between the house and the trees. Trees burn, barricades fall. Orange balls bounce off the house, disappear.

Wyatt watches Edward Coyle's men dying as if their defense weaponry is suddenly useless, as if all that is invisible, hidden, refracted, or disguised is suddenly made known to the Crist shooters, who react with the swift coordinated movement of a single being. His mind swirls from the effort to contain it all, from the effort to maintain this alien perspective.

All is black.

She's killed me. No time has lapsed. It is the same instant Anastasia turned her wand upon him. *She's killed me and I still love her.*

In the blackness, time passes. A lonely eternity. A place of perfect silence, marred only by his fading emotions, his final fear. And one memory. The memory of his own face, his head, his hair, his skeleton, his musculature, his nervous system, his skin, his physical being.

Wyatt gasps. He is naked, lying on the floor of the parlor in Victor's house, his back propped up against the cool stone wall. All of the servants are in hiding. A loud blast shatters one of the clerestory windows, the shards of melting lexan rain down upon the Oriental carpets.

Someone has dropped a wand nearby. It is just like his old sweeper unit. Wyatt picks it up, cradles it like a baby, sets it on *active,* lets it fall into his lap. He stares at it, then he looks up at the hole in the clerestory. Something below grabs his attention.

Wyatt does not move.

He is surrounded by visions.

Rafe is there, so is Jennie, the waitress from the Sector Twelve Grille, the flat-faced woman security guard from his tower, a scowling Bert Han.

Shit, Wyatt, Rafe screams at him from the foyer. *Shit. Maybe you didn't want to know. But don't tell me you didn't know. You were there. You were with that sack of shit when he killed us all. You knew. You might as well have done it yourself.*

You didn't stop him. You went along with it. You're as guilty as he is. Do you know how many died for this? Do you know how many more are going to join us?

Wyatt feels his right hand melting away, as if to scream: *Not me—I didn't kill any of them. See, I don't even have a shooting hand.*

You were the only one I ever loved, Jennie says sadly. *What happened to you, Wyatt? What happened to that sensitive, funny man I loved? Who are you? I don't even know you anymore. I don't even want to know what you've become.*

Wyatt feels the left half of his face melting away into an amorphous blob, hanging well below his chin, as if to deny himself, as if to say: *It's not me, Jennie. It's some kind of ugly monster born of the madness. Wyatt still lives. Waiting for you in that place. I'm still there, Jennie, waiting for you. Remember that place, Jennie?*

The visions fade—Rafe, Jennie, and the others who held their peace. They turn their backs on him in disgust, fade away. He is truly alone.

He hears the wands discharging outside, speaking to him in their own language. A language of crackling arcing bolts, sizzling fireballs. The shooting is more sporadic now. Two shots here. Another there. Silence. Another burst. Silence.

Wyatt shuts his remaining eye.

I remade myself from nothing. I can unmake myself again. I came back because I know nothing else. I can go find whatever else there is.

He hears the front door opening.

"Wyatt?"

The wand is in his left hand before his eye is open. It is Anna.

"Wyatt? I'm unarmed. Don't shoot me. Not until you

hear me out. Then shoot me if you must. It won't matter. I'm coming in alone."

He hears her soft footfalls on the blue Chinese runner, hears her swishing against the dried grasses in the Egyptian urn, sees her silhouette in the darkness across the room. Catches the bright sun-colored dress as she approaches, the orange sash.

She has something in her right hand. He raises the wand and levels it at her midsection.

Anastasia keeps on coming. The object is smaller than a wand. It is some sort of med-tech device. She stops about four feet away from him, kneels down, shows it to him.

"Why did you kill Victor?" he asks calmly.

"Don't you know?"

"Tell me. I want to hear you tell me."

"I killed him because he stole my childhood. Because he took liberties with me. Because he tortured and then killed my mother. Because he got Floyd killed. Because none of this can end so long as he's alive. Because so long as he lived, I would be imprinted to please him. But most of all, I killed him because he was ruining everything. His myopic vision and self-aggrandizement almost wiped out Crist Enterprises."

Wyatt laughs. "Almost?" he asks.

"We're Crist Enterprises now, Wyatt. You and me. Most of the servants and the techs are in the shelters below the house. We're down to about twenty soldiers here. They've already sworn their allegiance to me. They know what I am now. They're too frightened to resist me. What's more, they like it. Twenty men took out sixty without a single casualty. Edward doesn't have enough shooters left to try this again. Adolph is dead. Besides, the real chaos is just beginning."

Wyatt is careful to keep his thoughts suspended, careful

to give her no clues how to play him. He keeps the wand leveled at her. He wants to blast her. He wants to hold her.

"What's that in your hand, Anna?"

"It's what this is really all about, Wyatt."

"That would be . . . ?"

"The first of the new genes."

"You're the one who took Jennie away from me, weren't you? You made her the offer to disappear into The Archives without telling me. It was you who took that first embryo. Is that thing in your hand what's left of it?"

"No. That embryo was useless. The healing factor did not appear in it. This came from another embryo—ours."

"You were pregnant and aborted?"

"Yes."

Wyatt says nothing. He lowers the wand. He watches Anna sliding toward him on her knees. Her eyes never leave his. Twin pools of iced jade. He feels her warm hand upon his shoulder. Watches her press the device hard against his upper arm. Feels a sudden lancing pain.

"It will take a few moments, Wyatt. You'll understand everything then."

Wyatt knows he has blacked out, but he has no idea for how long. Anna is cradling his head against her breast when he awakens, gently stroking the melted mess that is the left side of his face. He hears a thousand voices gibbering out banalities, feels ten thousand fears, desires, excuses, lies. He listens to countless explanations of nothing in particular.

What is that? he cries out in his mind.

That's all of it. You have to learn to buffer it, to hear it selectively. I'll show you how.

What have you done to me?

What have I done to you? I've made you the first of the new

320

men, Wyatt. The first of those who will survive the death of this age, forge ahead into the next one. It's almost finished out there. The topsoil is gone. The machines that hold the ozone layer in place will not work forever. The stockpiles will last for another hundred and fifty years at most. The resources are scattered; the manpower needed to extract them no longer exists, because there is not enough food and potable water to sustain them. The crop seeds we plant are growing weaker and weaker. Soon, they will no longer be able to reproduce themselves.

What are you talking about?

You're like me now. You live more in mind than in body. But you still have a body. More importantly, you can have any body you can imagine, any one you need, so long as you fashion it according to the laws of biology and genetics. You can repair any damage, even return from the dead. I wanted you to see that for yourself. Our men will see that in a few minutes. Soon, everyone left will know about it. No one will dare oppose us. Like me, you can travel mentally, move through your thoughts, hear whatever you need to, once you've learned to filter out the noise, focus your attention. It will be much easier than learning to rebuild yourself, I'm sure.

Why did you shoot me?

To show you what you still haven't grasped. There is no limit to what we are, to what we can become. To show you that for all intent and purpose, we have become immortal.

What were you saying about chaos?

I couldn't let them wipe us out. Edward Coyle made too many deals to blame him alone. They were all in on it, all the major players. Victor made too many enemies. The rest of us were seen merely as extensions of Victor. Edward had to agree to stamp us out to become Chairman. He agonized over it for two days. I called you back the moment he decided. The only way for us to emerge dominant is to set all the rest of them upon each

321

*other, by feeding their petty jealousies and fears. I've already
done that. Most of them are so weak they can't tell their own
thoughts from the ones I put in their minds. Edward is fighting
for his life now—a losing effort. If he survives, I'll send another
Enterprise at him. He's got fewer men than we have to defend
him right now. He didn't really expect to send in the second
wave against us. That was an act of desperation. Two minutes
after he hit us the second time, someone else hit him. The entire
Heartland has turned upon itself. There is civil war raging everywhere while the city sleeps as usual. That is what you are
hearing. We've already won our battle. More to the point, we've
already won the war. There is no place for the survivors to turn
but here. They can't kill us, they can't surprise us. We are the
future, Wyatt. The two of us, and anyone we choose to take with
us. You and me.*

Anastasia smiles, revealing her perfect golden teeth.

I really hate those teeth, Wyatt thinks.

"I know," she says aloud and laughs.

Anastasia pulls her cheeks in, as if she were sucking on a
lemon. She draws her thin lips into her mouth, rolls them
out, grins again. There is no hint of gold anywhere. Even in
the semidarkness, Wyatt can see her teeth are perfect and
white.

"You took . . ." he gestures at the implement in her
hand, ". . . too," he says.

"Of course. You don't think I'd let you go it alone, do
you? You've got my telepathic gene, I've got your regenera-
tive gene."

Wyatt lets the wand slide from his hand onto the floor.

Anna stands up, leaning him gently back against the
wall.

"That was you on the train, after Victor cooked Sector
Twelve," he says suddenly. "That was you posing as Jennie."

"I had to let you find her, Wyatt. Find her, get her out of your system once and for all. She's an idealist; there is a place for her in all this—but not at the top. That's for us. It always has been. At first I thought it was only the gene, I admit that. I wanted you for that, when I heard about you through Adolph Void's people. But the moment you walked past Tassy, Sonja, and me, watching that insipid woman with her beauty tips on the screen, I knew that it would take both of us. There's no more mystery about what happened to Jennie. There's no more questions about who's who or what's what. Now you know anything you want to know. You know what's real, what's pretense. So stop playing the lost little boy and grow up. Nothing's over. It's just beginning. So get off your butt, pull yourself back together, make a strong showing for the men outside. We've got a world to remake—and no one will follow a weakling."

ABOUT THE AUTHOR

Paul Bates works in construction management, writes slipstream fiction, and lives on a wooded acre in eastern Massachusetts. His notion of heaven is to be well into the composition of his next novel with occasional breaks for long swims and Indian cuisine. His idea of hell is having writer's block and attending cocktail parties.